THE GIRL BEHIND THE WALL

BY

QUAYE COLEMAN

&

ASHLEY ANTOINETTE

IF YOU WANT TO SEE A GIRL FIGHT FOR HER RIGHTS,
PICK THIS BOOK!

-QUAYE

"To all the parents who want to share their love of reading with their child. This one is for you. Let's tap into our imaginations and explore a new world together."

-xoxo- Ashley Antoinette

PROLOGUE

I hate the color red. I mean, I absolutely despise it. I wish I was like other girls and I had a bubbly anecdote that explained my distaste for it. Other girls would say it was too boyish. It would be cute to say it was unflattering against my skin. It would be appropriate for a 17-year-old girl to be addicted to its paler counterpart, pink, therefore, red and every other color was hideous to me. There is no cute tale to accompany my reasoning, however. Red is the color of blood. It was the color of *his* blood. Blood I had spilled. There had been so much of it. I never knew how much blood people have inside them. It was everywhere. On my hands, on my clothes, stuck in the cracks of the soles of my shoes, crusted in my hair. I could even taste it in my mouth. When I close my eyes, I don't even see black behind my lids anymore. I see red. Blood and red and I hate it. Let me take you back to when red was just like any other color. Before that day. Just before…

CHAPTER 1

NEELY

Ma! Where is my uniform skirt?!" It was an ordinary day. Our house was hectic in the mornings. There was always something missing, always noise…mostly, from my 10-year-old brother, and always crowded. The King's household was everything but organized. I lived with my parents, and my little brother, Mario, and we were the most chaotic example of love that ever existed. There just wasn't enough room. Our three-bedroom, 1200-square-foot house felt like a box, and with the temperature of the last days of summer still lingering, it made the house feel even smaller. Not even the boxed fan that sat in the window could cool down my room, and the busted AC that daddy never got around to fixing was nothing more than a tease. A bead of sweat formed at my brow and I could feel my straightened hair begin to recoil into its natural state. "Great!" If I didn't get out of the furnace of a house soon, my hair would do a magic trick and abra-cadabra into an afro.

"Neely! Look in the basket in the hallway. The clothes are clean; they just aren't folded!" My mother yelled back. I grimaced because I had reminded her. "And why aren't they folded?! I asked you to do that last night!"

"Sorry, mama! After school! I promise!" I walked right into that one. I dug through the clothes and pulled out my skirt, then stepped into it. It was anything, but stylish, but it stopped bullying…at least that was what the rulebook said. If everybody wore the same thing, then no one would be taunted for their inability to afford name brands. It was such crap. Kids just found other stuff to bully you about. Like stuff you couldn't change…like your personality, but it was the rules and society had become full of rules. There were so many rules nowadays that it no longer felt like we had free will. I looked in the mirror, and sure enough, my hair was kinking up. I sighed, threw on a head-band to tame the curls threatening to make an appearance, and then bolted down the stairs. Not paying much attention, I stubbed my toe on a skateboard.

"Damn it Mar! Why is your stuff all over the floor?" More organized chaos. That was just us. Every morning, moving around one another, or tripping over each other, with habitual expertise in the tiny house.

"Language, Neely." My dad said it more to appease my mother than to actually chastise me and threw in a wink. He cursed like a sailor. It was where I got it from. I was his oldest child and although I was a girl, I couldn't be more junior-ish even if I was a boy. We were just alike, and, in a house, divided, we were always on the same side of things. I was in love with him the way most little girls were with the main man in their lives, but even deeper than that, we were best friends. My dad just got me, and when I needed advice, I didn't run to my mama like most girls; it was always dad.

"Yeah, language Neely," Mario mimicked. Little brothers were annoying, or maybe it's just mine, with his big head and even bigger mouth, and ears that stuck out so wide that he appeared he might take flight…yep, I'm sure it's mine.

I hugged my dad and stuck my middle finger up at my little brother behind my dad's back. My mother turned from the stove, just in time to catch me. She gave me a look, but didn't snitch. Black people never snitched.

"Sorry, daddy."

"Will all of you keep it down? I'm trying to listen to this," my mom said.

The hologram that showed on the wall played the news and my mom struggled to turn it up. My mom hated that thing. She would talk about the days of televisions, only because she wasn't savvy enough to change with the times. It was 2035 and my mother was still stuck in a time warp. She was so old school that it was embarrassing. She drowned us out with the coverage, as she maxed out the volume.

"The Democratic Party of the House of Representatives will bring the zoning bill to a vote today. Democrats would like to abolish zoning laws, which would allow the integration of all people once again. Zoning began in 2020 when President Trum signed it into law as his solution to police brutality…"

My dad turned it off.

"Dalton, I was watching that," she protested.

"I know you want things to go back to the way they used to be, but I for one, am fine with the way it is now, damn it," dad offered.

See, the language, I was definitely my father's child.

"I don't know. It would be kind of cool to live outside this box they put us in," I chimed in.

"That's because you weren't around back then…" He paused, as a somberness filled his face. "…when cops were putting bullets in black men for no reason, or when kids were being killed for having toy guns. It's best to be amongst our own kind. I sleep a lot better at night."

My eyes hooded because my dad spoke of those times often. Before zoning, before I was born, he said things were bad. We learned about it in school. Trayvon Martin, Tamir Rice, Sandra Bland. Their names were in all the history books, but when my dad spoke about it, it felt different. It brought tears to his eyes and my dad never ever cries, so it must have been bad. I couldn't help but dream about what it was like back then, though. It had to be better than being zoned. It was basically segregation all over again. I read about that even further back in the history books, but zoning seemed worse. Now, every race lived within a zone. All Black people were zoned with Black people, all Hispanic people with Hispanics, all White people with Whites, all Asians with Asians, all Middle Eastern people with Middle Easterners, and the Native Americans all lived on their reservations. If you were mixed, you were put in Zone 5 and no one in Zone 5 was allowed to procreate. It was basically a grave-yard. Only one generation would live there. There was also

Ground Zero, but no one lived there. It was where artificial intelligence models were created, a world of robots where Silicon Valley used to be. Intermingling outside your zone was a crime and punishable by death. President Trum created a world where diversity didn't exist. I went to school with black people, church with black people, bought our groceries from black-owned businesses. Everything was black. For us, by us. It didn't matter that some of us were African, African American, Haitian, Jamaican, Guyanese, nope. They didn't separate us that way. We were all just black. The purpose was to ensure that the neighborhoods were policed by men and women of the neighborhoods. That's what the law said. To Trum's credit, the police brutality stopped because there were simply no white police officers in our zone; no accidental slips of fingers on triggers because some white boy was scared when he encountered the big, scary, black, male species. Still, America, the land of the free didn't feel so free. It felt like concentration camps. Another horror I had read about in a book. President Trum turned the world upside down decades ago and it hadn't been right since. Every zone had its own governing laws, but was also held to federal laws. Black people decided black people's fate, but if you broke federal law, you were tried in The Panel. Back in the day, the judicial system was so skewed that it was set up against people of color. Old white men made the laws, old white men upheld the laws, so every brown, black, or yellow face that entered courtrooms were punished, hard. It was just a jacked-up system. President Trum changed the entire judicial system. Your own people judged you, but if you broke federal law, you didn't sit in front of one judge. You sat in front of them all. One judge from each zone sat on The Panel. So, if you messed up and ended up there, your fate wasn't in one person's hands. The Panel decided your punishment together, but nobody wanted to end up in front of them. There was only one panel, and they were so overloaded with cases that it took years to get in front of them. You would likely die in prison while awaiting judgement before they ever saw your face. Nope, black folks handled our dirty laundry in house.

I arose from the table, grabbed my bag from the floor and kissed my dad on the cheek. "See you later, papa bear."

"Have a good first day, baby girl," dad called back.

"I will. Bye, ma. Bye, chump." I flicked Mar's ear on the way out.

"Yo' mama!" He shouted, in retaliation. I snickered when I heard the "Ow!" that followed, as I slid out the door because I knew my mom had slapped some sense into him. "Damario, watch your mouth. Her mama is your mama, so how smart is that?" I heard her fussing him out all the way in the front yard. I loved my family. I loved them with everything in me, but I couldn't wait to break free; but somehow, I felt limited, like there were places I couldn't go and people I couldn't meet, simply because they didn't look like me. Fear had driven us to an odd place.

I was a black girl with almond skin that darkened to a creamed coffee brown in the summertime. Despite the occasional pimple, it was skin that I appreciated, skin that didn't show blemishes, skin that was rich like those caramel candies that filled giant heart boxes on Valentine's Day. I had kinky coils that framed my face like a lion's mane when wet. It was thick like the fog that settled in the air after a rainy morning, and known to break through any hairbrush that dare tried to tame it. On the rare days that I won the battle, it fell down my back, pressed straight. That was my intention today, to be silky and polished for the first day of senior year. The heat and my hair had other plans. Black girl problems. I loved everything melanin. The way we spoke, the way we dressed, the way our bodies moved when we heard music we liked, even the way our skin deepened a shade at our elbows and knees. Being black was lit. Perhaps, I was lucky to only know a world with zones because my mother didn't love her blackberry tinted skin as much. She was almost ashamed of her hair, often calling it nappy and anything reminiscent of being too urban. She called it ghetto, as if she was measuring black people against another type of people's standards. See, her mother and grandmother remembered a time without zones…a time when assimilation was required, so Valencia King had some remnants of self-hatred. Still, I couldn't help but wonder what it was like back then. How dope would it be to have friends that thought differently than me? Looked differently than me? Everyone I knew shared the same ideology because we were all from the same place. It was boring. Words like "diversity" and "inclusion" had been forgotten because it simply no longer existed. President Trump had started the notion of building walls to keep people out, but one wall had turned to two, and two to four, and four to eight. Before anyone knew it, walls were the norm and it felt like they were more for the purposes of keeping us in. Each zone was walled off; although there were ways around them, not many dared to leave. If you were caught out of zone, it was breaking federal law.

Beep! Beep!

I turned at the sound of the car horn to find Minnie. If loyalty needed a personification, she was it. She was my best friend. In my small world, she made it feel large. I swear, her brain was like an encyclopedia. She just soaked stuff up like a sponge. We talked about places we would go if we could, things we would do. Sometimes, we just sat in the library at school, looking at old books of the seven world wonders, dreaming about what it would have been like to see such incredible things. I hopped into her smart car, remembering my mom's words about technology. *"I don't want no car that I can't control. A smart car! I remember good ol' gasoline was all a car needed to get you where you needed to go. Now, it's uploading and downloading, software and megabytes. That's not a car, it's a god damned computer, is what it is."* Ma could curse up a storm too if you got her worked up enough, which was on a rare occasion.

"You ready for the first day of senior year?" Minnie asked. Her dark eyes sparkled against her opal skin. Her long locs were pulled up into a high ponytail, with gold ribbons intertwined in them. She had glowed up. Her glasses had been replaced with contacts and her braces had come off over the summer. My girl looked good, and I don't mean in a snack kind of way, Minnie was looking like an entire meal… loaded baked potato and all.

"Am I? Are you?!" I shot back. "Look at you! You look amazing!"

If she was lighter, her skin would have flushed red. Minnie's shyness didn't allow her to receive compliments without embarrassment and I laughed at her discomfort. "You better get used to it girl because you look great!"

We rode through Zone 7 and it was like a festival of black magic. The elementary kids didn't start school until the following week, so they were out in the street, burning off as much energy as they could in the meantime.

"Look at little Dehja, out here like she's grown, with her stomach out," Minnie said. The 12-year-old pre-teen wore French braids down her back as she stood, wearing a cropped top with one hand on her hip, waiting for her two sidekicks to turn the rope so she could jump. I don't know what she thought her hand was resting on because despite her desperation to be grown, all she had was bone. Her hips hadn't come in yet. My mom called her a "fast-tailed little girl" but little Dehja wasn't going through anything out of the ordinary. I was rolling up my shirts and sticking out hips that didn't yet exist, too, at her age. It was just a part of growing up, and little black girls loved to rush the process. My mom always says, "you don't know how good it is to be a kid until the years have already passed you by."

Mrs. Green waved as we drove by. The old lady came out every day in a purple flower housecoat and rollers just to sweep the curb in front of her house. She was everybody's grandma around Zone 7. Nobody, especially the youngsters, dared to disrespect her and if Dehja and her homegirls kicked up too much noise, she would curse them out for making too much racket. Her words…not mine.

The one thing zoning forced us to do is to strengthen the black community. Everybody knew everybody. It was a close-knit zone because we had learned that it was better to stick together than to let outsiders divide you and pick you off one by one. We were stronger in heritage now that we were forced to be. Zone 7 was a world of its own with beautiful, African and Caribbean roots fused with African American culture. The ride to school was like passing a parade, each house offering a different presentation of what it meant to be black.

"What do you think it's like out there? In the other zones?"

"I don't know," Minnie mused. "There could be dragons on the other sides of these walls, and we wouldn't have a clue."

"You've been watching too many archives, Minnie."

That was the one thing about Minnie. She loved watching old movies and television shows like *Lord of the Rings* or *Game of Thrones*. All the old remnants of pop culture, music, movies, and shows, even books, had been archived digitally. Most people never indulged in them, but it was Minnie's favorite pastime. She believed in those worlds almost as much as she believed in the real one. She was a certified geek. See, the bullying for stuff you can't change! Even I do it sometimes, but hey, she was my geek, and we are a pair. Buy one, get one free. We arrived, and I stepped out the car.

Hamady High School. This building and I had a love/hate thing going on. The campus was massive and sat on a green lawn over almost five acres of land. The sea of kids hustling outside was hard to navigate as we made our way inside.

The open-air buildings made school feel less prison-like, and everyone was alive with chatter, an excitement that only came with the beginning of a new school year. In a month or so, we would all hate it again, but today, I was eager to see people I had lost touch with over summer break. Minnie and I stood in line, placing our backpacks in a bin on a conveyor belt before walking through the full body scanners. I stepped inside and held my hands up as the machine whirled around me.

"No weapons detected," the computerized voice announced. I bounced out and retrieved my things and waited for Minnie before merging into the crowd.

"Soouuuuppp!"

The call of the frat boys rang out through the hallway, as the AKA's came stepping down the corridor in a line, everyone made way for them. The African King Association was the crème de le crème of African associations. My dad was a part of something like this back in the day only he called it Greek life, which was crazy to me because we weren't Greek. The African Kings symbolized a lineage of royalty that trickled down all the way from the Motherland. They were traditionally trained in Motherland war antics as an ode to the past, and their strength symbolized warriors that came before them. They were an elite class of black men and although they would never use half of what they learned;

the AKA's were fit to rule nations. It was tradition. One that we respected, and they may not ever rule over kingdoms, but they reigned the school. I found them kind of corny in that super cute, entitled, they can have any girl they want including me, kind of way. They were all charm, muscles, brains, and finesse. Okay, if I'm honest, I had a thing for one of them, the leader, Shakir, but he never looked my way. So yeah, I was a bit bitter about that, but I digress. He stopped right in front of Minnie and I as he grunted and beat his chest, then went through a series of stomps and claps to match the beat of his brothers. I smiled and rolled my eyes when he invaded my personal space to roll his body against mine. He was a tease. He knew I liked him. He had to know. He had caught me in the dreamy, fixed stare one too many times not to know, and he never made a move. I went to walk away, but felt him grab my waist.

"Hey!"

I was hoisted up on his shoulder, caveman style, as the crowd cheered. Minnie included. We all flowed towards the gym, where the marching band was playing in full force. He placed me on my feet, and looked down at me, smiling before his brothers joined his side in a straight line. Again, they stepped, this time to the beat the band was playing. Minnie found her way to my side and I couldn't maintain my tough girl act. This was what senior year was all about, the beginning of the year's antics, the pep rally. The energy was crazy, and the entire crowd grooved with the AKA's and the band as they fell in line, rocking from side to side to the music. It was dope. The entire gym was alive as the AKA's created a pulse for the rest of us to vibe to. The music vibrated through my body. I could feel it. It lived inside of me, making my heart race as I fell into rhythm with the group. I didn't look forward to school any other day, but the first day was always amazing, especially because it was my senior year…I was finally at the top of the food chain.

BRINGGGG!

The sound of the bell was barely audible over the music. First period was starting, but no one seemed to care. The majorettes only continued into their next routine, as the drumline went crazy, and the AKA's began to freestyle. It wasn't until the principal walked into the gym with a bull horn did we begin to disperse.

"I've got detention passes for every student I see loitering after second bell. Break it up and let's get to business." His voice blared, and I rolled my eyes. "You ready to break out?"

Minnie nodded, and I glanced over my shoulder once more at Shakir. He winked, and my heart stopped. Attention. He was giving little ol' me attention. I blushed as I pushed my way through the crowd and followed Minnie into the hall.

I felt the vibration of my channel and I quickly opened my bag to remove the device. It was a transmitter, something like an old school iPhone. My dad still had one of those things packed away in boxes somewhere. Channels were similar, but much doper. They were thin, like the protectant I saw my dad pull off his old iPhone screen, and practically weightless. It was for calls mostly, face to face scoping, texts, and some web browsing. Each zone was allowed limited interscope activity. Interscope was the third-generation internet, only it was all monitored by The Panel and access was restricted. Over the summer, I had figured out how to bypass the firewalls and get to the black scope. It was a secret network and I had found friends from other zones. We had been group scoping the entire summer, and there was one boy in particular that I spoke to the most. I smiled when I saw the message he left.

First day of senior year blows. It's soooo white.
Wish you were here to add some black.
Then we could live in the gray.
-xoxo- Liam

It was an inside joke of ours. We video scoped for hours about how life was too black and white. If we could, we would live in the gray together. It was a fantasy of another world, of another life, another time…one where I didn't have to break laws to contact a boy I liked. It was crazy because he was zones away, tucked all the way in District 1, but he knew me better than anyone around me. He, too, hated the walls, hated the separation.

"Umm…what are you reading?" Minnie asked, as she took my channel from my hand. Her eyes widened in alarm as she read the message. "Neely! Is this the black scope?"

I snatched my channel back. "Don't make a big deal, okay?"

"It is a big deal," Minnie's voice was barely above a whisper. "Do you know what will happen if you get caught on there?" Minnie asked. "It's fed law…"

"I won't get caught." I couldn't keep the tremble out my voice because I had thought about the possibility before, and I was crazy scared to do it, but it was my only connection to Liam. No way was I giving it up. "I have friends from other zones on there. It's all I've got outside these walls."

Our conversation ceased when we arrived at first period, Mr. Snell's poli-sci class. Minnie gave me a skeptical shake of her head, but dropped it as we walked through the door. We sat in the back row because although Minnie was a geek, we weren't completely uncool, and Mr. Snell began his lecture.

"Welcome to political science," Mr. Snell began. He was everybody's favorite teacher. The guys liked him because he was cool. He wasn't an artifact like the rest of the staff at Hamady High. He was old enough for us to take him seriously and young enough to still relate to our vibes. His 25 years didn't seem so far off. The girls liked him because he was nice to look at. His caramel skin was wrapped around a solid build. He had to play football back in the day because he was deliciously fit. His dark, deep-set eyes were penetrating, and he wore his hair cut low. He dressed really cool, too. He always wore jeans with fresh sneakers and button-down shirts, no tie, of course because ties were for old people. He always wore a blazer. I guess to remind us that he was, in fact, an adult. He was handsome and single, at least he never wore a wedding ring, so that's what everyone assumed. Every girl in the senior class hung off his every word. "This year, you will learn about the world around you. Political science is more than just studying government and law. I like to teach you how the law has been applied to your everyday life and how it has affected our zone, our people throughout the course of time."

I was already tuning him out. "We're going to take a look at the way government prohibits us from leaving our zones. We'll learn if it's constitutional or not? We'll learn about the Articles of Confederation. That governing document from the past would be the key to changing our current society if we knew where it was. Have any of you ever heard of the Articles of Confederation? Who knows what it is?" Mr. Snell began.

Minnie's hand shot up.

"The first written Constitution?"

Minnie always posed her answers as questions. She wasn't the most confident, despite being the smartest in the class.

"That's correct. The Articles of Confederation went on to become the U.S. Constitution after some ratifications. Historians propose that key pieces were redacted during President Trum's four-year term. It allowed him to break laws to make new ones. Your assignment is to find out which laws President Trum violated."

My channel vibrated again, and I pulled it from my bag, hiding it in front of the Kindle device that contained the class' textbook. Amazon had been thriving in the world for decades, always standing the test of time.

I opened the group scope.

The Vietnamese girl with slanted eyes, short bob cut hair, and red-painted lips popped up on her screen. She had two fingers in the shape of a gun pointed to her temple.

Kill me now. First day of school is the WORST.
-xoxo- from Zone 2

Sydney Tran, better known as Syd, was nuts. She was the daughter of the Asian Panel seat and even she hated the walls.

Another vibration followed, and this time it was Jesus Rodriguez. The Cuban kid from Zone 4. I couldn't contain my amusement as the photo of him smoking a joint popped onto my screen. Marijuana was another thing that stood the test of time. His caption read, *Botany Class.*

KNOCK IT OFF. DON'T SCOPE DURING SCHOOL. ARE YOU GUYS TRYING TO GET US CAUGHT?

That was Aziza, the Iranian girl from Zone 3, and her all caps were intentional. She was screaming. My fingers danced across the screen as I added.

I promise you guys are more interesting than all the kids at my school combined. Wish we could meet face to face.
-xoxo Zone 7

THAT'S NOT POSSIBLE
-xoxo- Arti

Arti was a cool kid, but he was overly cautious. He never put his zone in fear of being caught.

Why is it impossible?
Zone 1

"Ms. King, are we interrupting something? You know the drill. No channels during class. Hand it over."

My heart fell into my stomach. No, it went deeper than that. It fell out of my body. It was beating on the floor because if my messages were discovered my entire world would end. Mr. Snell approached, and I tried to close the screen I was in, but my channel froze. I tapped so hard; my fingernail chipped. Come on. Close. Please, close. One last tap and the screen went black and I sighed in relief as he snatched it from my hands.

"You can have it back after class," he said.

My eyes met Minnie's and she shook her head. We both knew how close I had come to getting caught.

An hour later, I was walking out of class with my channel in hand. I pulled Minnie into the closest restroom.

"Oh, my God. I can't believe that just happened. I almost died!" "You're playing with fire," she responded.

I pulled out my channel, and opened the device, catching up on the group scope thread. I had missed hella messages, but before I could get caught up, a hologram of Liam's face popped up off my device's screen.

"Are you crazy?" Minnie asked, eyes bugging out of her head. "He's face scoping you?"

"Lock the bathroom door."

As soon as I heard the lock click, I clicked the green button to answer.

"So, are you in?" Liam asked.

"I missed half the convo. My teacher took my channel. In for what?"

"We're meeting up in person. Do you know how to get underneath the wall?" Liam asked.

"Yeah, under the sewers, right?" We had discussed this many times, our grand escape, but never did I ever think we would actually go through with it.

"You can't!" Minnie was the angel over my shoulder trying to stop me from making a mistake.

"Who are you?" Liam asked.

"I'm her best friend, Minnie, and no way is she doing this," Minnie whispered, harshly. "Are y'all smoking 'shrooms or something in Zone 1. Are you white boy wasted or something?"

"Minnie's right," I agreed. "I'm not coming." Minnie's sighed in relief.

"*We're* coming," I clarified.

Liam smiled and gave her a wink. "Living in the gray?"

"Living in the gray," I repeated.

"I'll send you the deets in the group scope. Later."

His hologram disappeared when he ended the scope.

"Neely, no!" Minnie said, firmly.

"I'm going, Minnie, and so are you. Aren't you tired of wondering? Don't you want to see another zone for yourself? See the world through your own eyes instead of settling for pictures in a book. We'll be back before anyone even notices we're gone. Please, be my Louise?" I put my hands together praying as I pleaded with her.

"You didn't even see that archive," Minnie mumbled.

"But you did, and if Thelma goes off the cliff…"

"Louise goes off the cliff," Minnie finished.

I jumped for joy, as I screamed in excitement. I was finally breaking out of Zone 7, even if only for a little while.

CHAPTER 2

NEELY

Time had never been so torturously slow. Each minute that ticked by felt like hours, as I waited for my parents' bedroom light to turn off. Even after it finally went dark, and the house grew still, I waited a while longer to make sure no one would awaken. Sliding out the bed, I grabbed my backpack and made sure my flashlight, my channel, and a change of clothes were inside before slipping out the second-story window. Thank God I used to be a tomboy. I had practiced climbing the oak tree on the side of the house long before it became my escape route. I carefully placed each foot from memory, using the branches for balance, as I made my way down. When my feet hit the ground, I looked back up for reassurance and froze for a few seconds. All was silent. I took off running up the block where Minnie was waiting for me. She couldn't take her car. If her mom awoke and found it missing from their driveway, it would be a dead giveaway that she was gone. Instead, we trekked on foot, all the way to the edge of Zone 7, where nobody ventured besides zone officials and workers. It was so dark that I could barely see more than a few paces ahead of me. The yellow light was swallowed up by the black of the night. I don't think I've ever seen a shade of black so deep as the one that cloaked the sewer's entrance. It made all those childhood feelings of the boogey man come rushing back to me. The storm drain was locked, but the bars gating was wide enough for our narrow bodies to squeeze through. The squeal of rats at our feet sent Minnie into a frenzy. I swear she could be so prissy at times.

"Shh!" I chastised.

"I'm sorry! It's disgusting down here!" she snapped, as her leather combat boots trudged through the ankle height of water. "How do you know which way to go?"

"Syd's father is on The Panel. She broke into his study and sent a copy of the underground sewer maps of each district. Hold my flashlight," I handed it over and retrieved my channel from my bag. I copied it and sent it to Minnie's channel as well. It illuminated in my hands. I quickly pulled up the map and looked around. It was harder than I expected to gather my bearings. It smelled like day-old trash that had been left to fester in the summer heat. It took everything in me not to throw up. My heart galloped inside my chest. I couldn't tell if it was from fear or exhilaration, but it made me feel alive. It was like for 17 years I had been in sleep mode and someone had finally activated my life. Some people were just made to live without boundaries. I was one of them. I was a dreamer and I had been waiting for this moment of discovery, for this venture beneath the walls for years. No one knew about the sewer tunnels under the wall. The few who had tried to venture outside of their zones had tried to climb them. Syd was the architect of this plan. She had access to private files because of her father's position on The Panel, and we were exploiting it for one night of freedom, one night of cultural inclusion. I was psyched. "This way," I announced. I sounded more confident than I felt, but I knew if Minnie sniffed out even the slightest insecurity in my plan, she would abandon it. We walked through the sewer close to an hour, sometimes in circles, even though I insisted that I knew what I was doing. I hoped I knew. I marked our path along the way in red lipstick, that way our return trip would go smoother. It was quite easy to get lost in those tunnels, never to be heard from again and just as I began to feel that tickle of worry that made tears sting my eyes, we stumbled upon the exit Syd had suggested. We opened the steel door. It was so heavy, and hadn't been opened in so long, that it took both of us pulling with all our might to get it to crack even a bit. We rushed through it and then collapsed on the other side. The other side! We had made it, and as we sat heaving against the outside of the wall, a smile spread across my face. This was it. We were outside of Zone 7. I stood to my feet and took it all in, but it was too dark to make much of what was in front of me. Still, the air felt easier to breathe, freer, and I marveled it all the same.

"What now?" Minnie asked.

"There's an abandoned energy station about two miles north. Liam says we can't miss it."

"Two miles! What if someone sees us?" Minnie shouted.

"They'll certainly hear your big mouth first!" I snapped, covering her mouth with my hand. The areas between zones were called Interzones and they were always patrolled. "We'll stay off the main road. No one is out at this hour. Syd says Interzone patrollers make their rounds every hour on the hour. As long as we are out of sight when they pass by, we won't get caught. We'll be low-key."

"And the monsters?"

My chest tightened. It was the other thing that kept us all inside the walls. Humans were no longer at the top of the food chain. After decades of pumping animals with steroids for mass production, the animals began to mate and mutate. Humans tried to regulate their growth, and when it got out of control even tried to stop it, but it was too late. The damage couldn't be reversed. All of a sudden, what used to be a figment of a child's imagination was suddenly real. Monsters were born. We tried to keep them at bay. Hunting season came each year when the leaves turned from green to orange, but it was no longer legal to hunt any pure breeds. The hunters went after the monsters. The only animals that still lived amongst us were the ones we kept as pets, but the ones that were a threat to us dwelled outside the walls. They roamed between zones freely until they were killed by hunters or died off on their own. Some people thought that the mutated species were a myth. My dad thought it was a tale concocted by The Panel to keep the people zoned by using fear. Not many people had ever encountered a monster. I had never seen one, but I also had never stepped foot outside my zone. I could feel the adrenaline pumping in my veins. Maybe I hadn't thought this thing through, but I was the kind of girl who hated to admit when I was wrong. "Stop worrying. You're going to make me nervous. We'll be fine."

I led the way with fake confidence, appearing cooler than I felt. I was terrified. The darkness outside the zone seemed to be blacker than anything I'd ever seen. Without the city lights, it felt like we were the only people in the world. The sound of crickets surrounded us so loudly that it felt like they were playing a concerto that would be the soundtrack to my demise.

"What way is north?" Minnie asked. I looked to the sky. The stars were so hard to see. My parents often talked about a time when they were younger, they would sit under the stars all night. My mom said no great love could begin without looking up at the stars together, but I couldn't see them. So much pollution covered the earth now that the stars looked like specks, no longer shining brilliantly as my mom had described. They were no longer sonnet inspiring, but good enough to gather my bearings, however.

"This way."

"This stupid white boy better be worth it," Minnie fussed, as she followed me, tripping along. The Interzone was untamed land. It was a mixture of old highways that had been abandoned long before, and forest that had grown over them. The trees stretched high into the sky like skyscrapers growing through concrete. The road that snaked through it was a two-lane highway. I hugged the shoulder as I led the way. I really should have been off the road completely, but I was terrified of what lived in the depths of the forests. I would rather battle patrollers than monsters, so I didn't let the shadows completely envelop me as I walked.

"You don't know him. He's everything, Minnie. We would scope for hours every day. I can talk to him about anything. He just gets me, you know? Haven't you ever met someone that made you feel like your version of crazy was sane?"

"You can't feel that way about someone you've never even seen face to face. It's not real. What are you going to do? Sneak outside the zone every time you want to see him? He's white. You're black. The zones exist for a reason. You know what happened when we were all allowed to co-exist. Black people were killed. Killed by white people!" Minnie didn't get it. I heard her. I knew the history, just like everyone else, but who wanted to live like that? Sectioned off to avoid being hurt? To avoid the bad people? Everyone couldn't be lumped into a group. Bad. White. Killer. No! That was bull. I remember reading about black people killing black people too back in the day. The history books detailed those times as well. Some city named Chicago used to be called *Chi-raq*. Another, called Flint, had 20 murders in one summer! Those were black folks killing black folks, and you didn't see us sectioning ourselves off from ourselves? I just didn't get it. Zoning laws made zero sense to me.

"Liam's different. I have to believe that there are people in Zone 1, white people, who are different. We let one stupid president separate us. He made everyone think that the color of our skin mattered, and he was orange for God's sake!"

"Well, maybe color does matter, Neely! Maybe we're in

Zone 7 and this boy is in Zone 1 for a reason! Not everyone is supposed to get along."

I spun on my heels to face her. "We don't all have to get along, but we are all better than this. We're all human."

"I think that was the problem back then, Neel," Minnie said, as she passed me. "They forgot that black people were human. They shot us down like we were monsters."

I knew when I had no wins against Minnie. She had some personal issues regarding the subject. Her grandfather had been a victim of police brutality and her family held grudges. I could argue until I was blue in the face, and her opinion wouldn't change. So, we both just shut up.

"Get down," I hissed, as I saw the headlights to a car in the distance.

We slid down the steep bank on the side of the road.

"The flashlight!" I whispered. Minnie scrambled, across leaves and through a brush, as the yellow light illuminated into the air. She dove on top of it, covering it, as I waited to hear the car pass.

"Please, let him pass, please let him pass," I prayed. If I had seen the car's headlights, it was possible that the patroller might have seen the glow of the flashlights. When I heard the car door, my heart stopped. Creeping deeper into the trees, I hid behind one, but Minnie couldn't move. If she did, the light she was covering would give her away. Darkness enveloped her, and I could barely see the outline of her body if the patroller shined a light her way, we were done. The patroller went to his car and turned on a light, sweeping the area. I ducked behind the tree as it passed me by.

SCREECHHHHHHHH!

The sound was like ice and I froze, instantly, luckily so did the patroller's light. He whipped it toward the direction of the sound.

SCREECHHHHHHHH!

The patroller got in his car and sped away and I ran as fast as I could to Minnie's side.

"What is that?" Minnie wailed.

"Turn off the light," I warned. The quiver in my voice revealed my apprehension.

SCREECHHHHHHHHH!

"Is it a monster? It's a monster, isn't it?"

"I don't know," I whispered, but I did. We both knew. "Minnie, we have to run, and we have to do it in the dark. The light will just attract whatever is out there."

"I want to go back. Please, please, let's go back," Minnie cried.

"We're closer to the energy station than we are to Zone 7 now. If we can just get there, we'll be okay. We'll figure out how to get back when we meet with everyone else," I promised. "Now, let's get out of here. We have an hour before the patroller comes back around."

We took off running as fast as we could, lungs burning, as I kept whipping my head back to make sure that we weren't being chased.

"I think I see it!" Minnie called out. When I looked ahead, I slowed, laughing as a smile broke out on my face.

"We made it," I said. Minnie was bent over, her hands gripping her knees, as she gulped in air.

"Come on, we're almost there," I said. We walked the rest of the way, approaching the barbed wire fence that surrounded the tall factory. It was a remnant of a civilization that no longer existed. A time when people lived in the Interzone and the plant used to power everything around it.

"Over here!" Minnie called, as she climbed through a hole in the fence.

I followed and looked up at the tall building. The windows were broken, and it had been tagged with spray paint. I wondered by who. No one came out this far.

A light shined on us from behind and I turned, holding my hand up to shield the blinding beam.

"I didn't think you would actually have the balls to show, Zone 7."

"You want to get that light out of my eyes?" Minnie shouted.

"Oh, my bad," he said. He lowered it and it was the first time I was introduced to someone who didn't look like me.

"What's up, Jesus?" I smiled a mile wide. I took him in, observing him from the top of his low-cut head to the bottom of his Converse covered feet. He was slightly taller than me, and that's saying something because I'm tall for a girl, 5' 7''. He was cute in that, *I'm the most popular kid at school,* kind of way and from the charming smile he gave us, I knew he was aware.

"She's your babysitter?" Jesus said, with a nod to Minnie.

"My best friend," I corrected. "This is Minnie. Minnie, this is the dopest Puerto Rican kid I know."

Jesus laughed. "I'm the only Puerto Rican kid you know," he said.

"Exactly."

"Let's go find the others," Jesus said.

He climbed through a broken window and we followed. The factory was dark and wet. Despite the heat outside, there was a chill in the air.

"It's a real palace," Jesus said, as he wandered into the hallway.

"Hello!!" he shouted.

An echo returned. "Hello! Hello! Hello!"

"Shh…your voice carries in here. We'll have to be careful," I warned. Hands covered my eyes from behind.

"You wouldn't want to get caught."

I recognized his voice. It was him. It was Liam. I turned around and he held out his arms. I walked into them without hesitation. The hug was brief and friendly. He let go and slapped hands with Jesus.

"Glad you made it, my man," he greeted. He turned to Minnie. "The infamous bestie."

Minnie giggled. I laughed because I had never heard her giggle before, not like that. It was shy, but flirty and mixed with a whimsical blush that her dark skin didn't reveal. Apparently, Minnie liked that white boy's swag too. Liam had that effect on people. All he had to do was say hi for girls to feel special like that hello was the most special of all the hellos in the world. *Oh my God, I love himmm.*

"Where's Syd, Aziza, and Art?" I asked.

"They're already here. Upstairs," Liam said. "Come on."

He could have said, "Come on, let me lead you to trouble" or… "Come on, follow me off a cliff, and I would have been right behind him. I was so excited to see my friends, so geeked to smell them, touch them, hear them in real life. Our friendships had developed over scopes. We had gotten to know each other through pictures and videos, but this was the real thing. Never could I have known that Liam wore cologne by just speaking through our channel. I couldn't see that he had perfectly tanned skin and that there were specks of blonde in his brunette hair. Face scoping didn't show me that his eyes were green. I had been dreaming of a white boy with hazel eyes for months only to find out they were green. So, nope, nothing beat this connection to people different than me. I had never even assumed that Jesus would have an accent. We had only sent messages in the group scope, so I had never even face scoped with him. He was cool and his thick, Spanish brogue gave him character that I would have never imagined. We climbed to the top floor.

"I guess the gang is all here," said Aziza, with sarcasm. She hugged me first, then Jesus. "Who's this?"

"Minnie." Minnie held out her hand, with her name, and Aziza laughed.

"It's not a job interview, Minnie. What kind of name is that, anyway?" Aziza asked. "And I thought the idea was to keep this under the radar? We don't even know you. You should have come alone." Her eyes dared me to challenge her before I could get a word in.

It was the first time in my life that I thought about what I would say before I said it. Under normal circumstances, I would have checked her because I believed people established a pecking order at the very first meeting. She was trying to chump me and the black girl in me wanted to unleash my tongue and tell her about herself, but I had a stifling feeling inside. It was something I hadn't ever felt before. The need to not show all my blackness to people who didn't look like me because they probably wouldn't understand. It was odd because I was holding back, only giving these people, I called my friends, a glimpse of who I really was. I wasn't sure they could handle me at one hundred percent potency, so I dialed it back; filling myself with pieces of each of them, interacting with them on their level, of on my own. Somehow, it felt like black girl Neely would be frowned upon. It left me speechless because I didn't know how diluted Neely should respond.

"Excuse her, she was raised with wolves," Syd interrupted. "I'm Syd." Syd stuck out her hand for Minnie and Minnie shook it. Syd rolled her eyes at Aziza. "See, that's how people with manners greet one another."

Aziza stuck up a middle finger. That was another thing that hadn't change over the years. It was, is, and will always be, the universal symbol for screw you.

"Where's Arti?" I asked.

"He's not coming," Liam said. "He couldn't sneak out."

"What zone is he in?" Minnie asked.

"No one knows. He won't tell us. Just in case we're caught, he wants to protect himself," Syd piped in.

"Smart kid," Minnie mumbled.

Jesus held out two cases of beer. "Are we partying or what?"

"Yeah we are!" Syd exclaimed.

Jesus tossed a bottle my way and I caught it out of mid-air, as Liam came up behind me to grab one of his own. I didn't drink, not normally, but tonight was special. It was a celebration of freedom, of discovery. To that, I could drink. We all huddled in a circle. "To a life without limits and a life without walls," Liam said, raising his drink in a toast. We all drank to that. We sat in a circle, eyeing each other curiously.

"Why don't we play a game?" There was something mischievous about the way Liam proposed it and I looked up at him in intrigue.

"What kind of game?" I challenged.

"Truth or dare," Liam stated. "This might be our only night we get to be around people of a different race. We should make it one to remember."

"Okay, truth or dare?" I asked him.

"Truth," Liam answered.

"Is it true that white boys have small…"

"Whoa!!!" Liam held out his hand in protest, as the rest of the crew burst into laughter.

"Brains!" I finished. "I was going to say brains!" I held out my hands and shrugged, while feigning innocence.

"I can't speak for us all, but I have plenty of smarts, thank you very much," Liam defended, as a hint of amusement danced in his eyes.

"My turn," Aziza chimed in. "Truth or dare?" Her gaze was fixed on Minnie.

"Truth," Minnie countered.

"Is it true that you have lions as pets in Zone 7?" Aziza asked.

Minnie scoffed. "What? Do you think we wear Kente cloths and put bones through our noses too?"

Aziza shrugged. "I honestly don't know. I've heard so many rumors…"

"We're regular people, just like you. No lions," Minnie informed.

"Okay," Syd interrupted. "Since no one is obviously going to choose dare, why don't we just go around and tell one thing about ourselves…"

"Or… why don't we just cut to the chase and do something that will make us remember this night forever?" Jesus said, as he stood up and walked over to the glassless window. There was a bungee hanging out of it and my eyes followed it to the pole it was anchored to in the middle of the room.

"No way," I protested.

"I'm in," Syd added. "I'll even go first."

There's this feeling you get right before you're about to do something stupid. It's a gut-wrenching notion that makes you feel like you have to throw up. I climbed to my feet and walked over to the window, hanging halfway over the ledge, to analyze the fall.

"We're at least 20 stories up. If that thing doesn't hold, there's no surviving that fall." I couldn't believe the words had come out of my mouth. Minnie was normally my voice of reason, but the ground looked so far away, and the bungee looked so old. There was no telling how long it had been rotting in this building.

Jesus pulled the elastic cord with both hands, testing it. "It'll hold," he said. He scoured the room for the rest of the pieces, finally locating an ankle harness.

"Screw it! Hook me up!" Syd's eyes were wide with excitement.

"The Asian girl is an adrenaline junky, huh?" I asked.

"Absolutely," she agreed. Jesus wrapped the harness around her ankles, securing the straps tightly. I wasn't even the one going first, but my heart was going wild.

"This is crazy," I whispered.

"This is living," Liam cut in. Syd climbed up onto the ledge, and before any of us could make the decision that this was foolish, she jumped.

"Woo!! Hoo!!!!!" Her voice carried through the night, as we all raced to the edge and looked over. "Ha! Ha!" she laughed she bounced up and down, each drop causing me to close my eyes in hopes that nothing would go horribly wrong.

"Help me pull her up!" Jesus said. He and Liam pulled together, until Syd was in our reach. The rest of us pulled her into the window and she fell onto the floor, panting.

"How was it?" Aziza asked. I could see the anxiety dancing through her. Even Minnie had started gnawing on her fingernails, a nervous tell she did when she was either afraid or lying.

"Incredible!" Syd said, breathless. She reached for her ankle and released the harness. "Who's at bat?"

For some reason, Liam looked directly at me. He grinned and shot me a wink. "I'll do it."

"That's what I'm talking about!" Jesus said, as he hit his chest in excitement.

Liam sat on the ledge of the window and Jesus put the harness on Liam's ankles.

"I'm all good?" Liam asked.

I was like a deer in headlights, I watched him.

"On the count of three," Jesus coached…

"One," Aziza piped in.

"Two," Minnie added. I snapped my head in her direction, surprised she was even taking part in the antics.

Before anyone could say three, Liam rolled backward out the window.

"Whoa-ho! Woo!" There was no fear in his voice. All I heard was laughter and happiness. I had never heard such an uninhibited sound. It sounded like freedom. I was here, in the middle of the night, bungee jumping with my melting pot of friends. When his cord lost momentum, it took three of us to pull him up. He ran a hand through his perfect hair when he was back on his feet. His smile was contagious. I beamed as he walked directly up to me and grabbed the sides of my face. "Best feeling ever."

"Okay, I'm next. If I don't get it out the way, I'll never go." My voice shook, as I removed my backpack and handed it to Minnie. I couldn't pretend like I wasn't afraid, but I had to get it over with. No way would I be the one to punk out. Liam removed the harness from his ankles and attached it to me. My eyes teared and I pursed my lips before blowing out a sharp breath. My chest seized in absolute warning.

I swung my feet over the edge and looked down. The height alone made me dizzy.

"I don't know if I can. I can't, I can't." I was freaking out until I felt Liam's lips on the back of my neck.

"You can," he urged. I squeezed my eyes shut and I jumped.

"Oh, my godddddd!" My stomach plummeted, tickling all the way down and when the cord sucked me back up, I opened my eyes. "This is amazing!" I shouted, with laughter. I plunged like a yoyo, bouncing a few more times as the momentum waned. When I looked down toward the ground, all the fun stopped. Flashing red and blue lights glowed outside the gate and the sounds of a police siren filled the air.

"Someone's here!" I shouted. "It's a patroller!"

Syd's head popped out the window.

"That's not a patroller. That's a cop!" she hissed.

I panicked. Cops made patrollers look like mall security. They were the highest level of enforcement within the zones, and if we got caught, the rest of our lives would be ruined.

"Pull me up! Pull me up!"

"We've got to get out of here!" I heard them take off. Dangling in mid-air, I felt each second tick by torturously slow.

"We can't just leave her!" That was Minnie's protests.

"Minnie! Liam! Pull me up!" I cried. There was hesitation as I dangled there, then Liam looked down at me. I stretched my neck upward, meeting his eyes.

"Don't leave me!" I pleaded.

Liam nodded. "I won't. I promise."

CHAPTER 3

LIAM

Go! Get out of here!" I shouted to the others, as I pulled on the bungee cord to pull Neely back up. I could hear the footsteps of the officer echoing up the abandoned stairwell. He was getting closer and I didn't have much time. There was no point in everyone getting caught, but I couldn't leave without her.

"What about you?" Jesus asked.

"I'll be fine! Just go! There's a storm drain at the south entrance, right where the forest meets the fence. We'll meet you there. If we're not out in 15 minutes, run!"

Minnie hesitated as Jesus tried to pull her away.

"I'm not leaving her!" Minnie shouted.

"Just go! We'll meet you guys! I promise!" I urged. I could see her reluctance, as Jesus dragged her away, down the opposite stairwell. I struggled to pull Neely up, my hands climbed over one another, as I inched her up.

"Hey, kid! Put your hands up!"

I stopped pulling, but my hands held tight to the cord, I looked at him. His gun was drawn, and I looked from the rope to him, then from him to the rope.

"Don't make me shoot you, kid! Put your hands up!" His white face was beet red, as he gave the order. There was a gun in my face, I was out of zone, yet the threat didn't seem real. I still felt entitled to live, to breathe, like who was this guy to shoot me? My life mattered. My life was valuable. I belonged to someone. I had people who would demand answers if I was harmed. No, his bullets weren't meant for people like me. I knew it, and so did he, which is why the trigger had yet to be pulled.

"Liam!"

The sound of Neely's voice caused the officer to scoot toward the ledge. His gun was still pointed, as he eyed me, then peered over the edge, only allowing enough time for a quick glance. It was the distraction I needed to take off. I let go of the bungee cord and bolted. I didn't think he had the gumption to shoot me in the back. The sound of Neely's screams pierced the air, as she took the plunge all over again. I raced to the floor directly below Neely and looked up as the cop began pulling her up by the cord.

"Liam!" she yelled. There was fear in her voice, fear that sounded different than what I was feeling. She was screaming for her life.

"Unhook the harness!" I shouted. Her eyes filled with terror.

"I can't!" she screamed. The cop was pulling her up, inching her closer and closer toward the window. If she didn't release the harness, she would be caught, if she did, she would free fall.

"I'll catch you. You have to trust me! You know what happens if we get caught."

The tears in Neely's eyes shone, as she stared at me. She reached for her ankle and pulled at the buckles.

"Agh!!!"

I barely caught her outstretched hand at the fingertips, and she hung wildly, kicking her legs, as she looked at me in dismay.

"Argghhh," I grit my teeth, as I reached down with my other hand. The jagged glass from the bottom of the broken window sill dug into my stomach, as I pulled her up. Her feet slid against the side of the building, as she tried to help, tried to gain a footing.

"I don't want to die!" she cried out, as we struggled to keep our hands connected. I could feel her slipping. The look in her eyes told me she could too. I put all my weight on the window sill, as the glass stabbed into me, and I pulled. She came through the window, and we fell backward. I landed on my back and she landed on top of me. I was stunned, as I looked up at her.

"I thought you were going to leave me," she said.

"Never," I replied. Our eyes locked and I swear my heart skipped a beat. I had never seen eyes that matched that color of someone's skin. She was dark and there was a depth in those eyes that had me stuck. Neely was the prettiest girl I'd ever seen. I knew it from face scoping, I had noticed it instantly when she would send selfies to the group scope, but seeing her in person, up close, was like watching the sunset. A photo just didn't do it justice.

"We've got to go," she whispered urgently, as she scrambled to her feet. I grimaced, as I stood, gripping my stomach, and then pulling away a wet hand.

"You're bleeding!" she exclaimed.

"I'm fine! Go!"

We ran toward the stairwell, but the barrel of a handgun stopped us in our tracks.

"Get your hands up! Both of you!" the cop said. "On the ground." With Neely at my side, the look in his eyes had changed. Gone was the man who was reluctant to kill. He almost sneered at Neely. He kept the handgun trained in her direction. Her hands shot into the air. My hands were at my side, but Neely's were high, palms facing forward. She steeled in place as if it was instinct for her to assume the position. I smelled trepidation. That moment when you know your life is about to change. This was it. What should have been a night of fun had gone horribly wrong, but still, I couldn't regret it because I had seen the sunset up close. I had basked in a shade of melanin so rich that it felt like some of it had rubbed off on me. She was brilliant. Neely was worth it.

"On the ground! Don't make me say it again!"

Neely was shaking. I could see her trembling, as she lowered to her knees. The officer dug his boot into her back, forcing her face to the ground hard.

"Hey, bro! She's down! You don't have to do all that!" I shouted, as I lowered onto my stomach. Our faces were flat on the ground, gravel dug into my cheek, and my knees scraped the concrete.

"We're just out here fooling around!" I shouted. "Is this really necessary?" It all felt like overkill to me. I wanted answers. I wanted to know why he had us face down like criminals. Why was the loaded gun in his hands? We were kids. He couldn't feel that threatened by us. What was this about?

"Liam, please, pleeaase, be quiet. Just do what he says."

I stared in her eyes. Neely was crying. The vulnerability in her voice caused her words to rattle, as she choked them out.

"It'll be okay," I whispered. I don't even think she could see me through the tears clouding her vision. Her lip quivered, as the cop moved on to her. He bent over her and ran his hands up her body. She squeezed her eyes shut, sobbing, and I watched as his hands lingered in places he shouldn't touch. Between her legs, he lingered, rubbing, groping, squeezing, as grunts of sick satisfaction escaped his lips. He was disgusting.

"Yo! Man! Stop touching her like that!" I protested.

The cop sneered and returned his focus to me, patting my body quickly and nowhere near as intimately as he had done to Neely. He pulled my channel from my pocket and checked my identification.

"Liam Witten," he said. "Get up!"

I stood and went to help Neely.

"Just you!" he stated. I dusted myself off and looked him in the eyes. "You're a long way from Zone 1. Get out of here and don't let me catch you out here ever again. Forget about tonight." The cop jammed my channel into my chest. I couldn't believe I was getting a pass.

"Come on, Neely!" I bent down to help her up, but the cop pushed me away.

"I didn't say she could go. Get out of here! I'm taking her into custody!"

"What? That's not fair! Just let us go! We won't come back!" I reasoned.

"You either get out of here or you're getting locked up with her!" the cop barked.

Neely was sobbing, face down on the concrete floor, and I looked down at her in pity.

"I'm not leaving her! So, arrest me!" I stuck my wrists out. No way could I sell her out like that. I had invited her here. This entire rendezvous was my idea. I heard the click of the safety on the gun being released, as the cop held it point blank to my head. It was a sobering moment. My life didn't flash before my eyes. I didn't think of everything I had yet to do. Things just slowed down, as if someone had hit a slow-motion button on my life. I analyzed the entire situation in a millisecond because that was all the time I had before this trigger, this gun, this coward ended me. If I hadn't realized how bad things were before, I knew now. I understood the look I had seen in Neely's eyes. It was like she knew all along that things would end deadly with this cop as if she were predisposed to unjust punishment, or at the very least, had expectations for it. I didn't live in a reality where cops put guns to the heads of teenaged kids, or where they could run their hands over the private mounds of the flesh of young girls. The look in Neely's eyes told me she did. The feel of the gun against my head told me, I now did as well.

"Go back to Zone 1 and pretend like you were never here. I'm trying to cut you a break, kid."

I backpedaled with my hands up, as my eyes bounced from Neely to the cop, back to Neely. It was so messed up. I was being let off and Neely was taking the fall for everybody. I did the only thing I could. I ran.

NEELY

He left me. He freaking left. I felt the cop plant a knee into my back, as he hovered over me. The heaviness seized my lungs, crushing me, killing me. I couldn't breathe. It was like I was sucking air through a straw and the desperation to just suck in one gulp of air made me panic. His hands between my legs made me cry even harder. This wasn't an arrest. This was an assault. Suddenly, the words of my father popped into my mind. This was the misuse of power that he had warned me about. White cop. Black girl. Alone. I knew I wouldn't come out of this unscathed. This cop was putting mental chains on me, taking me back to a time when his entitlement to my body was his right instead of his crime. A feeling that hadn't existed for me within the safe walls of Zone 7, filled me for the first time. Inequality. This encounter, this one man had knocked down my self-worth and implanted an inadequacy inside me that I had never known. I wasn't aware that my melanin was a weapon. It was like yielding a knife, or a gun, when in the presence of cops like this one. I was his target and I was trapped. Liam had been let off with a warning and

I was about to find out the price to pay for daring to defy the rules. I grit my teeth, as he pulled at my pants.

"Please. Don't do this," I begged. "Please." I felt the air on my skin, as my pants were pulled down beneath my thighs, and then felt the kiss of cold steel against the back of my head.

"Don't move. You stay right here." His voice was cold, but the lust I heard in his tone was terrifying. I'd rather have him pull the trigger than to do what I thought he was about to do. I heard the sound of a buckle, as he undid his belt.

"Aghh!" He was tackled to the ground and I rolled over to find Liam grappling with the cop. The gun slid across the concrete. Liam grabbed a pipe from the floor and swung it, hitting the cop square in the face, but the man was twice Liam 's size. It stunned him, but didn't stop him. I hurriedly adjusted my clothes, as I watched in horror as Liam swung again. This time, the cop caught the pipe, snatching it from Liam 's hands and rushing him. Liam 's back was against the wall, the pipe was against his throat, as the cop pushed with all his might.

"You shouldn't have turned back, kid," the cop sneered.

I rushed to the gun. It was like I was moving in slow motion before I could even think about another solution, I aimed. I pulled.

BANG!

The cop fell into Liam and they both crashed to the floor. Liam scrambled away from the cop, as he gripped his throat, gulping in air. The gun suddenly felt heavy and my hands released it, sending it to the ground. I covered my mouth in horror, as blood pooled beneath the man.

"What have I done?"

Liam rushed to my side. "Is he dead?" I was distraught. I was sick. I could feel it in my stomach. The dread.

I walked over to the cop and watched as Liam leaned down to check his pulse.

"He's alive!" Liam said.

I didn't know if that was a good or bad thing, but I couldn't leave him there. I couldn't just walk away. I knelt at the cop's side.

"We have to help him," I shouted.

My knees landed in the blood. It soaked through my jeans, as I pressed my hands into the hole in his uniform, trying to stop the bleeding. There was so much of it. There was too much of it and it gushed through my fingertips. "I shot him! If he dies, that's murder!" I screamed. "Help me!"

Liam stood back; his hands fisted on the sides of his head in distress. "We can't, Neely. We've got to go." He pulled at my arm, but I snatched away.

"I can't!" I shouted. He was a bad man. He was the worst type of man, but I wasn't like him. I couldn't just let him die.

"You have to!" Liam said. "He's the only person that can put us here. If we don't leave now, right now, Neely, our lives are over. We can't save him." I stood. I knew what he said was true and I closed my eyes. I could see my entire life flash before them. It wasn't a cliché. It really happened. I wasn't the one dying, but I may as well be because nothing after this day would ever be the same. Tears streamed down my face. "Come on." Liam pulled me away and I let him. I don't know why I felt guilty leaving him there. Had Liam not come back, I was certain the cop would have hurt me, maybe even killed me because the way he put his hands on my body was such an abuse of power that I don't think he would have left me alive to tell about it. Still, I felt like the scum of the earth walking out. I couldn't help but take one last look at him. That officer was danger personified. I had seen up close exactly what my dad had recounted in his stories. "F*$% the police," he often said. "F*$%, f*$%, f*$% the police." I had even heard him say it in a cadence, dismissing it as a song from the *good ol' days*," but I heard the conviction in his tone when he said it. He meant those words and as I thought about the way the cop's hands felt against my skin as he forced my jeans down, I concurred, I understood. It was "US" versus "THEM."Cops like the one I had encountered were the reason why zones existed, but if I gave into the notion that separation was okay, then Liam would be lumped into the "THEM" category and that was someplace he didn't belong. Helplessness seized me, as I ran behind Liam gripping his hand tightly, as I tried to keep up. I don't even know how my legs held me up. They were shaking, my entire body trembled. I couldn't stop the quake of emotion that was spilling out of me. Liam stopped running and turned toward me. He cupped my face and said, "I'm not going to let anything happen to you. I swear. Everything will be fine." When he swiped my cheek with his thumb, I realized I was crying. My one interaction with an officer outside my zone had rattled me to my core. I felt violated, I felt terrorized, like someone had broken into the comfort of my home and stolen my sense of security. In a way, that was exactly what had occurred. My peace had been tainted, my self-worth diminished, and this was only from one encounter with one cop. I couldn't imagine how people of color used to feel when this was an everyday occurrence. I couldn't even fathom feeling safe if I had to trust my protection every day to men like that one. "Come on!" I followed because I couldn't go back. I couldn't rewind. I couldn't erase the chain of events that had led to this point, so instead of going back, I went forward. When the crack of lightning illuminated the sky, tears began to pour from the sky, or at least that's what it felt like. My pain was palpable, and the universe could feel it. Melodramatic, maybe but hey, what 17-year-old girl doesn't think the world revolves around her? Liam ran so fast that my feet couldn't keep up. When we got to the gate, we half slid, half fell down the slope before running into the storm drain.

"Neely!"

When I saw Minnie, I rushed into her arms, embracing my friend for dear life.

"Please tell me you have my bag," I said. My channel was inside, and if it was found in the building with the body, there would be no point in running.

"Of course," she said, handing it over. I slid the backpack on my shoulders, sighing in semi-relief. That was only one of many worries.

"Was that a gunshot?" Aziza shouted.

"Bro, is that blood?" Jesus asked.

Syd shined her flashlight over me.

"Oh, my God! What did you do? What happened up there?" Syd asked.

"He attacked Neely. He had his hands all over her, and when I tried to stop him, he attacked me," Liam's words ran out his mouth so quickly as if they wouldn't believe his explanation.

"I shot him," I stammered, as I held onto Minnie.

"It was self-defense!" Liam was the only witness to the act that would ruin all of our lives. Aziza's hands flew to her mouth, in stun, as Jesus bent down in disbelief, his hands rested on top of his head.

"This is bad. This is really bad," Syd said. "This was supposed to be fun!"

"What do we do?" Minnie asked.

"What do you mean *we*? She killed that cop all by herself. That has nothing to do with the rest of us," Aziza snapped.

"Hey!" Liam shouted. "If Neely hadn't pulled that trigger, then that cop would have killed me. He would have killed her too. I saw what he tried to do to her. He couldn't let me walk away after that. She had no choice!"

I was grateful that someone was still on my side. I understood their reluctance. Nobody wanted to be associated with what I had done. I didn't even want to be me right now.

"We all just need to get back to our zones and pretend like this never happened. We take it to our graves. We don't tell anyone about this. Not our parents, friends, no one."

"I'm not covering for anybody! I didn't have anything to do with this!" Aziza shouted.

"We're all in this!" Liam shouted.

"Umm, guys…" Minnie couldn't get a word in edge wise.

"I didn't want to hurt anybody!" I shouted.

"Umm, guys," Minnie's timid words were ignored, again.

"Yeah, well, shot a cop! You can't expect us to go along with that!" Aziza was the only one protesting, but I could tell Jesus and Syd shared her sentiments.

"Umm, guys!" Minnie was louder, more forceful this time.

"What?!" We all snapped at her in unison.

"What's that sound?" Minnie's eyes were wide and alert as we all froze to listen. The trickle of the water in the bottom of the sewer had been the only sound I had noticed before, but this sounded like something was moving, scratching along through the tunnels and splashing along the way.

SWOOSH! SWOOSH! SWOOSH! The sound seemed to echo off the wall. We were standing in an apex that connected four sewage tunnels and I couldn't tell where it was coming from. The fear of the unknown made my throat go dry, and I swallowed down the ball that had suddenly lodged there, stopping my voice.

"What is that?" I managed. The hair on the back of my neck stood as the sound stopped. Nobody spoke. We all stood paralyzed, bracing ourselves, as if we were playing chicken with whatever was in the tunnels, trying to see who would retreat first…us or it.

SCREECHH!!!!

It was the same sound Minnie and I had heard before.

SWOOSH! SWOOSH! SWOOSH! Whatever it was, it was on the move again. We shined our lights down the corridors, frantically searching for the direction, desperate to find the origin of this noise.

SCREECHHHHH!!

This time, we all turned in the same direction. The sound was right on top of us, and as we all pointed our lights together, it became crystal clear.

"Run!" Jesus shouted. Liam took my hand and led the way as we took off, stumbling in the dark, as our flashlights bounced off the wet walls.

SWOOSH!! SWOOSH!! SWOOSH!! SWOOSH!!!

"What is that?!" I shouted, afraid to look back as I ran as fast as I could. Had I seen what I thought I had? It was some creature, some monster, a snake, but no, snakes didn't have teeth, snakes weren't that big or black. It wasn't a snake, but it was something and it almost filled the width and height of the sewer; its body sliding through the sewer tunnels just barely fitting. Our heavy steps splashed through the dirty water. I was slowing Liam down. The others passed us, running full speed as he tried to compensate for my speed by dragging me along. I could hear the snapping of teeth as it lunged at us, trying to catch me, the weakest link between its rows of sharp teeth. Suddenly, the cop seemed like the least of my worries.

"Leeches!" Jesus shouted. "Go! Go!"

My heart burned in exhaustion as I struggled to keep up. We all had heard of the things that lived in the sewers, but it was supposed to be a myth, they weren't real. The dog bones and dead squirrels that had been turning up by storm drains for years had been dismissed, but this was real, this was very real, and I cursed myself for daring to even sneak out of bed tonight. Thinking I could leave my zone without consequence was stupid. I couldn't die down here. No one would ever find me. My parents wouldn't even know where to begin looking. I'd be more bones at the edge of storm drains that people dismissed. An opening was up ahead. I could see the moonlight shining through the gated exit ahead, but it didn't feel like I would make it. I could feel this thing crawling down my back, so close to catching me that I could feel gusts of wind from its mouth each time it clamped down in an attempt to catch my feet.

"Run, Neely!" Liam shouted. The others were already at the storm drain, slipping through the gate to safety, one by one.

"Run! Go! Run!" They all shouted, but I knew I was in trouble just from the tone of Minnie's cries. It was like I picked hers out of the crowd to focus on and the shrill in her voice told me I wasn't moving fast enough. I made the mistake of glancing back and my mouth fell open in horror as I stumbled. The feeling of my hand slipping from Liam's terrified me and I hit the ground hard; the shallow, dirty water doing nothing to soften the fall. When I looked up my breath caught in my throat. Liam stopped running and I looked back at him as he halted, feet spread, one foot facing away from me, the other toward me in indecision. Panic spread across his face.

"Go!" I shouted.

"Neely!" Minnie cried.

SCREEECHHHH!!!

The leech was on top of me. Hovering above me as it stopped right in front of me. It was inches from devouring me as I sat, leaned back on my elbows, heaving in terror, as I waited. I closed my eyes, feeling the warmth from my tears that slid down my face.

SCREECHHH!!!!!!!!!

The sound was deafening and then it was gone. I opened my eyes, as Liam scrambled to pull me to my feet, but I couldn't will my body to move. I just backpedaled, stumbling with every step, as Liam pulled me through the murky water. I gaped at the black hole where the monster had retreated. I fell to my hands and knees as soon as I was on the other side of that gate, gasping out of disbelief that I was even still breathing. Minnie threw her arms around me.

"It just stopped! It just turned away!" Syd shouted, in disbelief.

Liam stood above me, pulling air into his lungs, as he rested his hands on his knees. I looked up at him in disbelief.

"You didn't leave me."

"I told you, never," he replied. The sound of sirens rang out in the night air. "We've got to get out of the open. We'll figure out how to get back to our zones, but first we have to get off this main road." He held out his hand, and I grabbed it, allowing him to pull me to my feet, we all began to walk into the trees. Minnie hesitated, and I stopped to look back at her.

"If that thing was in the sewer, what do you think is out there? Maybe we should turn ourselves in and just explain to the cops what happened," she reasoned.

"They won't listen, Minnie," I pleaded. "Liam probably can beat this. Syd's dad is on The Panel, she'll be fine, but you and I, and even Jesus... we'll burn for this. We have to keep moving."

Jesus piped up. "She's right."

Minnie nodded and reluctantly followed us into the woods. Each of us holding a different terror in our hearts.

CHAPTER 4

NEELY

We walked so deeply into the forest that we could no longer hear the sirens. We were silent. The only sounds that could be heard were the wild ones around us.

"Yo, this is far enough. We don't even know where we're walking to. We need to get back to our zones," Jesus said.

I looked up at the moon, I stepped over to the lake it reflected over. Liam walked over to my side. It seemed that was where he was most comfortable, next to me, and I was grateful because he calmed my fear.

"Umm, guys. We're in trouble," Syd said. She pulled her channel from her bag and held it up for us to see. We all gathered.

"A federal police officer was gunned down this evening in the Interzone. This is a live event and the shooter is still at large. The police have no suspects at this time, but they are canvassing the area around the old energy station. The Panel has ordered a count of each zone to find out if there has been a breach outside of zoned areas and to help bring this heroic officer's killer to justice."

My heart sank, as I stared at the news report.

"This is bad," I whispered, as I put my hands on top of my head in dismay. "This is really bad."

"There is no sneaking back now, patrollers and cops are going to be everywhere! We won't make it back without being caught," Aziza shouted.

"And it's only a matter of time before the count is off and they know exactly who's missing. We're screwed," Jesus added.

"What do we do?" Minnie asked.

"The news is wrong! They're lying! He was all over her. He was going to…"

"We don't have proof! The way it's being reported, it looks like you shot a cop in cold blood!" Aziza argued.

Our channels rang out, one by one, individually, and I snatched mine from my backpack to silence it quickly. Arti's face was on my screen. I accepted the face scope.

"Please tell me that what I'm watching on the news isn't you guys," he said. "What is all over your face?"

His tone was playful, but when I didn't return his joking sentiments, his face turned serious.

"Wait a minute. Please, tell me you guys didn't!"

"*We* didn't do anything," Aziza stressed. "Neely killed the cop."

Arti stood and ran to his room door to close it. He brought his face close to the channel and lowered his voice. "What do you mean?! How did this happen?"

"It was self-defense," Liam corrected. "The cop attacked us."

"Good luck with that story," Aziza shot, sarcastically.

"What is your problem?" Minnie shouted, as she pushed Aziza.

Aziza pushed her back. "My problem is all of this! All of you! I can't be involved in this!"

Liam and Jesus struggled to pull them apart. "You're already involved. In a few hours, our names will be all over the news. Just let me think," Liam said.

"You need proof. Were there functional cameras at the energy station?" Arti asked.

"I don't know," I whispered. "It was abandoned. I didn't think to look for cameras."

"I didn't see any. The place was pretty busted," Jesus said.

"This is a digital age. There are cameras everywhere, even when you think there aren't. I'll hack into the federal database and see if I can scrape together footage of the attack," Arti said.

"You can do that?" I asked.

"I can try," Arti responded.

Liam added. "We need you to do more than try, Arti. Our lives depend on it."

"I'm on it. In the meantime, stay off the roads. The areas they are searching are closer to the roads. I'll keep you guys updated. Be careful."

Arti disconnected.

"Even if he comes up with something we're still on the hook for being in the Interzone," Aziza said. She was a *glass half empty* kind of girl, but I couldn't say I blamed her. She was scared. We all were.

"We've got to get to Zone 2," Liam said.

Everyone looked at Syd. "Your dad. He can help. If we get the evidence, he can help us prove it was self-defense," Jesus said, hopeful.

Syd nodded.

"There's no way we can get there tonight. I would rather navigate these woods in the daylight. We don't know what's out there. Whether we like it or not, our names will be discovered after they finish sweeping each zone. We have to make our way to Zone 2 and when Arti finds footage, we'll find a way to sneak in and show it to your father."

I could have picked a million holes in Liam's plan, but I remained silent. It was the only one we had and even if I didn't think it would work, we had to try.

"And what do we do tonight? We are in the middle of nowhere," Minnie said.

"We make camp here and we sleep in shifts. At day break, we head to Zone 2," Liam said.

"My dad will help us. I know he will. We just have to make it there," Syd assured.

"How? The quickest way is through the tunnels under the zones. They'll be swarmed with patrollers and cops," Aziza protested.

"We'll just have to find another way in," Syd said.

"We should sleep. Not all at once. I'll take the first watch. You guys try to rest," I offered. Liam walked over to me.

"I'll take the first shift with you," he said.

We sat on the ground, as the others tried their best to sleep.

"How screwed are we?" I asked.

"Pretty screwed," he concurred.

"Challenges build character." I smiled because it was the answer my dad always gave my mom when things seemed tough. God, I missed them. I wondered if I would ever make it home to them, home to that little, crowded house, home to my zone where I was safe behind the walls. My laughter faded, as I thought about what I had gotten myself into, what I had gotten us all into. "You think we should have just stayed behind the walls?" I asked.

Liam gazed at me, and I couldn't break the stare if I tried. "Is this where the guy leans in to kiss the girl?"

He smirked. "Maybe if you weren't covered in mud and blood," he said. "Come on. Let's get you cleaned up." We walked around the rim of the lake. We were out of earshot of the others. I knelt to splash water over my arms. Out of nowhere, he nudged me, sending me flying into the cold lake, face first. The shock of that first contact of water on dry skin was exhilarating. It made me feel alive.

"I'm going to kill you!" I shouted, with laughter as I splashed him. He took off his shirt and stepped out of his jeans, exposing his strong body. He wore his athleticism well. He ran into the lake before diving underwater. I swam toward him laughing, as he pulled me under. I bounced up, flipping my hair backward, as I reached for his neck, squealing from the frigid temperature.

"This is the part where the guy kisses the girl," he said. I looked up at the sky, hoping for those stars my mom told me about. There wasn't one in sight. I focused on Liam.

"Not quite," I returned, inching out of his reach and wading back toward the shore. When I could stand, I splashed my skin with water, making sure to get clean before climbing out. I took my backpack and hid behind the trunk of a tree, as I hurried into my change of clothes.

Wringing the water out my curly hair, I put it in a bun on top of my head. Liam came out the water and dressed quickly before we rejoined the others. Liam's energy was magnetic. I gravitated towards him. Even as we sat, in silence, my hand found its way to his. We were too sleepy to make conversation, so we just sat there with my head on his shoulder, and our fingers intertwined. Black skin on white skin, touching freely for the first time in decades.

"Neely?"

I looked up at him.

"I know you're at the center of all this. I know out of us all you'll be judged the most and it's all built on *bs* prejudice. What I'll never understand is how people look at you and feel hate. Your skin, the shade, the tone, I've never seen anything like it. It's beautiful. You're beautiful. It's the world that's ugly. I just want you to know even when we turn ourselves in, even when it gets bad and all eyes are on you, I'll be right there with you. Maybe this was supposed to happen. Maybe something drastic needed to happen. Maybe we use this, use you, to get people to change. Maybe you and me, we bring this whole jacked up system crashing down," he whispered.

It sounded good, but I knew it probably wouldn't end up that way. Still, it was a nice thought. It was a dream. "Maybe, one day," I sighed.

Liam placed a finger under my chin and tilted my head. We were so close that I could feel his weighted breaths.

Butterflies tormented my stomach. This bond, this chemistry between us was electrifying. It made me feel like I was falling, terrifying me yet exhilarating me all the same. "But there are no stars," I whispered. "My mom said all first kisses should happen under the stars."

"Yeah, there are. They're in your eyes," he said, as his lips touched mine. I closed my lids and he was right, there they were…stars.

"Aghh!!!" The scream broke through the still night, destroying our moment, and I pulled away. I jerked out his embrace and looked across the lake to the camp ground. I saw flames dancing in the darkness, surrounding them.

"Are those torches?" I whispered in angst.

I took off in their direction, thinking of Minnie. She was only out here because of me, because she was being a good friend, following me, being loyal to me and if anything ever happened to her…God, I didn't even want to finish the thought. Liam was on my heels. The darkness and the sounds of the waves gently lapping the shore concealed our approach. I stopped abruptly, about 15 yards away from the campground and hid in the brush of the trees.

"Those aren't cops," I whispered, eyes wide as I took in the scene. Men with sage colored skin circled our friends, holding them hostage with spears. Their torches cast an eerie glow, their grunts of aggression caused Minnie and the rest of the crew to huddle together, back to back, forming a circle.

"It's The Navarra," Liam replied.

"Is this native land?" I asked, my eyes widening in fear. The natives governed themselves. They followed their own laws, living on reservations and The Navarra Tribe was the most lethal of them all. To walk onto a reservation uninvited was dangerous. "Liam is this…" I turned to him and my words glued themselves to my throat. He was hemmed up by a man with black face paint, warrior markings, I had learned in some book I had read. The glint of a knife shined, as it pressed into Liam's neck, a small trickle of blood flowed. I lifted my hands, palms forward, in submission.

"Please. We're just passing through." I don't even know how I found my voice to say those words, but it was all I could manage before I felt a strong hand grab my waist from behind. My mouth and nose were covered with a cloth before everything faded to black.

A throbbing pain coerced me to open my eyes and when I did, the world swayed back and forth. I squinted, trying to stop the swaying and make sense of what I was seeing. Everything was upside down. Or was I upside down? As I came to, I felt the tightness that shackled my ankles. As I shook the haze from my mind, I realized I was bound at the feet; a thick tweed rope burned into my skin as I hung from a tree. I twisted frantically, as I scanned my surroundings. My friends were all hanging in the same position, they were not yet conscious. The throbbing in my head matched the cadence of the drums that echoed through the trees. The men who beat them were bare chested, cloth draping their bodies as the sun glistened over their strong chests. Their bald, shaven heads were terrifying, only a strip of hair decorated their scalps; it was braided down their backs with intricate feathers intertwined. The rest of the tribe was gathered around us, encircling us, as they looked up at us in awe. One man stood directly in front of them all. A headpiece full of brilliant colored feathers adorned his head, his long black hair was centered parted and fell over his shoulders all the way to the ground. A bird, the biggest one I had ever seen, sat atop of his left shoulder. "Is that a bald eagle? Where are we?" I whispered, as I peered straight ahead. I didn't recognize these woods. The trees were red and stretched as far as I could see. The clearing that this tribe stood on seemed to be the only place where trees hadn't grown.

"I am Adoeete, chief of The Navarra people. You are a foreigner on Navarra land. Who sent you?"

"N…no…no one," I stammered. "It was a mistake. We didn't know we were trespassing."

"Cut her down," Adoeete's voice bellowed over the entire forest. I saw a man point a bow and arrow toward me.

"No! Wait!" I flinched. He released it, sending an arrow flying directly at me. He hit the rope with ease, sending me plummeting to the ground. I screamed. I was at least 30 feet in the air. Unlike the bungee jump, this free fall would kill me. I heard a whistle leave Adoeete's lips, the bird left his shoulder and flew toward me. My eyes had to be playing tricks on me because I could have sworn it became larger, almost quadrupling in size. It snatched me out of midair, capturing me between its talons. Terror gripped me, I held on tight as the bird ascended to heights unknown. I could barely breathe, the wind whipped through my hair from the speed. I looked around frantically, trying to recognize something, anything, that could give me any indication of where I was. It all looked foreign. I didn't even see any walls. Even the energy station had disappeared.

"Whoa!" Gravity shifted and the eagle plunged suddenly. "Ohhhhhh mmmmm geeeeee…." It was like the drop of the steepest roller coaster ride, only I wasn't wearing a seatbelt. I pinched my eyes closed, but when I felt his talons opening, I screamed. "Wait! No!" We were closer to the ground, but still too high for me to fall. I held on with all my might, but when I felt my feet begin to dangle, my grip began to slip.

I plummeted to the ground, screaming the entire way. "Aghh!!!!!" The fall knocked the wind from my lungs.

"Please. We just want to pass through. We meant no harm," I said.

I was under the scrutiny of his intense gaze, as two members of his tribe pulled me up. Standing me on my feet, they held me up, one on each side.

"Wall people have no place here. To infiltrate our land, violate our rules, is punishable by death. The last time our people allowed that, your kind brought war, disease, and cursed our tribes. Any last words before you are judged by Navarra Law?"

"We're kids. We don't want war. We don't want anything. We just want to go home," I pleaded.

BRNNNNNNNNNNNNN!

The horn that blared through the air caused the entire tribe to form a tight circle around me and the chief.

Thunder and lightning ripped through the sky, suddenly, the entire tribe looked up. I turned to my friends, who were still unconsciously swinging from limbs of trees by their feet. Every member of the Navarra tribe lifted their eyes to the sky, and when I lifted mine, bewilderment filled my heart.

"What the…?"

The sky rippled like waves in the water. I saw police officers walking above us in the sky. My mouth was fixed in an *O*. I was stupefied. It was like I was looking through a two-way mirror, watching the police scour the area where my friends and I had been captured. They were around the lake, but it played out like a movie above my head in the sky. "Where are we?"

"You see what you've brought here?! Invaders!" Adoeete barked. "Cut them down. Cage them until I return." His stare was on me, again. I couldn't respond because I knew he was right. I had lured the police onto their land inadvertently. They were searching for me, a cop killer. I waited for his wrath, but when his eyes turned red, I was mystified because he disappeared before my eyes. Suddenly, my arms were free; the men beside me had disappeared as well. In their place were three bald eagles, soaring upward into the sky. I was apprehended by tribesmen, but I no longer cared. My feet shuffled, as I kept my eyes on the sky, on the men who had transformed into birds right before my eyes. I shook my head. I had to be dreaming. This couldn't be real. Maybe I had hit my head harder than I thought when I was shot down from the trees. Maybe all of this was a dream; the entire night, from the cop killing to me escaping my zone, but the feeling of doom in my gut told me that this was very real. I didn't know how, but I was discovering that the impossible was possible. I was thrown in a barricade made of logs that had been bound by rope, and I watched between the tiny spaces in between the wood as my friends were shot down one by one. When they were thrown inside with me, Minnie ran to me, hugging me, as she cried. "Where are we?" she yelped.

"I don't know," I answered, truthfully. "But we're in trouble."

Liam looked at me, stared right through me, and I shook my head as a tear slipped from my eye. "We're never going to make it home," I whispered.

"Did you see their daggers?! One of them has a necklace of teeth, human teeth!" Jesus shouted.

"Shut up before they come in here and add our teeth to the collection!" Aziza snapped. It was the first time all night I had agreed with her.

"What do we do?" Syd asked.

I had no answers, but my heart settled slightly when Liam said, "We stay calm. We can't panic. If we panic, we die." He sounded calm. At least one of us was level headed because I was freaking out.

The ground began to rumble, and I held my hands out in an attempt to keep my balance, as the dirt floor dissolved into shades of blue. Clouds were under our feet. The sky was under us. Wonder filled my eyes. This had to be a dream. No way was this real.

"What's happening?" Syd screamed. I peered through the slits of the barricade again, as I saw the three eagles shoot up from the ground, or was it the sky? I didn't quite know. What I thought was up could be down. What I thought had been the sky before, had turned to water, and now the earth was turning to the sky. I was losing my mind. None of it made sense. It was illogical, impossible…it was magical. "He's back," I whispered.

"Who?" Liam shouted. I pointed to the sky as the birds soared above us.

"Him," I said. Adoeete landed in human form right in the middle of the imprisonment, cracking the ground, which had restored itself to dirt and gravel upon impact. I was too enthralled to be afraid and too afraid to be this enthralled. I didn't know what to feel. My feelings were just as mixed up as my directions.

"You and your friends are murderers. You killed a cop. A white cop. Those men are here for you." He motioned toward the sky, and we looked up to see visions of police officers leaving the space where we had camped. The landscape of our makeshift campsite looked completely different than where we were now.

"I'm hallucinating. This can't be real," I whispered.

"We aren't murderers," Liam said. "Just let us go. We won't come back to your land. The man who was killed was the bad one. We're just trying to expose the truth and clear our names. We hurt one of them, but he tried to hurt us first. We're just trying to get to Zone 2."

I was thankful that Liam hadn't singled me out. He hadn't fed me to the wolves, not even to save himself. The truth was, I was the only one who carried the burden of murder on my shoulders, but he hadn't pointed the finger. None of them did. Maybe, despite our differences, despite Syd's fear, Aziza's abrasiveness, and Jesus' doubts, perhaps we were friends. Our differences divided us until we had no choice but to stick together. Now we stood, terrified, but united as we awaited Adoeete's response.

"Please!" Syd added.

Adoeete was silent, as he took us in one by one, judging us, sizing us up because it was clear that wherever we were, he was in charge and he alone could decide our fate.

"Our way of life is sacred. Our ways, our practices; the society we've built is meant for our knowledge only. Every foreigner who has ever stumbled upon us has been put in the dome. No one has ever survived," Adoeete said. "One of you will face one of my ballplayers. If you win, you may go free. If you lose, you all die."

"I'll do it," Liam said, his chest puffed up in bravery, as he stepped forward.

"Always the arrogant class, your kind," Adoeete said, as he stared at Liam in contempt. He turned, and as he walked out he added, "The choice is not yours to make."

CHAPTER 5

NEELY

The sun blazed above us, shining brightly in the sky. It was too beautiful to burn this bad, but as we lay trapped behind the wooden walls, the rays seared us. I gazed up, there wasn't a cloud present to offer a bit of relief. The heat was so intense, I could see waves in front of my vision. We were silent as we lay sprawled about, awaiting the unknown.

"Everything will be okay," Liam whispered. I nodded, but I wasn't sure. I had no idea how we would make it home. It felt so far away that it seemed impossible to get back. I leaned my head against his shoulder, and he nuzzled my face. I enjoyed a brief moment of comfort, but it was short-lived, as the door to our prison opened and a woman walked through. Her wrinkled skin and long, white hair made her look mystical. Her eyes were like white marbles, there was no pupil, no color, and she leaned onto a wooden cane, her long fingernails scratching the sides. The handle of the cane was carved in the shape of a snake and it seemed to be the only thing holding her feeble frame up.

"Line them up at the temple of the sun," her raspy voice

sent a chill through me, as we were corralled from the ground. With spear toting warriors surrounding us, we were escorted out and across the field. We stumbled along, we stepped into the trees, following the old woman. My mouth fell open when I noticed where we were headed.

"Is that a pyramid?" I whispered. We stepped onto open land and three structures loomed above us. I sucked in a breath. "Oh, my God." I stopped walking, causing the others to bump into me.

"Keep moving!" one of the warriors barked. I was stuck in place, as I took in the detail of each structure. The markings on the stone were exquisite and it rose hundreds of feet in the air. A steep staircase ascended all the way to the top, where a rectangular watch tower crowned the structure. "I said move!" The warrior turned his spear, hitting me with the blunt end, and I shuffled along until we all stood in front of the beautiful edifice. We lined up side by side in front of it, as a figure appeared at the very top. The sun was so bright that I couldn't make out who it was, but I recognized the intricate feather head dress he wore. It was Adoeete.

"We have intruders on our land," he said. "We must have a ballplayer's ritual to decide their fate. We will let the gods choose one to elect into the ceremonies. Blind them!"

Warriors came directly in front of us. They held out their hands, revealing red dust, and before I could ask what they were doing, it was blown into our faces.

"Ah!" I cried out, as an intense burning invaded my eyes and I fell to my knees. The sound of drums erupted, and I struggled to peek through the stinging. Women surrounded us, dancing, thrashing, contorting their bodies in ways I had never seen, to the cadence of the drums. Water leaked from my eyes and I doubled over, placing flat hands on the ground as I shook my head.

The music stopped so abruptly that I forced my eyes open, fighting the pain, as I looked up at Adoeete who was descending the steps one by one. It seemed the closer he got to the ground, the darker it became, and I glanced at the sun to see that it was darkening as well. It was like someone was placing a dark circle over it.

"It's an eclipse," Syd exclaimed.

The sun was covered completely, cloaking us in darkness; and as it passed, a single beam of light streamed through an opening at the top of the pyramid. It crawled down the side of the pyramid.

"Neely," Jesus said. I looked to my right and he stared at me in awe. Aziza stood on his other side, doing the same. I turned left and Liam, Minnie, and Syd were all focused on me.

"What!" I shouted. I looked down at myself and saw that I was draped in light, the beamformed the shape of a snake, and I was standing in the clutches of its mouth. Everyone else was still covered in darkness.

"The gods have spoken. Take her!" I was snatched by the elbows, a warrior on each arm, as I was dragged backward.

"What are you doing to her?" Liam shouted.

"Neely!" Minnie cried. As the eclipse passed and the light was restored, I saw that my friends were surrounded by spears as I was carried away. The drums had started again, followed by a processional, as the entire tribe followed behind me. Adoeete and the old woman were last, walking behind the warriors who held my friends prisoner.

I was taken to an open field where two walls framed me, sitting like bleachers on the sides of a football field. The grass that had once grown there was beaten down into dirt, only peeps of green sprouting in odd places remained. The walls were oddly shaped like waves of the ocean, they curved inward and a circular hoop hung from each side.

"What do you want from me?" I yelled, turning in surprise when I heard my own voice return.

"What do you want from me?"

"What do you want from me?"

"What do you want from me?"

The echo carried as clear as day across the entire field.

Adoeete and the old woman climbed the stairs on the side of the wall and sat in stone chairs at the top, looking down over me.

"Speak your name for the gods!" Adoeete shouted.

The wind carried his voice three times.

"Speak your name for the gods!"

"Speak your name for the gods!"

"Speak your name for the gods!"

My eyes fell upon my friends who were being escorted to the top of the adjacent wall. I was horrified when the warriors forced them to kneel and placed their hands and heads through a contraption that kept them in place. A man, wearing red facial and body markings, stood with a long machete in hand.

"Please! No!" I screamed.

"Please! No!"

"Please! No!"

"Please! No!"

"Your name and tribe!" Adoeete demanded.

"Your name and tribe!"

"Your name and tribe!"

"Your name and tribe!"

I was bawling. I couldn't stop myself from falling apart, as I glanced back at my friends.

"You can do this, Neely!"

I closed my eyes at the sound of Liam's voice.

With each echo, I took a deep breath.

"You can do this, Neely!"

"You can do this, Neely!"

"You can do this, Neely!"

With a trembling lip, squared my shoulders. I didn't know what to say. I was just Neely, a teenaged girl from Zone 7. What did they want from me? I was just a stupid girl who had done a stupid thing that had landed me here, but I had to say something. I had to say anything to save my friends, to save myself.

"Neely King. Tribe of the melanin people! Dark skin! Light heart! Clear mind!" I shouted, remembering something my mother had told me when I was a little girl. *You're a part of a Melanin Tribe, Neely. With beautiful, dark skin, an open and light heart, and a brilliant, clear mind.* I had never thought of the words she had spoken to me until now. My words echoed, and I looked at Adoeete with pride, as he stood.

"Neely King, of the melanin people, you will battle for your life. First, to pass the weight of a new born child through the canal will be the victor!" As his voice echoed, I looked toward the circular rims that jutted from the sides of the walls.

What the…? The weight of a newborn child? I was lost, but I had to try. My heart pounded, as adrenaline filled me. When I saw the old woman stand beside Adoeete and lift a black, circular ball above her head, I frowned. *What was this?*

"May the will of the strongest warrior prevail," she rasped, as she held it over the edge of the wall, releasing it and sending it tumbling to the ground. As her voice echoed, three, Navarra warriors stepped into the dome. They wore loin cloths around their waists and ceremonial feathers were braided into their hair. Their bare feet, kicking up dust, as they hooted in unison.

"Choose two," Adoeete said, as he nodded towards my friends.

I looked up. I had no idea what to do. I scanned them quickly, remembering conversations we had participated in over the summer. Syd was a scholar and band geek; no way was she the woman for the job. Aziza was a cheerleader and we all know that's not a real athlete. Minnie had asthma; she would be useless. That left the boys.

"Jesus and Liam!" I shouted.

They were released, and they walked down the stairs, as my echo filled the air once again.

"Can we do this?" I whispered, as they made their way to my side.

"Yeah we can," Jesus replied, with a confident grin. I nodded and looked to Liam who shot me a wink. The drums that rang out around us only heightened the angst in my belly, as I looked around at the Navarra Tribe who had circled the dome. The warriors rolled the ball down the center of the field and Liam bent to pick it up. He tucked it like a football player, and we all took off running. I winced, as one of the warriors collided with Liam, hitting him so hard that Liam went flying into one of the stone walls.

"No hands!" he growled. He beat his chest, roaring loudly, before heading back to his side of the field. Jesus and I ran over to Liam.

"Are you okay?" I asked.

"I'm good!" He said. "That ball weighs at least ten pounds. How are we supposed to get it up there through the hoops without using our hands?" Liam asked.

Jesus smirked, as he held out a hand for Liam, pulling him to his feet. "We use our feet," Jesus said. "Their ball. Let's play."

I ran over to our end of the field. "Like soccer?"

"Did you see that hit?" Jesus asked. "This is soccer on steroids."

I reached up, tying my hair in a bun.

"Screw it," I said. "It's all or nothing." I picked up the ball and rolled it down the field and then went running after it. When the Navarra warriors reached it, they kicked it toward the wall, causing it to bounce off the sides. They thrust their hips, passing it from one to the next. The way their bodies contorted to catch the ball, without ever using their hands, was spectacular, but they underestimated us. Liam was an all-zone defensive end in football, and he was zeroed in on the warrior with the ball.

CRASH!! The hit he put on the Navarra warrior laid him on his back.

"Oohh…" I grimaced because I knew that there was no getting up after taking a hit like that.

"Yes!" Jesus shouted, as he quickly stole possession of the ball. The remaining two Navarra warriors double teamed Jesus, but the footwork he used while standing in one place only frustrated them. The ball may have been heavier than a soccer ball, but Jesus was skilled.

"Neely, go long!" he shouted.

I ran, and Jesus kicked the ball down the field, passing it to me. I wasn't agile like Jesus, but years of running track had me quick, as I ran up the field, passing the ball from my left foot to my right. "Off the wall!" I shouted, as I kicked the ball against the stone, sending it over the head of the warrior who blocked my path. Liam leapt and bounced the ball off his chest before kicking it back to Jesus. Jesus and his fancy feet finessed the warriors all the way down the field, before he shouted, "Neely!" He kicked the ball, sending it flying toward the wall and I ran, using the wall for leverage, as I jolted off it with one foot and kicked with all my might with the other. My foot connected with the 17-pound ball with so much force that I hit the ground with a thud. The entire tribe grew quiet and the drums stopped, as the ball went through the hole.

"Yes!" Jesus hissed. I managed to my feet, my ankle throbbing, as Liam ran to me at full speed, picking me up and spinning me around. We looked up at Adoeete who was standing.

Liam placed me on my feet, and I limped forward a few steps.

"Release them!"

"Release them!"

"Release them!"

Minnie, Syd, and Aziza were allowed to stand.

"Neely, of the Melanin Tribe, I grant you and your friends safe passage through Navarra land," Adoeete announced. As his voice bounced off the walls, the girls ran up to the rest of us and we hugged. "Now, we will accommodate our guests properly."

I yelped in surprise as we were lifted in the air in celebration and I couldn't help but laugh as we were carried toward a large bonfire that burned in the distance. "We did it!" I shouted in triumph. We were placed on our feet and we danced with the tribe, as the circle cast an amber glow against our skin. We ate a king's feast, dining and laughing with The Navarra. Somehow, we had passed their test and were now welcomed with open arms. The sunset and Adoeete showed us to our sleeping quarters. We each had our own room inside the large pyramid and as I sat in the open window, staring out at the vastness of the reservation, I was enthralled. Wherever we were, it was beautiful and unlike anything I had ever seen. A knock at the door caused me to turn away from the majesty of the unsoiled land. Adoeete stood in the entryway.

"Neely. May I enter?" he asked.

"I'm the guest," I scoffed. "This is your land, your home."

Adoeete stepped over the threshold. He was always serious, always intimidating. I had to remind myself that he no longer meant me any harm.

"No one has ever come to our land and won in the ball player ceremony," he said. "Today, the serpent god fed on you. You are chosen, Neely."

"Chosen?" I laughed it off, scoffing, dismissing the notion.

"People. Humanity has been waiting for you, for a very long time. We've lost our way. That is why my people conceal ourselves here. Using ancient, mystical ways, we go unnoticed. There is no brotherhood outside our world. Blacks don't like whites, whites don't like browns, browns don't like yellows. Men have contaminated animals, food, and air. You are the instrument of change. Neely, queen of the melanin people."

"Me?" I asked, eyebrows raised. "I think you are mistaken, Adoeete. I'm nobody. I'm no one's queen."

"Nature submits to you. Elements will bend to your will. This is about more than proving your innocence. Men will unite at your feet. Humanity will align behind you. You hold the key to our future. When you realize the power you hold, you will fix all that is broken. It is in you. You come from a bloodline of kings who brought men together through peace."

He seemed to speak in riddles, and they were complex ones that I couldn't decipher. "You are on a quest to clear your name, but danger lies ahead of you. You will need to know how to defend yourself, to get to the place you seek," he said. "The Navarra can teach you, train you and your friends if you would like."

I thought of the cops that we would have to get by to make it to Zone 2. I thought of the threats that awaited us. I wasn't in a position to turn down anything that could help us get to where we were going. We would need to know how to defend ourselves if cornered. "We would appreciate that. Thank you, Adoeete."

"No, thank you, Neely," he responded. He motioned for the clothing that lay at the foot of the bed. It was a tribal dress, similar to what I had seen on The Navarra women, and I nodded my head in appreciation.

"Thank me? For what?" I had done nothing but bring confusion to his land. I was the last person that deserved his gratitude.

"For all that you are about to do," he responded. I watched him leave and then I laid down on the bear skinned covered plank that would serve as my bed for the night.

As a heaviness took over my eyes, the last thing I whispered was, "unbelievable," before drifting into a well-deserved sleep.

CHAPTER 6

NEELY

The cold kiss of steel against my throat jolted me out of my sleep. My eyes popped open as I felt the point of a blade, as it pressed lightly into my skin. I stared into the eyes of a Navarra warrior, as he loomed over me.

"Rule number one. Only close your eyes around people you trust," he said. He withdrew his knife and I scrambled away from him, as I held up a hand in defense, while reaching for my neck. I pulled back a bloody hand. "Just a little nick to remind you to stay sharp."

"Who are you?" I asked, panting. There was panic living in my chest. It had moved in and settled there the moment I pulled the trigger of that gun. It had been paying rent ever since, extending a lease on my heart every time a new challenge presented itself. I was in constant fear and as I stood bracing myself for him to attack, I realized Adoeete was right. I was defenseless. I had no control over whether I lived to tell my truth or let my name die attached to a lie.

"Alo, son of Adoeete, prince of The Navarra Tribe," he announced, as he lowered the blade. "Someone tells me you and your friends need to learn to fight. Come on." He grabbed my hand and pulled me to the terrace, where we looked out over the village. Without warning, he pulled me to his chest, closing his arms tightly around me, and dove over the edge.

"Agh!" I screamed.

"Rule number two, trust your allies," he whispered, calmly. Suddenly, he transformed into an eagle and I was sitting safely inside his talons, as he flew me across the village. I laughed, in sheer amazement, as I stood. For the first time since being taken by The Navarra, I wasn't afraid, and I marveled at the land beneath me. In this hidden world, life was untainted. The grass was green and wild, with yellow dandelions growing about. It wasn't cut in perfect, uniform lines, the way it was required to be kept inside the zones. It wasn't poisoned with pesticides to keep the dandelions at bay. It was high and blew with the wind. There were no concrete buildings, no cars, no man-made signs telling people when to stop and go. Wild horses raced in teams below and my eyes gleamed at their powerful strides, as the wind blew through their long manes. It was breathtaking, and as Alo neared the waterfall I opened my arms, laughing as he flew through the brisk water. He landed on the other side, and by the time his talons hit the ground, he was in human form again and I was on the ground, soaking wet. "That was incredible!" I shouted. I had never felt so alive. I heard voices and I stood to my feet, following the echo bouncing off the walls to the cave that hid behind the falls. I stopped, mid-step, when I stumbled upon my friends, learning to fight, each with a Navarra warrior guiding their every move.

"It's about time you joined the party," Liam called out. The warrior training Liam, flipped him, knocking the wind out of him, as he landed hard on his back.

Alo whispered in my ear. "Rule number three, never get distracted during a fight," he said.

Alo reached down and extended a strong arm to Liam, pulling him up.

"I'm going to teach you all to fight," Alo said, as we crowded around.

"Fight? Fight for what? We're just trying to get home." Minnie's apprehension seemed to be the consensus. Aziza and Syd nodded in agreement. If we could make it back to Syd's father without incident, that would be ideal.

Alo's eyes rolled to the back of his head, the pupils turning white, as his head fell back. A hologram appeared in front of him. His thoughts playing in front of us, as if we were watching a movie screen. The Navarra people were full of mystique. They did unfathomable things and I was in awe of them. How they had hidden their gifts for so long, I had no idea, but I felt lucky to be allowed to witness them and live to tell about it.

"What is this?" Aziza asked, defensively, as a broadcast played in front of us. Four faces were on the screen. Mine. Minnie's. Jesus'. Aziza's. The words WANTED FOR MURDER was plastered beneath. The cop's face appeared on the screen next.

"Officer Brian McDugley was a decorated officer who served in the Interzones for over 15 years…"

"It's the news story. Our faces are all over the news," Jesus said, as he watched, horrified.

"They're making this cop look like a fallen hero! He tried to rape me!"

Images of the officer with his family, in his uniform, holding babies, flashed in front of us, as the report continued. *"The five suspects are wanted dead or alive. They are considered armed and extremely dangerous."*

"My face isn't up there," Syd whispered.

"Must be nice to have a daddy in high places," Jesus sneered.

"Or to be white," Minnie added. "Liam's face isn't up there either."

"The media skewed the story. They control the narrative," I whispered, in disbelief. Black people were thugs, brown people were illegal, Middle Eastern people were terrorists. That was the caricature history had painted us in for decades, and as I looked on in disbelief, I knew we needed Arti to come through with that footage. If not, The Panel wouldn't think twice about locking the three of us away and throwing away the key. We were screwed.

"I don't care what that says. We're all in this together," Liam said.

"It isn't your face on the broadcast," Jesus stated.

Alo closed his eyes, when they opened, they were restored to normalcy. He stood in the middle of the circle we had formed around him, turning to look at each of us.

"To get home, you will have to put up the fight of your lives. We are going to teach you how."

Through the falls, walked six warriors, ready for battle. They surrounded us and Alo laughed. "Let's fight."

"Hmph, hmmph, hmmph," I grunted, as I blocked Alo's assault. My forearms ached from every blow that landed against them.

"Where's the counter?" he yelled, full of aggression, as he backed me against the wall. His forearm pressed against my throat and he glared at me.

"Take it easy!" I shouted, growing frustrated with training.

"I am taking it easy on you, Neely, because out there they want to kill you. Now, again," Alo said, as he released me.

I doubled over, breathing hard, as I balanced my hands on my knees. The sting of tears burned my eyes. This was too hard. This was torture. I looked around and saw each of my friends battling against their own warrior. We had been fighting for days, behind the waterfall, in the sun, and I was worn. I stood straight up and readied my stance because although it was hard, it was also necessary. I attacked, and Alo rolled over my back, disorienting me, before catching me with a firm kick to the back of one knee that sent me crashing to the ground.

"Again," he said. "You attack with your entire body. Your arms, your legs, your head, even your fingernails are weapons,

Neely, use them. I'll call out your weapon and you attack."

I nodded, as I struggled to my feet. Sweat dripped in my eyes, as I took my stance. "Jab, duck, jab," Alo called out.

My fists flew as I followed each command.

"Each blow should land like it's your last, Neely. Like you won't get a second chance," Alo said. "Harder!"

"Kick, Kick, roundhouse," he ordered. His words were faster than my movements, and by the time I got to the roundhouse, Alo swept my leg that was planted from underneath me. I hit the ground so hard that all air escaped my lungs.

"You need to be fast," Alo said. "On your feet."

I was slow to get up, and before I knew it, Alo's machete was coming at my head. I rolled to the side and stood, as his machete hit nothing but ground. "So, you can move quickly!" he badgered. His baiting set me on fire, as I rushed to my feet.

"Roundhouse!" My leg swung powerfully into the air and he caught it, as I knew he would. When he pushed it to the ground, I used the momentum to lift my left leg in a roundhouse, catching him in the side of the head. This time, it was Alo that went to the ground. His machete clanged against the dirt and I reached down to pick it up. I stabbed it toward him, only missing him by an inch, before I stood straight up, heaving. Everyone stopped fighting and looked at us in shock. Alo lay on his back in stun. A smile parted his lips. It was me helping him up this time.

"Not so slow after all, huh?" Alo asked.

Laughter filled me. It was a small triumph, but after getting my butt kicked under the hot sun all day, it felt damned good.

"I think you've earned dinner," Alo said. "We're done for the day," he announced.

"Thank God," Syd exclaimed.

Alo looked at me. "Climb on," he said, turning his back to me. I smiled because I knew what was to come. I jumped onto his back and he ran full speed through the waterfall and off the cliff. I didn't close my eyes this time as we plunged.

When his arms turned to wings, there was no surprise this time. I was learning The Navarra ways. I dug my fingers into Alo's feathers, as I held on for the ride. This was why I had wanted to see the world outside my zone. It was more than I could ever imagine. The limits of my imagination could have never stretched this far. The wind on my face took my breath away, as I marveled at the vistas below. Alo did tricks, angling his wings at 90 degrees and spinning around, giving me the thrill of my life. I had never felt so free. This was living. This was exploration. This was what happened when people weren't afraid of each other. When we ignored skin color and connected on a deeper level than simply a common skin tone. Every single person I had met, since stepping outside Zone 7, was cooler than everyone I had known and been forced to be around my entire life. Not because of any other reason than because I had been able to choose the company I kept, and through our differences, I was learning.

"Show off!" I yelled, as I laughed. I glanced behind me and saw my friends, soaring on the wings of the warriors they had trained with. We were flying. It was incredible. It was something each of us would remember for the rest of our lives and something that only our little group would believe. We shared the experience; only us and it would bond us forever. We landed; and this time, I dismounted, jumping down just before Alo hit the ground.

"Clean up and come join our tribe for dinner," he said. "The mothers of the tribe have washed your belongings."

I nodded, as I watched Alo and the other warriors leave.

"Do you really think a little bit of training is going to help us make it out there?" Minnie asked.

"I don't know," I answered. I was skeptical myself, but adding that to our pooling doubts wouldn't do any good. The less we believed we could actually pull this off, the more impossible it would become. "I hope so." I headed toward the pyramid. "I'll see you guys at dinner."

Gloom hung in the air like humidity after a good rainstorm, as I entered my temporary quarters. The tribe was alive in the field below me, dancing, and eating. Loud drums and the sounds of flutes serenaded the air, as a huge bonfire illuminated the night. It was a boisterous celebration, but I wasn't in the mood much for partying. I could see the others below, blowing off steam, as The Navarra taught them native dances and painted markings on their faces. A small smile graced the corners of my mouth, looking at Minnie smiling as she danced with some of the women below. She looked so carefree like she was having the time of her life. I had never seen her laugh like that before. I, on the other hand, had so much weighing me down that all I felt were tears stinging my eyes. We were all in jeopardy for leaving our zones, but the greatest crime was the dead officer that resulted from it. That was my crime and mine alone. I couldn't shake the smell of his blood from my mind. It smelled like metal, like an old penny, and I had been sick to my stomach ever since. Every time I thought of his hands on my body, and what was about to occur if Liam hadn't stopped him, it sent a chill down my spine. My entire life was at stake and it felt like I had made an irreversible mistake. If I had just let that cop do what he wanted, if I had just laid there and endured it, maybe we all would be at home in our beds by now. Fighting back had made things worse. Sometimes, the path of least resistance was best. I remember my mother saying that black women were the most neglected in the world. That we weren't appreciated, that our voices went unheard, that our cries were muted. I never understood that until that cop put his hands in places that no one should touch. No matter how loudly I screamed, he seemed to not hear the anguish I felt. Even now, after the fact, I would be vilified because no one would believe the truth.

"I thought you might be hungry after all that training, you know?"

I turned toward the door. Liam entered, and filled the room with charm. He was good at that…at making me forget whatever I was thinking about before he infiltrated my space. *Did he know he had that power over me or was it unintentional?* I couldn't tell, but I smiled, as I joined him on my bed.

"I was pretty good, right?" I beamed, as I took the plate from his hands.

"You're amazing," he said. I got lost in his eyes. Those emerald pools of confidence put butterflies in my stomach.

"Can I tell you something?"

"Anything," he replied.

"I'm terrified." It was my first time admitting it aloud.

Liam took the plate from my hands and set it aside, and then slid his hand over mine. "You're going to make it through this. We all are. I promise, and I'm not into making promises I can't keep."

"Listen, if something happens to me. If I don't make it, I want you to tell my mom and dad…"

I was interrupted by a kiss. His white lips on my dark ones. The eyes of the world would have a fit if they could see us. Everything I had been taught about cross breeding and keeping bloodlines pure, seemed foolish in this moment. The chemistry I felt between us couldn't be common, it felt too special, too rare to be an everyday occurrence. Right then and there, I determined that love didn't have a color. It didn't live within boundaries and I wasn't sure if it existed between Liam and I, but that kiss…sheesh, it had to be a distant cousin of love if not the real thing.

"If you don't make it, I don't make it, so I can't play messenger. I'm right here with you, Neely. No matter what, until the very end of this thing." He caressed my cheek. I lowered my eyes to my lap. No one had ever looked at me like that…admired me like that. In a world where the standard of beauty matched his skin tone, his eyes, his hair texture, somehow, he was taken with the contrast of me. The black girl with big, kinky, coiled hair. I was his opposite, and in that moment, I had proof that the saying was true. Opposites did attract.

"Hmm hmm."

We both looked up at the sound of another presence interrupting. Alo stood, food in hand.

"I see I'm too late," he said, holding up the plate. "He who feeds the pretty girl first wins."

I blushed and stood to my feet. "I umm..." Why was I stammering? And why were the butterflies back? Alo stood tall with his broad shoulders, defined build, copper skin, and long, jet-black hair. Yep, opposites definitely attract. The room suddenly seemed too small for the three of us.

"How about we all go eat dinner together? Fresh air sounds great right about now."

I toyed with my fingers and looked back to Liam, and then lifted my eyes to Alo. These two were completely different, and certainly disagreed on most things, but apparently melanin was the one thing they had in common.

"Yeah," Liam nodded. I couldn't descend the steps of the pyramid quickly enough. I was glad that our time with The Navarra would be short-lived because with the two of them so obvious in their affections, I would feel torn and that was the last thing I needed to focus on.

I was inside my head the entire evening. It was hard for me to feel anything other than dread. We sat around the bonfire as Adoeete and the elders sat above us in stone coliseum seating, as they watched over the antics.

"Walk with me," Alo whispered into my ear, as he stood from his seat. The others were distracted, as they mingled with the tribe and I slipped away, following Alo into the shadows of the trees that surrounded us. Everything about The Navarro land seemed to be more abundant. The grass was greener, the sky bluer, the sun brighter, and these trees were so massive and so tall that the moon was hidden out of sight.

"You're afraid?" Alo asked.

"Huh?"

He stopped walking and turned to me. "I said, you're afraid."

"Are you asking or telling me?" I chuckled.

"I'm asking to see if you will admit the truth. I already know the answer," he said.

"What are you a mind reader, too?" I rolled my eyes.

Alo smiled. "You don't have to read minds when you can read people. Your actions speak what your mouth is afraid to."

He placed his hand on the large trunk of the massive oak tree in front of us. "Let's go."

"Go where?" I frowned. Alo was full of mystery. Whenever he spoke I was always left with questions. He never divulged information for my comfort. He was vague as if his every thought was a puzzle I had to solve. He didn't answer with words, he just began to climb.

"I can't climb this!" I yelled at his back.

"Because you're afraid?" he countered.

I stepped back and glanced all the way to the top. The canopy was so high that I couldn't even distinguish where the leaves of the trees ended, and the sky began. The height was dizzying and unlike Alo, I couldn't fly. If I fell…

"You can talk yourself out of anything if you ponder it long enough. Sometimes, you just have to do it," Alo yelled. Every muscle in his body flexed in cooperation as he began to ascend the huge tree. I huffed out my uncertainty. My internal alarm was telling me to turn back and go to my room, but we were so deep in the forest that I wouldn't be able to find my way out alone. I had to go where Alo led me and he was going up. I reached up, planting my fingertips in one of the grooves in the side of the tree and started the climb. It took all my effort, every single ounce of strength I had to keep reaching and planting one foot on top of the other. I knew it was taking me a bit of time because the moon moved across the sky, giving me a beautiful clock to mark my pace. I turned to see my progress. The ground was so far away that I snapped my head forward and pinched my eyes closed.

"Now, why would you go and do that?"

Alo's voice was above me and I peered up at him, glossy-eyed, fear-filled. He was about ten yards ahead and sitting comfortably on a long, thick, branch, that extended out into the air.

"You never look down," he said, with amusement dancing at the corners of his lips.

"This isn't funny, Alo. I don't think I can make it."

"You won't if you think you won't. Your mind is powerful. Your thoughts are road maps to things not yet attempted," he said.

"Help me!"

I was losing it. He was speaking in riddles and I was hanging off the side of a tree.

"Look at me." His voice was so calm it was irritating, but I obliged and lifted my eyes to meet his. "You don't need my help. *You* can do this. You'll have to do a lot more out there. You have to believe you can. If you don't believe in you, how are your friends supposed to? How is the world supposed to?"

He spoke with conviction, as if he had known me my entire life.

"Speak it, Neely. Say, I can do this."

I can do this…I can do this. He couldn't hear me repeating it in my mind, again and again, but for some reason, he didn't interrupt. I grit my teeth, as I reached for the next branch. The rough bark bit into my soft hands, as I wrapped my hand around it, holding on for dear life. My arms were dead, but this wasn't a task I could quit halfway through.

"I'm almost there," I whispered, aloud.

When I felt my hand inside Alo's, I sighed in relief. *Thank God*.

He pulled me up and relief turned to anger, as soon as I was perched safely on the limb. It was wider than my entire body and gave me a false comfort because it was so sturdy it felt like I was on solid ground. "You could have just helped me!" I shouted.

"Then you wouldn't know your own strength. You would only know mine," he replied.

I gazed at him. The charm I initially found in his philosophy had become annoying.

"How old are you?"

"I've survived 19 trips around the sun," Alo replied.

"You're only 19 and you speak like a grandpa. No more riddles with me, Alo! I'm tired of thinking," I spat.

Alo laughed, bringing those dark eyes down bashfully before blinking them back up to me. "You got it, Neely," he said. "Come on. I want to show you something." He stood and pushed through the giant leaves of the tree, as he made his way further out onto the limb. I stood, slight angst in my belly, as I followed him. When I broke through the bushel of leaves, I was struck with amazement.

"It's beautiful, right?"

Beneath us was the Navarra reservation. As far as the eye stretched, I took in the wonders that were shadowed in darkness, slightly illuminated by the moonlight in the sky.

"Wow." It was all I could manage. The untainted nature below was like real life art. I had never seen anything like it.

"How does your land look like this? I've never seen trees so tall or grass so green."

"We feed the land, so the land feeds us. We don't take more than we need. It's a mutually beneficial relationship," Alo replied.

"This place is like a different world. If I could, I would stay here forever."

"The Interzones used to look like this," Alo said. "The Zones too. People have a way of exploiting and abusing the very resources they need. Greed is a dangerous beast. It has pushed people to take more than they need. That is why we don't allow outsiders on our soil."

"Except me," I interjected.

Alo smirked and nodded in agreement. "Except you."

"I have no idea what's waiting on me out there. I'm in a lot of trouble." My reality was sobering. I had broken federal law and killed someone. I would have to atone for that. I just hoped I didn't end up paying with my life.

"Your journey will be hard, and it will seem impossible, but when it's all said and done, it will be worth it," Alo said. I could feel the emotion welling in my chest. I was overwhelmed thinking about what I had done, about how my parents were doing, wondering if I would ever see them again. Wondering if The Panel would be sympathetic. I had so many worries and no reassurance for any of them. I closed my eyes, and pulled my bottom lip into my mouth, as a tear fell down my face. A calloused hand, Alo's hand, cupped the sided of my face and his thumb wiped the tear away. "You are going to be okay, Neely. As long as you remember to look up and not down, look forward and not backward, you will not fall. You can do this."

"I can do this," I repeated, with a nod. I sniffled and wiped the wetness from my nose, before looking away in embarrassment.

"Neely of The Melanin Tribe," Alo commented.

"You know that's not a real thing, right?" I laughed, grateful for the relief in tension.

"I hope I'm there to witness the moment you realize that it is," he replied. "Let's get back. You have an early morning tomorrow."

"More training?"

He nodded. "More training."

I trained hard, we all did. Fighting against The Navarra, despite the fact that we were ruled by fear, Alo told me we had to get used to the feeling of being hit. "They should hurt, but not hinder you. Absorb the blows and retaliate immediately," he said, sternly, in my ear. He made us punch the steely abdomens of tribe warriors because, "connecting with muscle is painful. You need to know how and where to hit a man to bring him to his knees," was his advice. We even cut through beef with machetes because, "just in case things get out of control, you need to know what it feels like when a blade penetrates flesh," he said. We used rodents for target practice, as we learned to shoot guns with precision. I learned to move without a sound, keeping my feet light, as I ran through The Navarra forest. I walked across wire thin ropes at dizzying heights. I swam through freezing waters and held rocks at the bottom of lakes to teach me how to hold my breath for extended periods of time. I did things I never thought I could, and I wondered if the magic of The Navarra would rub off on me when we were off their land because being amongst them made me feel invincible. We ran, we fought, we caught bees through the tips of daggers with one throw. Ten days passed before it was our time to leave. I would have lost count if I hadn't been keeping track of how many times I'd watched the sunrise. I was sure we weren't ready, but it was time for us to move on. We had no more time to spare. The stories being broadcasted had only sensationalized as days passed. Riots and protests demanding justice had erupted in Zone 1. White supremacists were demanding justice. If I didn't clear my name soon, I would be tried in the court of public opinion, and they would sway the outcome of The Panel. I was afraid to leave the safety of The Navarra land, but I knew I couldn't avoid reality forever. My parents were probably worried sick. I was desperate to hear their voices and to tell them my version of the story. I wasn't completely innocent. I had pulled the trigger, but I was acting in defense, or more so reacting to his offense. That was my right as a woman, to say no, to not have the hands of men in places that I hadn't approved. He had violated that, and although I hadn't meant to kill him, I did. *None of this seems fair,* I thought.

"You have grown strong in your short time here."

I turned to Adoeete's strong voice. His face revealed no pride, but I could hear it in his voice.

"It doesn't feel like it. This entire thing seems hopeless," I admitted. "I'm just one person. We're just kids."

"All it takes is one person to change the world, and it looks differently through the eyes of the young. I told you, you are chosen," Adoeete said.

"How does this place exist?" I asked, as I looked out over his reservation.

"The Navarra is rich with history, rich with beliefs, and rituals that we pass from generation to generation. Our shaman blesses us with an ability that makes us one with the world around us. It is just our way. It has always been our way. I hope you will respect what you have learned here and not share what you have seen."

I nodded. "I promise."

Adoeete reached for his neck and pulled one of the many necklaces that dangled. He held it in both hands as he slipped it around me. I fingered the long tooth that hung from the center of it. "For protection during your journey. It will come to your aide when you need it most."

He went to leave, and paused, as he turned around. "If you want to blend humanity, you have to locate the articles," he said.

"I don't want to do anything, but clear my name," I said.

Adoeete chuckled. "In time, you will see you are meant to do much more. Remember what I said. The articles are the key."

Adoeete with his unsolvable riddles, I supposed. He exited, and I blew out the candle, turning the room black, as I prepared for bed.

CHAPTER 7

SYD

Drip. Drip. Drip.

My eyes fluttered into consciousness, as I felt beads of water land on my forehead and roll down the sides of my face. I sat up abruptly, in panic, as I looked around. "Guys!" I shouted, my voice echoing, bouncing off the walls of this dark place. "Where are we?" I whispered. I had fallen asleep in a room in the high pyramid on Navarra land and awoken here, a black, drafty... "Is this a cave?" I asked, ducking fast, to evade the shrieking bats that darted above my head. My eyes adjusted to the darkness and I could see the silhouettes of the bodies lying on the dirty ground. I rushed to them, shaking them awake.

"Get up," I urged.

The fog of grogginess lifted as they sat up.

"What is this place?" Minnie asked.

Liam arose from the ground and walked toward the amber glow coming from the mouth of the cave. The brilliant hues of orange and yellow crept over the horizon, as the sun began to rise. "There's our campsite," Liam pointed out, as he stood on the edge. "They brought us back."

We joined him, standing side by side, looking at the land below us. Neely reached for her backpack and pulled out her channel.

"What are you doing?" Aziza asked.

"I need to scope my parents. Let them know I didn't do this. I need to tell them I'm okay," Neely urged.

"You can't scope anyone. Now that they know who we are, our channels are probably being tracked. We have to keep them powered off until we make it to my father," I said.

"What now?" Jesus asked.

"We get to Zone 2," Neely asserted.

There was determination in her voice, like our time with The Navarra tribe had put confidence in her. We were all stronger, all tougher, but Neely somehow looked taller to me, like she knew we would make it through this. I, on the other hand, still felt small. Like, no way would we ever make it to my father without being caught. I knew if I could just make it home everything would be okay, but I had to get there first.

We began the descent, climbing down the jagged rocks. Our silence, a dead giveaway to our uncertainty. I had never wanted to see my parents' faces more in my life. They had always sheltered me, always protected me. I was the only child and no others would follow me. My mother and father had mixed me up in a test tube. His sperm. Her egg. A huge incubator for 40 weeks and I was born. In vitro fertilization had birthed an entirely new way to bring life into the world. No one used that method anymore. Ex vitro had taken its place. The growth of a fertilized egg outside of the womb. That's how I came to be, and it made me feel like a science experiment. I was the only viable egg my mother could produce, and it made me their most prized possession…their most expensive investment. I knew it was the reason why my face hadn't appeared in the broadcast. If I was implicated in this crime, it would not only be a disappointment to my family and break my mother's heart, but the science behind ex vitro fertilization would come into question. My bad decision making would be under a microscope to determine if I was genetically susceptible to commit violent acts. The science of my very existence would come into question. Me getting busted wouldn't benefit anyone; not The Panel, not the scientists and doctors who made me, not my mother. My father would never allow anything to happen to me. My name would never be mentioned with the others; my presence at the crime scene never be revealed. He would make sure of it, and once he heard the truth, I knew he would take care of my friends, too. I just hope Arti comes up with that proof. If he doesn't, it will be our word against the images of a dead cop that the news has been playing on a loop.

"Aghh!"

I didn't even realize I was falling until it was too late. I was jarred from my thoughts, as the rocks beneath my feet came loose and I felt my back skidding down.

"Syd!" Minnie shouted. I reached out, my arms grasping for something, anything to slow my descent. I slid down the steep cliff, the skin on my back and arms burning, as I hit every jagged rock on the way down. Finally, my hand caught onto something. I looked up, thanking God for the old root that was sticking out from the sides of the mountainside. The momentum from the fall jerked me, violently almost causing my hand to slip.

"Help me!" My legs swung wildly, and I tried to plant my feet, tried to find a foothold, but it was too steep to gain traction. My feet just kept slipping, kicking down eroded rocks.

"Hold on!" I looked up and could barely see the faces of the others, but I heard Liam urging me not to let go. I looked down at the dizzying heights and the rocky bottom below. No way would I survive that fall. There was nothing to break the impact.

"Get me down!" I cried, as my fear of heights convinced me that I couldn't breathe. The lump in my throat seemed to suffocate me, as I gasped for air. I squeezed my eyes so tightly that tears fell down my cheeks. "Okay, okay, okay, okay," I whimpered. "You're not going to die. Your friends are going to save you. Just breathe. Just breathe." I glanced down. Huge mistake. "I'm going to die!" I shouted.

"No, you're not! Hang tight," Minnie yelled. Unless Liam had wings, there was nothing he could do to help. Where was The Navarra when you needed them? *The whole man turning to giant eagle thing. Yeah, I could use that right now.*

I could feel my hands slipping.

"Syd! You have to climb! Look down!" Jesus called. I turned and the sight of a cop aiming his gun at me urged me to reach for a piece of rock above me. If I didn't climb up, I would be shot down.

BANG!

"Agh!" I shrieked, as the dirt a few inches from me crumbled as the bullet hit it. My arms burned, as I released the branch and reached for the next indentation I felt above me. It was barely enough to hold on to, but I dug my hands into the mountain, gripping it, as I pulled myself up a few more inches.

BANG!

NEELY

"We have to do something!" Minnie cried. "He's going to shoot her!"

"No way, that there's just one cop. If he's all the way out here, there has to be more of them close by. We have to go," Aziza reasoned.

"We're not leaving her! I'm going to go get her. I can bring her up on my back, but I'm not bulletproof," he said.

Jesus took off running, full speed, down the sharp path that led to the ground below. I didn't know what to do.

"Be careful," I shouted, as I peered over the edge at Liam who was making his way down. Every rock he touched peeled away, crumbling to the ground. It was a guessing game, as he tried to plant his feet and hands in the right spot. "We can't just stand here." My eyes widened, as I remembered the gift Adoeete had given me. "The knife!" I exclaimed. I pulled my bag off my shoulders and pulled out the hand carved blade.

"What are you going to do with that?" Minnie asked. She was panicked. We all were.

"I'm going to do what they taught us," I responded.

"You're going to throw it? At the cop?" Minnie's bewilderment played on her face. "We're too far up for you to aim. You'll never hit him."

"I can't not do anything!" I shouted. I looked down the side of the mountain, finding a ledge below. "There's a trail there. If I can get to it, I'll have a better shot. I'll meet you guys at the bottom."

"How are you going to get to it? It's at least a 20-foot fall!" Aziza asked.

I thought of Alo. "I can do this," I whispered, and before I could talk myself out of it, I jumped over the edge. I gripped the handle of the knife, as the blade dug into the dirt, slowing down my descent, slightly. My body scraped every rock and branch on the way down and I grimaced in pain, as I felt the skin burn from the friction. I arched my foot and let gravity drag me for 20 feet toward the ledge. I hit it hard. The entire left side of my body was bruised and bloodied, but I had no time to register the pain. I gripped the knife and set the cop in my sight. "Breathe, aim, throw," I whispered, repeating what Alo had trained me to do. I flung it with expertise and when it pierced the cop between his shoulder blades, he dropped the gun, falling to his knees.

"Wow! I did it," I whispered in disbelief, as adrenaline pumped in my veins, exhilarating me. Using trees as target practice was one thing, hitting a moving target that had a gun in his hands was another.

"Climb, Liam! Climb!" I shouted. I peered back at the cop, but Jesus had made it to the bottom and was holding him at gunpoint.

Liam put Syd on his back and began the climb back to the top. He groaned with every inch he climbed, every muscle in his body strained from the extra weight he carried. I didn't know if I was standing there enthralled at the sight or if I really wanted to make sure they made it to the top. When Liam and Syd were safely at the top, I ran down the trail, headed to the bottom.

Jesus stood with the cop at gunpoint. I put a foot to his back, forcing him to the ground, face down, and snatched the knife out his back.

He grimaced as Jesus bent down. "How does it feel to have a boot in your back?" Jesus asked. "Huh?!" he shouted. He pushed me out the way and put his foot on the cop's back, adding pressure. "You can't breathe, can you? Let me hear you say it! Say it! I can't breathe!"

"Jesus!" I shouted. "You're going to kill him! This isn't us! We aren't killers!"

Jesus pushed me off, as the others emerged from the trail.

"Say it," Jesus said.

The cop's face was blue, and his eyes bulged.

"What are you doing, man?" Liam asked.

"Say it!" Jesus demanded. The look in his eyes was pained,

passionate, as he inflicted this punishment, but I didn't understand what Jesus was punishing this cop for.

"I," the cop could barely make out the next word. "Can't." His mouth opened, struggling to release. "Breathe."

Jesus jumped off the cop and stormed off, swiping tears of frustration from his face, as we all stood there in shock.

I picked up the gun on the ground and Liam reached into the boot of the cop, pulling out another pistol that was holstered there.

"We've got to go," Minnie whispered.

Syd stood, with her hand over her mouth, gaping at the scene like it was a car accident that was hard to tear away from.

"She's right let's get out of here," Aziza agreed.

Liam pulled my hand and I reluctantly followed him into the trees, as we all went after Jesus.

"What was that back there?" Liam asked, as we finally caught up to Jesus. He jumped up from the boulder he sat on, as he pointed a passionate finger toward the direction we had just come from.

"That is what they did to my father! He went hunting five seasons ago, but the monsters he encountered weren't crossbreeds. They were cops! White cops like that one! All they saw was a Latino with a gun and they threw him to the ground. One of them put him in a headlock and handcuffed him, while his partner put a boot in his back to keep him down. He couldn't breathe. He shouted it! He went without oxygen for three minutes! By the time they got him to the hospital, he was brain dead. He's been a vegetable ever since."

We were silent. I blinked away tears. We hadn't discussed stuff like this over scopes, and I suddenly realized we only knew one another on the surface. We each had histories, secrets, and things that we struggled with. We had only shared the good stuff, but it was the not so good that truly told a person's character. How could I tell him not to be angry? Not to hate? I understood his pain. It was written in my DNA, but saying all cops were bad was the same as saying all blacks were thugs or all whites were racist. It simply wasn't true, but logic could never win a battle with emotion, so instead, I offered, "I'm sorry, Jesus." It didn't quite seem like the right thing to say, but it was all I had. He shrugged and flung the gun holster over his shoulder before walking off.

"Let's just keep moving. Let's catch up with Jesus," Liam insisted.

His hand found the small of my back. It always seemed to, and it always had the same effect. It somehow made me feel safe, despite the dangers that faced us ahead. The hand of a boy I liked, gracing my skin, taking control, was enough to calm the anxiety dancing up my spine. We walked ahead, clearing the thick bushes and trees out our way, as we stayed off the main path.

"Whoa, whoa!" Liam said, stopping mid-step, as he put a finger to his lips. We all stopped behind him. He slowly pulled down a large leaf, peeking out into the clearing. What I saw made my heart collapse into my stomach. A patroller had Jesus at gunpoint and nine other patrollers stood, armed. Liam came close to my ear. "I'm going to go around and catch them from the back. You can do this," he whispered. He handed me the gun in his hands. "Shoot to kill, Neely, because they're going to do the same to us."

I nodded, as he began to slink through the trees. Aziza, Syd, and Minnie looked to me. I handed Minnie the gun. She was the best shooter. Alo had said so, and we were in a situation where we couldn't miss. I wasn't sure I'd hit the patroller holding Jesus hostage on the first shot, and I didn't want another body on my conscience. So, I put my money, and the burden, on Minnie.

"When you shoot, they'll scatter," I whispered. "We separate them and take them out one by one."

Minnie aimed, but I could see her hand shaking.

"Can you do this?" Aziza hissed. Her eyes were wide, as Minnie lowered the gun in exasperation.

"If you give me space!" Minnie bit back, barely keeping her tone down.

Aziza backed up and I focused on the patrollers, as Minnie aimed quickly and pulled the trigger.

BANG!

The patroller dropped as Minnie's bullet hit the center of his forehead.

"I did it?! I did it!" she shouted.

"Yes! You did it!" I yelled. I sprang into action, tossing the knife with precision.

"Two down," Syd said.

The patrollers scattered, as Liam emerged from behind,

running to snatch the guns off the men that had fallen. Two patrollers attacked him, and I ran full speed to intervene.

"Hmmph," my first blow landed to the back of one of the men's heads. He spun quickly, but I ducked, anticipating the reaction and following my instincts like Alo had taught me. I heard him in my head. *Right hook, left jab, low kick, leg sweep.* The patroller went down…hard. I delivered a final blow to his larynx, leaving him writhing on the ground. My adrenaline pumped, as I spun to find the next patroller, aiming a gun right at me.

Rat, tat, tat!

The patroller fell before he could even pull a trigger, and behind him stood Aziza, holding a gun with a shaky hand.

"Duck!" I shouted. Aziza reacted. That was one thing The Navarra taught us to act without thinking and I was glad she had learned the lesson because if she hadn't, the patroller would have ended her. I pulled The Navarra blade from my waistline and launched it, hitting the patroller in the neck. I looked up to see Liam and Jesus going blow for blow with patrollers. They quickly got the best of them.

"That's only half of them," I said, breathlessly. "Where's Minnie? Where's Syd?"

I ran toward the trees where the pair had been hiding, but they were gone. The only remnant of them was the gun Minnie had in her possession before she was taken.

"Neely!"

Minnie's voice cut through the air and I turned in a full circle, trying to pinpoint which direction it had come from.

"They're gone!" Aziza panicked.

"Agh!"

Another scream, this time belonging to Syd, pointed us in their direction. I grabbed the gun off the ground, and we took off, one after another, racing, and hoping we were headed the right way. My lungs burned, but I refused to stop running. I had gotten Minnie into this. No way was I letting her be taken away by these men. Who's to say these men would even turn her over to the cops, or that the cops would do the right thing? After my run in with one, I didn't trust them and out of everyone, Minnie was my best friend. She had known me my entire life and I would ride for her harder than anyone. There was no slowing down. There was no giving up. I had to get my best friend back. The trees cleared, and we were running toward a road, where I could see squad cars waiting.

"We can't let them make it to those cars!" I shouted. I stopped running and aimed the gun toward the cops.

I didn't want to hurt anyone else, but no way were they taking Minnie. I had to stop them, by any means necessary.

I pulled the trigger.

MINNIE

I ducked as I heard the bullets ricochet off the squad cars. Resisting was easier said than done. I tried my hardest to pull away from the officer, but the gun jammed in my side was all it took for me to comply. How had I ended up here? Running for my life, while Neely used me for target practice. I knew the bullets weren't intended for me, but I was too close for comfort. My heart pounded and the closer I got to the police cars ahead, the greater the ache in my chest became. If they got me in the back of that car, I didn't know if I'd ever be free again. I could fight, and risk being shot, or cooperate and face the unknown. I wasn't a risk-taker by nature, but I was stuck between a rock and a hard place. I closed my eyes, dreading the anticipation of how badly this could potentially go.

Just do it. Just do it, just do it. I tried to hype myself up in my head, but still I was being pulled toward the squad car. My body was frozen with fear. *You have a right to defend yourself. If they take you, your entire life is over.* I pivoted, taking the officer by surprise, as I snatched from his grasp.

BANG! BANG!

By the time he fired, I was already behind him. I kicked his knee cap in, sending him crashing to the ground in a kneel, and then wrapped my cuffed hands around his neck.

I pulled with all my might, as he sent wild shots into the air, flailing madly in an attempt to shake me from his back.

"Neely!!!" I shouted. The man bent down and flipped me over his shoulder. My back hit the ground with force and my foot smashed against a boulder. Pain shot up my entire leg, and before I could even think to move, I was staring up at the federal agent over the barrel of his gun.

"Say goodbye," he wheezed, winded, as he massaged his neck with one hand, holding a steady grip on the trigger with the other. There was so much pain; my foot, my back, and I was anticipating more to come. I was waiting for the bullet that would end it all.

His finger moved only a hair and I closed my eyes.

CLICK!

My eyes popped open.

CLICK! CLICK!

The man shook his arm as if he could will bullets into the chamber. It was empty. I rushed to my feet, but quickly realized my left foot was hurt worse than I thought. I could barely hold myself up, as I stood there, squaring off with a man twice my size. The gun was tossed to the ground. He attacked, but I sidestepped as his fist barely missed my face.

"Agh!" I shouted at the radiating pain from my foot, but I couldn't take pause. I ducked under his arm and used my leg to sweep his feet from underneath him. It was his turn to see how that ground felt, only, it didn't seem to affect him as much.

Is he a freaking ninja or something?

A kip-up put him back on his feet, and I stumbled backward in surprise. The look in his eyes told me that I had thoroughly pissed him off. He swung. I dodged the blow; my ankle screamed in protest as I stumbled. He swung again. I slapped his hand down, redirecting the force of the punch toward the ground. My hands were blocking and redirecting his blows, just as quickly as he delivered them. My eyes bulged at his strength. There was no way I would win by going toe to toe with him, especially on an injured foot. I remembered the teachings of The Navarra warriors who had trained us. "The best offense is defense." With my hands cuffed in front of me, all I could do was bob and weave.

"You can't hit little ol' me, big fella?" I baited the cop, frustrating him. His face reddened in anger as he swung another punch. I evaded left, he swung again, I dodged right. I could feel the heaviness in his swing. Each time he missed, I could feel a kiss of wind on my cheek where his punch was meant to land. I would have to be careful because all it took was one to connect to put me out. "You're slow, old man." My goading was intentional. The more I provoked, the harder he attacked, and I needed to tire him out if I was going to win any kind of physical battle between us. On top of that, my hands were bound, so I was at a huge disadvantage. He jabbed left, my head went right, he switched hands, I took a half step back. I thanked God for the years of ballet and gymnastics because I was light on my feet, making me hard to get ahold of. He was winded. I could feel the difference in the punches he tried to throw. They weren't as strong, and I kept evading until I saw my opening.

Left punch.

I lifted my cuffed hands, allowing his blow to land right against the metal, before rolling my wrists around his arm as hard as I could. I heard the snap. Everyone heard the scream that followed.

Jesus finally reached us and hit the agent in the back of the head with a gun, knocking him out cold.

"Good job, big guy," I said, sarcastically. "I did all the hard work."

The sound of tires screeching caught my attention and I turned to see Syd banging against the back window of a squad car as it raced away.

The others finally caught up. They were heaving in exhaustion, as we all stared at the car in horror. "What do we do?"

My question was met with silence and I turned to look at the others.

"She's one of us!" I shouted. "We can't just let them take her."

"And what would you have us do, Minnie?" Aziza shouted back.

My chest caved as I realized there was no saving her. Syd was at the mercy of the law and it felt like the first piece of our foundation had been chipped away. Once they began picking us off, one by one, it was only a matter of time before each of us were apprehended. A chill ran down my spine.

"The strongest weapon Syd has is her father. She will be okay," Neely whispered. She wrapped an arm around my shoulders. "Come on, Minnie. We can't stay here. It's dangerous. We have to go."

"I can't. My foot. I can barely walk on it," I said. "So, what now, Neely? Are you going to leave me behind too?"

CHAPTER 8

SYD

Nooo!" I turned in the backseat of the squad car and looked at my friends, as the cop sped away. Tears burned my eyes, as they diminished, getting smaller and smaller until finally they disappeared. A bulletproof partition separated me from the men upfront.

"Please! I am the daughter of Bao Tran. I demand that I be handed over to the custody of Zone 2!" I tried to keep the quiver out of my voice. It took all my will to add some authority to the words, but who was I fooling? I had no power and the men didn't even glance back at me to offer a response. I was used to my voice being ignored. In my zone, men were more respected than women. It was tradition for women to be demure, for women to be soft-spoken, and to make a home acceptable for a man to retreat to. It was just our way, so there was no sting behind dulling my voice. Even when I had strong opinions, I sometimes held back. I didn't want to seem aggressive, but as anger, fear, and adrenaline pumped through me in the back of that squad car, I couldn't play the passive role. I had to make them hear me because they were driving away from Zone 2, and after what happened to Neely, after the way she was almost victimized, I needed them to know that I was somebody who would be missed if anything happened to me. Not saying that Neely wasn't, but history had a way of repeating itself. Black people had been deemed invaluable before they had been regarded as less than human, three-fifths of man, or something crazy like that. History had raped, murdered, and disrespected people like Neely since forever. I'm sure that's what made the cop assault her in the first place. Nobody would believe her, even if he let her live to tell and if he decided to make her disappear, nobody would look for her. Her parents, sure, maybe even her zone, but white people would sweep her under the rug like they had done so many victims of police brutality before her. I could not become that victim. My father was somebody. I was somebody. They needed to know that. I lifted my foot and kicked the back of the seat so hard that the men jerked up front.

"I'm the daughter of Bao Tran, Panel elect! I demand to be taken to Zone 2!" I couldn't stop the tremor, but it didn't matter. I asserted my voice through the fear, which may not have been a big deal to some, but for me, it was no small feat. As a girl, sometimes the apprehension of standing up for myself stopped me from speaking up at all. Not this time. My need to be turned over to my father was great enough for me to stand my ground. No way could I allow them to not hear me. I wouldn't be bullied into submission, not when I knew my rights. I had the law on my side.

"You hear that? We got the daughter of Bao Tran in our custody," one of the men patronized.

The driver scoffed, but didn't respond.

"I am his daughter! Take me to Zone 2! I'm supposed to be reprimanded by my own people! Where are you taking me?"

The car flew through the Interzone, and as I looked around I realized the trees were becoming scarce. They were giving way to sand dunes and barrenness. *Are they taking me to the desert?*

"Where are we going?" The panic that set into my bones made tears come to my eyes, but I refused to let them fall. If I cried, they would know I was intimidated. They would know they had gotten into my head.

"Ordinance 777 of Federal Law states that any person apprehended within the boundaries of the Interzone must be delivered to the appropriate zone for processing," I shouted. I knew the law. I had been given Panel law from the time I knew my ABC'S. It was how I had learned to read. "I know my rights! My father will have your badges for this. Where. Are. You. Taking. Me?" I kicked the back of the seats in frustration.

"Hey!" one of the men reached through the partition and jammed an electrode into my neck. I was glad he chose that weapon instead of a gun. The old school billy club had been re-invented to send electric currents through its victims. It was another non-lethal precaution that had been instituted over the years after the walls went up. My entire body seized.

"Agh!"

It felt like a million tiny needles pulsated through my body. The cop turned up the voltage, as I writhed in excruciation on the backseat. My skin felt like it was being singed off, as the currents ripped through me.

"That's enough, man. You'll kill her, man!"

The prickling stopped, but the numbness of my body remained. I couldn't see straight. Everything was hazy in front of me, as I rolled onto my back, gasping for air. I wiped the slob from my mouth, as I grasped the edge of the window in desperation. I looked up at a large brick compound with barbed wire around it. We were in the middle of nowhere, somewhere in the Interzone, out in the desert, and I wasn't being taken home. "My father will…"

I felt the electrode once more, as it jammed deeply into my side and I couldn't hold the tears. This time, I wished the cop had used a gun. At least a bullet was quick. This mobile electric chair was inhumane. Whoever thought it was a just punishment, had to be on the side of the law that would never experience this. The pain. The burn. It was unlike anything I had ever had to bear. It was cruel and unusual. I had read how this was safer for citizens, how it was less deadly, how it improved police liaison with the residents of each zones, but it was all a lie. Now that I felt it, now that I was being skinned alive by electricity, I knew that this was just a torture device. This was equivalent to a whip a slave master used to use to keep his slaves in line, just because it wasn't a bullet didn't make it better. I grit my teeth to try to prepare for it, to try to brace myself and convince myself that I could take one more jolt.

"Aghh!"

The world went black. Black meant death. It felt that agonizing. Yes, I must have been dying. Nobody could survive that type of pain; no person should even inflict that much on another. Who was even mighty enough to be tasked with such authority? I gave in to the darkness and shut my eyes, knowing that they may not open again. Yes, this was death.

Long, slow, weighted. My eyes could barely function as I tried to make sense of what was in front of me as I came to. I blinked, repeatedly, trying to force my brain to speed up… trying to will my eyes to clear the haze that made everything so fuzzy. My cheek was flush against the concrete and my entire body hurt, as I planted my hands on the sides of my head to push up off the ground. It felt like I was in a box. The room was so small I could reach out and touch all four walls. It was too small to breathe, too small for the panic attack that I could feel building in my throat. *Just stay calm. Just breathe.*

"Let me out of here!!"

My voice echoed off the walls and I shrank to the floor, shriveling up in the corner. My arms around my knees, as I pulled them to my chest, was my only comfort. No one knew where I was. Not my friends, not my family. I rushed to the steel door and banged my fists against it.

"Let me out of here!"

JESUS

I was angry all the time. Literally, every minute of every day. Estoy enfadado! It was the reason why I had been desperate to escape in the first place. Zone 4 was home and I loved it, but I was fed up with the bureaucratic crap that went on inside those walls. Those walls may as well have been bars because Zone 4 felt like a prison. We got the worst of everything. The scraps. Our homes were rundown and old. The streets were full of potholes so deep that you would pop a tire driving down them. No grocery stores existed within Zone 4. They had all gone out of business due to a bad economy because there were limited jobs available, too. We had to grow our own food, and whatever we couldn't grow, we traded with one another. I had seen mi madre trade the cabbage and beet plants she was known for with other people around our zone. She would give what she grew, and in return, she would bring home corn, berries, and bread, or whatever else she could negotiate. It was our way…the only way that we survived, by depending on each other, but I didn't know how long it would last. Crops had been dying for weeks and mi madre said it was because of bad pipes under the zone that allowed lead to bleed into the water. Only lead could kill crops so quickly, she would say. So, we stopped using the water altogether. The Panel shipped bottled water to Zone 4 once a month. Every household was designated 100 free bottles each month to bathe, to drink, to cook with, to water our crops with…it was never enough, and we found ourselves rationing out the amount we used. It just felt like the end of days back home and nobody cared. How did The Panel expect us to survive without water? Without water, nothing could grow? Life couldn't grow! Our problems weren't even making the news. Our entire zone was in trouble. We couldn't live without clean water and The Panel wasn't doing anything about it. Sometimes, I thought they pumped our pipes with lead on purpose to get rid of us all together. That's what it felt like. Extermination. Like, we weren't important enough to save. Like our lives weren't worth more than their bottom line. Or like it would be beneficial to erase us, all together and just remove our culture from Zone 4 and call it their own. Before stepping foot outside the walls, I wondered if it was the same everywhere. Did the other zones suffer like we did? Were other kids reading out of outdated textbooks and being taught in schools where mice were on the attendance sheet daily? I wanted to see what the other zones were like, what the people were like; if all black people loved fried chicken. They didn't. I discovered because Neely cursed me out when I joked about it in our group scope. Were all Asian girls super smart? Syd seemed to be, but she kind of lacked common sense at times, which told me the stereotype just may not be true. Were all white boys douche bags? Liam certainly was, *LOL*…but he was my bro, and the more I got to know him, the more I understood that it was all in good fun. Were all Middle Eastern people hate filled? Nah, that one definitely wasn't true. The terror the media put into the atmosphere about attacks and suicide bombers was completely opposite of Aziza. She may have been outspoken, but she was crazy beautiful and caring. She was the only one I side barred with outside of the group scopes, and the way she showed compassion for me was anything but terroristic. Arti was…well… Arti was a mystery because he didn't share much about himself. Then, there was Minnie. I hadn't expected to meet her. Didn't know Neely would be bringing a tag-along, but she broke another stereotype. I had heard that black girls had bad attitudes. All I saw was light and loyalty when I looked at her. She was the nicest person I had ever met, and she was drastically different than Neely. She wasn't as outgoing, which told me that one thing I had heard about black girls was true. They came in all flavors. Neely was bold. Minnie was sweet. Both, equally dope, and crazy attractive. Meeting them, my new friends that felt like old friends, made me wish that these walls that started with President Trum had never been built. I wanted to live in a melting pot of all people, from all backgrounds, of all colors because life was simply more interesting when I had access to things outside my comfort zone. I remember when I first scoped with Liam, I looked on in amazement as he showed me his home and his room. Zone 1 had it all: shiny houses, restaurants, grocery stores, big campus sized schools. Liam took it all for granted, but I wanted access to those things. I wished I could live in a zone like that or that zones didn't even exist. Maybe then I could pursue nice things like that. In Zone 4, you got what you got, and you didn't complain.

"Hey, man! Where's your head at?" Liam asked, waving his hand in front of my face.

"My bad. Just thinking, you know?" I tossed my head in the direction of the girls. "How is she?"

"Her foot is bad. I don't know if it's broken, but it will definitely slow us down. She can barely put weight on it," Liam informed. "The real question is, how are you?" Liam gave me a look of confusion.

"Man, don't look at me like that." I had received that look before. I had seen that judgment in the eyes of others. That *'why are you so angry, kid?'* type of look. I detested it. "These cops, these patrollers, aren't the victims!" I didn't mean to bark at him, but there were things that Liam couldn't possibly understand simply because it wasn't his struggle to comprehend. It belonged to the rest of us, the ones with hints of color to our skin.

"They aren't all bad, bro," Liam said.

"Yeah, well you show me one that wouldn't shoot me first and ask questions later and I might agree with you. Your skin gives you the ability to be blind to a lot, and that's not on you, that's just the way it is. If you're brown or you're black, you're dangerous to them. You're guilty to them. You're suspicious to them. Before I even get the benefit of the doubt, I'm already pegged guilty to those cops."

Liam placed a heavy hand on my shoulder. "You probably would have said those same things about me before meeting me, bro. I would be a part of the *them* you're talking about, but I'm not like them. We believe the worst parts of each other and act like the best parts don't exist. I'm off that now. I think differently. Linking up with you guys has shown me *different*. I know I'm white, and I believe in the whole white privilege thing. I'll never say that doesn't exist, but I'm not like them and I know a bunch of other people from Zone 1, the majority of the people from my zone, aren't like them. Most of those cops and patrollers aren't bad people. We just live in separation and we don't know one another. People fear what they don't understand. We'll have to change that. I have a feeling that whatever this journey is that we're on is going to change that." His eyes drifted to Neely and I could see the admiration in his gaze. Liam and Neely. The energy between them was heavy, even I could feel it.

"She's going to change all that. We just have to help her." He held out his hand and I shook it, pulling him in and patting his back, like I did with my bros from Zone 4 because Liam was becoming one of my brothers, skin color couldn't get in the way of that. These people were becoming extensions of my family, not blood born, but man made. I hoped that Neely was the change that Liam spoke of because without change, I would eventually have to tell each of them goodbye.

NEELY

Minnie and I had never fought…like, not ever. Well, we fought once, way back in kindergarten, we both wanted to play with the jump rope at recess. It was how we met. Instead of fighting over it, we were forced to share, and we had been besties ever since. That fight had united us, this one felt different. This fight threatened to divide us. I felt horrible that Syd was taken, but what was I supposed to do? There wasn't much any of us could do. Syd's name wasn't even mentioned in the broadcast. I hoped her privilege meant she was protected because I hated to think of the alternative. Pondering Syd's fate made me think of my own and the inevitability of my capture. The shiver that chilled my spine made me quiver and forced me to my feet. I marched over to the group where Liam was putting a makeshift splint on Minnie's foot. The others were spread around, close enough to hear, but far enough to be engrossed in their own thoughts of doom. We were just waiting to be caught, we were exposed, out of the shadows of the trees where any patroller, cop, or fed could spot us.

"We can't stay here. We're like sitting ducks."

"I can walk," Minnie insisted. She struggled to her feet, and with one step, she was crashing to the ground.

"She'll never make it to Zone 2," Aziza said. "We need to find a place off the road where she can hide, while the rest of us go on. We can come back for her."

"We're not leaving her," I said. "That's not an option. We stay together."

"If you're the one who got us into this in the first place, please shut up," Aziza snapped.

I had to woosah because homegirl had been begging me to slap her since our very first encounter. I didn't want to go ghetto girl on her because, frankly, I wasn't even from the ghetto, but somehow in this group, I developed an urge to take it there. Maybe it was just something that was inside all black girls…like we could shred a person to pieces with just our words and attitude if pushed far enough. I hated when people pushed you over the edge and then played victim when you pulled them over it with you. I knew I would look like the bad guy if I went off on her, so I blew out air, clearing my chest of my frustration before I said, "We are not leaving my best friend in the Interzone alone."

"I can't walk, Neely," Minnie intervened, hopelessness in her voice.

I kneeled beside her and stared her square in the eyes. "We are not leaving you."

"We'll have to carry you," Liam interrupted. "Jesus and I can take turns putting you on our backs." He extended a hand to Minnie and she grasped it, her dark melanin forging a bridge with his opaque shade…an unspoken understanding…a silent promise. He nodded, as she looked up at him, reassuring her… reassuring me that he wouldn't abandon the group to save himself.

"If we can make it to Zone 4, my mama can help her," Jesus said.

"How are we supposed to sneak into Zone 4? How are we supposed to even sneak into Zone 2 now? Syd was our way in! She was our road map!" Aziza panicked. I could hear it in her voice, but I couldn't help but wonder if it was fear, or if she was just a natural, born jerk.

"I don't know much about Zone 2, but in my hood, it's plenty ways in. The Panel has water delivery trucks going in and out all the time. We hijack one of the trucks and drive it right through the import center," Jesus said.

"That just might work," Liam said.

With Minnie on his back, we disappeared into the folds of the trees, using the dense forest to conceal us as we made the journey to Zone 4.

CHAPTER 9

NEELY

All this felt impossible. It was like we were running in circles, just to avoid the inevitability of being caught. Carrying Minnie slowed us down, but it was the only way we could all stick together. There was strength in sticking together…confidence that reduced fear in unity, but I couldn't lie…I was still scared. Even if we somehow pulled off this trek and got our face to face with Syd's dad, I wasn't sure if he would hear us…if he would believe us…if he would put his neck on the line to help. Most people I knew wouldn't. Black folks minded their own business. I prayed he wasn't like black folks. In fact, I wanted him to be all up in my business at this point because I needed someone powerful to help me prove that what I had done was right, despite how wrong it appeared. With Minnie injured, we couldn't stop. We walked through the night to make up for the crawling pace we took during the day, but the woods were terrifying. They were full of whispers, alive with groans, with trees so tall that the wind whipped through the leaves, making a whistling sound that resembled screams. People didn't belong in the Interzone and I was on edge, waiting to bump into some type of deformed monster to pop out at any moment. The others must have felt the same because no one spoke. The tension, as we trekked through the Interzone, was thick. I almost feared that the monsters would know we were there just from our combined fear alone. It was palpable. It was real. If I could feel it, certainly unnatural beasts could as well.

"We're here," Jesus said. He peeked through the thick bushes that concealed us, and I peered through the hole to find Zone 4. The wall surrounding it was tall, but derelict, as holes where stone should be riddled it. It was worn down, damaged, old, but apparently effective. It stood tall and intimidating in the distance. "The water delivery truck will come this way. They'll use the main road. All we have to do is get them to stop."

"And how are we going to do that?" Minnie asked.

Aziza removed her hijab, revealing long, jet black hair that flowed down her back.

"Wow," Minnie whispered. "You're like a freaking super model."

Aziza shrugged. "If I'm going to die out here, I might as well say screw tradition, right?" She pushed through the bushes.

"What are you doing?" Liam was uncertain. Worry laced his tone and his scrunched, blonde brows revealed his apprehension.

"If the driver is a man, he will stop," Aziza said. There wasn't arrogance in that statement either, it was all fact. I knew Aziza was pretty, but as she ripped her shirt, shortening the fabric and revealing a toned, but curvaceous figure and rolled up her knee length shorts to expose her long legs. I realized she was drop dead gorgeous. She was the type of girl that teenaged boys ogled on posters behind closed doors.

"If the driver's a woman, she'll stop too." It slipped out, and Aziza winked, before replying. "Even better."

Is she a lesbian?

I smirked at her innuendo. Aziza liked girls! Who would have thought? No wonder she wanted to escape her zone. She had to feel stifled there. She could never be her true self in a traditionally Muslim zone. At least that was my assumption based on what I'd read in books, but assumptions…even my own were what had brought us to this place…to this separation…to this system that kept us fearful of anything different than ourselves. In that moment, despite the fact that I didn't like Aziza all that much, I decided to stop assuming and to get to know her in the little time we had with one another. Maybe beneath her attitude was just a girl fed up with suppression the same way I was fed up with oppression. Different struggles brought the same beast out.

"Woo!" I shouted, egging her on.

"Shh!" Minnie chastised.

"What? She's hot!" I defended, in a whisper, shrugging my shoulders.

"Let me find out you're fishing in the lady pond?" Minnie said, suggestively.

"I can assure you she isn't," Liam said, with a knowing smirk. The heartbeat that traveled from my chest to my stomach to my panties assured me I was straight.

"Let me find out you've dipped your toe in the white boy pond," Minnie added.

If I was white, I would have faded to red because I didn't know my attraction to Liam was so apparent. I planned to go diving in that pond. I planned to frolic in it, splash in it, who knows, maybe even skinny dip all up in that thang. He was the Zack Morris of my generation. I remembered the thump of my heartbeat when Minnie and I discovered the old-school show in the archive's library. I watched every episode with my head rested in my hands and my legs folded up, while hearts floated from my eyes. Liam gave me that same feeling.

"Guys! Here comes the truck!" Aziza hissed. "Get ready!"

Please, let it stop. Please, let it stop.

I prayed in my head again and again, as the yellow headlights neared Aziza, shining brightly. The hum of the semi-truck, as it approached, caused my heart to gallop. If the driver didn't stop, he would report Aziza as soon as he got through the gates of Zone 4. Everyone would know exactly where we were, and with Minnie's injury, there was no running to escape. "Come on, stop," I whispered. As if I had hummed a magic spell, the truck began to slow, and the squeal of its brakes rang through the air.

Aziza waved her hands above her head.

The driver cut the engine and it ticked to a stop.

Lights illuminated her, and she shielded her eyes. "Thank goodness you stopped! I need help!"

The driver stuck his head out the window.

"What are you doing out here? Are you hurt?" The bass filled voice matched his white, chubby, red haired, beard covered face. The flannel shirt and baseball cap he wore accessorized his stereotype. I'd put my money on it, he had a beer belly.

"I need help. Please." Aziza faked a limp, as she walked toward the driver's side of the door. A damsel in distress didn't quite describe Aziza. More like a seductress lying in wait. This man had no idea he was walking right into a setup. He opened his door and stepped one, heavy foot down onto the ledge of the tall truck. Only half his body was out. He looked down at Aziza and up at the wall ahead.

"You're out of zone. You don't belong here. You're not one of these wetbacks. You're one of those kids…that killed the…"

Before he could even conclude his revelation, Aziza grabbed the one leg that was out of the truck and yanked the trucker down with all her might. Liam and Jesus sprang into action, stepping out of the trees with weapons drawn.

Jesus hit the man with the end of the long assault rifle he carried.

"Christ!" the man howled, as he rolled onto his side, covering his nose with both hands. I was sure it was broken. He deserved it for the wetback comment.

"What do we do with him?" Aziza asked.

Liam cracked open the back of the truck and emerged with rope. He tossed it to Jesus.

"We tie him up. We aren't hurting anyone that doesn't threaten to hurt us first," Liam said. "He's just a means to an end."

"Did you hear what he said? Wetback, huh?" Jesus asked, pointing the gun at the man.

"You can't attack every single person who says something you don't like." I pushed his arm, messing up his aim. "They're words. You have to learn to control yourself, Jesus! If you hurt everyone who spews hate, you only prove them right…you give them exactly who they expect you to be!"

"Don't give me that *when they go low, you go high crap!* I ain't Michelle Obama! Sometimes, it feels good to go low. Sometimes, to get respect, I have to show them that I'll play as dirty as they will. You think they would hesitate to blow my head off? Or Neely's head off? No! The high road won't make them see us as human beings. In their eyes, we'll always be beneath them!"

Jesus' jaw was rock solid, as his temple throbbed. I never knew anger like that could live inside someone. I was his friend and I thought it was terrifying he got like this; the impulsivity, the lack of regard, and the absence of remorse. It was an insane cycle of ignorance. White people's disregard for minorities angered minorities and that anger terrified white people. We were terrified of what we created. How could we erase the misunderstanding? Jesus grit his teeth, as he stared down the gun at the trucker who laid on his back, hands raised, palms forward.

Jesus was a real live wire…a hot head and I could feel how much he wanted to punish this man. Jesus seemed to want to punish all white men. A few seconds passed, but they felt like lifetimes before Jesus lowered his gun. "Fine. We'll tie him up!"

Jesus and Liam restrained the man, muzzling him, before tossing him into the back of the truck.

"You keep quiet, and at the end of all this, we will let you go. You make one peep, and I'll show you what I think about your little wetback comment," Jesus threatened. I helped Minnie into the back, then climbed in with Aziza and Jesus. Liam slammed the door shut, cloaking us in darkness.

He would play the role of the driver. He was white. No one would bat an eye if he drove this water delivery through the gates of Zone 4. I sat in darkness. I couldn't even see in front of my face, as the bed of the truck swayed with every bump in the pavement. *What if they open up the back? Please, don't let them open the back. Why didn't we think of that?* Anxiety ate away at my chest. *God, what if the driver tries to scream for help?*

"Not one word." The threat came from Jesus, as he racked the gun. Guess he was worried about red head screaming, too.

The truck rolled to a stop and I closed my eyes. My steepled hands rested below my chin. *Come on, come on, come on.* I'd never prayed so much in my life until I ventured outside my zone. I needed to believe that there was someone or something guiding me through this thing because it felt impossible to get through it alone.

"Water drop off."

I noticed the quiver in Liam's voice, and I hoped his eyes didn't reveal his trepidation because even from the back of the truck, I could hear his uncertainty.

"Inventory list."

My eyes bulged at the stern voice that replied to Liam. Not being able to see what was happening in front of the truck was torture. Was there more than one man at the gate? Was he suspicious? Were things going smoothly? I had to assess the entire situation from the darkness in the back. I was a bystander in my own fate, and I hoped Liam could keep his cool to pull this off. I felt a squeeze of my hand and knew that it was Minnie. She was the best friend that caught your vibe without ever needing to speak. She was comfort and I gave her hand a squeeze back, as I held my breath in the dark.

"All set," I heard, and when I felt the truck move forward, I sighed. I had never felt relief like that, but I knew we were far from home free. All it took was for one person to spot us and the entire plan would implode. We drove for a while before the truck rumbled to a stop, and when Liam pulled open the back, light flooded the space.

"Hurry. We need to get off the road before someone sees us," he said, ushering us out.

"What about him?" Aziza asked.

"We'll leave him until we get back," Liam said.

"The heat alone will suffocate him if we close him in the back of this truck for too long," I countered. I had enough on my conscience. I didn't need more. This entire journey was supposed to be fun. It was supposed to be enlightening and expand my scope of the world, of other people, but it wasn't worth the tragedy that had occurred. I had blood on my hands and heart that I couldn't just wash off. "And we can't just leave a water truck on the side of the road. Is there a place we can hide it?"

"I know where we can take it," Jesus said. We all climbed out and into the front of the truck. Jesus took the passenger seat and we hid in the space behind them.

"There's a junkyard near my neighborhood. We can hide the truck there and tie the driver to the steering wheel until we return," he said.

I took in Zone 4 as we drove. Children played shirtless and shoeless in the middle of the streets. Piles of garbage were strewn about; colorful, three-story buildings provided homes only they didn't appear very homey. They were derelict, run down, broken windows, and raggedy paint made it seem like these buildings were barely standing. Clotheslines filled with colorful, but worn items hung from balcony to balcony. There was no grass, just concrete and speckles of broken glass that sparkled like diamonds all over the street.

"This is where you live?" Aziza asked, unable to mask her shock.

"How do people live like this?" Minnie croaked, her voice cracking in emotion, as we passed a stray dog that was starved to the point where ribs showed through his mangy fur.

"We manage," Jesus replied. "We don't have much, but this is home." His voice was full of pride and I had to blink away my tears. I would have never envisioned this level of poverty existed. I felt like a jerk for complaining about my little hot house.

How had The Panel allowed a zone to get this bad?

We pulled off the main road into a landfill where trash mountains casted shadows over the truck, as we maneuvered through. We hopped out and Jesus pulled the driver from the back, then secured him to the steering wheel.

"Hmmmm!!!" The man attempted to scream for help, but his muzzled mouth didn't produce much sound.

"You can yell all you want. No one will hear you out here," Jesus said.

"You don't need help," I said, staring him in the eyes. "Nothing is going to happen to you. We just need a little time to get help for our friend. After that, we'll let you go."

"This way," Jesus said. We climbed through piles of trash, covering our mouths and noses. The stench was overwhelming, and I gagged as my feet sank all the way up to my kneecaps with every step.

The hole in the fence led us out into an abandoned lot.

"My house is just over the train tracks," Jesus said. He almost had to yell the words. The chaos from the neighborhood in the near distance filled the air. The people were alive, laughing, and screaming full conversations over the dogs that yelped loudly. The sound of music, live drums, in fact, could be heard.

"Is it a parade?" Aziza asked.

Jesus smirked. "No, just another day. People praying, performing rituals. It's called Santeria. Everybody sacrificing something to receive something else."

"What are they sacrificing and what do they want to get?" Liam asked.

"Giving their souls for clean water, for better soil, for help…anything that will make this easier," Jesus said.

"Wow." It was all I had to give. I couldn't fathom the

desperation, but it was in front of my eyes clear as day.

Jesus approached the back of a building of row houses and a white pit bull lunged at us. I paused, mid-step, eyeing the beast that was only restrained by a rusted, thin chain. Anything with a red nose, blue eyes, and knife sharp teeth could rip you to shreds. The dog barked incessantly, sneering and lunging. The chain snapped.

"Run!" Liam shouted, but to our surprise, the dog ran full speed toward us but slowed at my feet. It sat on its back paws and lowered its head onto its front paws in front of me before offering up a whimper. It licked at the soles of my sneakers, as it sniffed me. I steeled in place. We all did.

"What do I do?"

I didn't want this thing to suddenly attack.

"That crazy dog has been chasing people around this neighborhood for years. The owner can't even control it. Guess you can," Jesus said, in amazement. I stepped around the dog and it stood. My blood froze in my veins.

"I don't think she's going to hurt you, Neely," Minnie whispered.

"Until it bites me," I shot back.

The dog snuggled against my leg and my shallow breaths filled in, as I extended a shaky hand towards its blocky head. I rubbed the top and the dog melted into my hand, moving its head all around and licking my fingertips.

I kneeled, smiling, as the beast jumped on me and licked my face. This was how white people treated their pets. Black folks didn't let dogs lick them in the face. I laughed, as the dog's tail flicked in excitement.

I stood to walk. My friends took timid steps behind me. The dog quickly joined at my side.

"Go! Get!" I shooed the beast away and it whimpered, frowning as if I was breaking its heart.

I started walking, again, and the dog followed.

"Get out of here, you dirty mutt!" I hissed.

The dog sat on its hind legs and lifted his paws.

"Aww, she's begging, Neely!" Minnie cooed. "She's cute!"

"She's a pit bull! There is nothing cute about a pit. They kill babies and tear grown men apart."

The dog turned its head as if it was feigning innocence.

I took a step, it trotted to catch up to me.

"Looks like she's yours now," Liam teased.

"Absolutely not!" I protested. We approached the back of the building, with the stupid dog in tow, and Jesus led us through a door covered in iron bars.

"What's that smell?" I asked. It smelled like gas or chemicals filled the air, like at any moment my lungs would fill with poison.

"It's just propane. We use it to cook. It heats the houses, makes the water hot…it's harmless," Jesus said.

Until someone strikes a match.

Red and black braided wire was exposed where sheetrock should have covered them. It snaked up the uneven concrete staircase that felt like they would crumble beneath our feet at any moment.

"Is this your house?" Liam asked.

"My abuela's," Jesus responded. "Mi madre comes here every day for lunch to check in on her. She has dementia, so even if she sees us, she won't be able to tell. Everyone will just think she's in one of her spells."

Is there any part of his life that's easy?

I didn't want to pity him because I knew he would hate it, but I felt sorry for Jesus. We were the same age, but lived drastically different lives. His was filled with struggle, survival, and loss. It didn't seem fair that a boy so young had so much weight to carry around on his shoulders. No wonder he was so pissed off. I'd be fed up, too.

We made it to a door on the second floor and he pulled open the wrought iron door that guarded a wooden one. He reached above the landing and pulled down a key, unlocking both, before ushering us all inside. He slammed the door on the dog, who whimpered in protest, before scurrying down the steps.

The house smelled like mothballs and was painted in puke yellow paint that was full of chips. A large picture of Jesus, or the image that we assumed to be him, was in a dingy, gold frame on the wall. A mantle filled with candles that had the same Jesus wrapped around them was front and center.

"Who's there?"

The frail voice came down the narrow hall before I ever saw her face. The woman stood no taller than a child, with jet black hair and wrinkled skin came hobbling out. The only thing that kept her upright was the metal walker that preceded her small steps.

"Abuela, it's me, Jesus."

His voice softened in a way I hadn't heard before. He was

gentle with her, as he guided her to the big, blue, tattered rocking chair in the corner of the room.

"Jesus?" Abuela asked.

"Si, es tu nieto, abuela," he responded.

"She doesn't remember me, sometimes," he explained. "You have a seat, abuela. Did you eat?"

"Who are all these people in my house?" she asked.

"These are mi amigos, abuela," Jesus explained.

He turned to us.

"What now?" Liam asked.

"We wait," he replied.

He pulled out a chair for Minnie, grimaced in pain. She lifted her pants leg to reveal that her foot had almost doubled in size. It was swollen and the skin on her ankle was turning purple.

"Mi madre will be here soon," Jesus said.

As if he had summoned her, a woman walked through the door.

"Mama, why is this door unlocked?" The woman paused in shock when she came around the corner to find us.

"Jesus!" she shouted, as she rushed to him, wrapping him in her arms. They had identical faces; same shade, same eyes, same nose. "What did you do, papi? The feds came to our house. Where have you been? I thought I would never see you again!" She steeled, as she gripped his forearms and her eyes cast onto the rest of us. "Who are these kids?"

"They're my friends, mama," Jesus said. "And we need your help."

He motioned to Minnie's foot, and his mother pulled in a

breath. I didn't see her let it out. Her chest puffed up, as she looked at each of us.

"Did you kill that cop?" she asked.

"Not me, personally, no, but I was there. The cop attacked my friend."

"He tried to rape me," I spoke up, my lip trembling. "I'm the one who shot him."

"But it was self-defense. We have a friend who can get the footage to prove that to The Panel. One of the girls who was with us is the daughter of Bao Tran," Jesus explained.

"Oh, mijo," she sighed, her eyes watering. "Why would you leave zone?"

"Look around, ma!" Jesus said, passionately. "We're living in hell. I just wanted to see what it was like out there. I wanted to see what they were like." He motioned to us. "Things just went horribly wrong."

She nodded and patted his cheek lovingly. Finally, she released the breath and her chest deflated. "Let me take a look at that foot."

She bent, and as soon as she touched Minnie's foot, she howled.

"Is it broken?" Liam asked.

"No, but it's badly dislocated. I'll need to pop it back in place."

"Wait, wait, wait," Minnie protested, she reached for her injury. "Will it hurt?"

The look on Ms. Rodriguez's face told us all that it would, but her mouth said, "Un poco, mi amor."

"Just a little," Jesus translated.

Minnie nodded. "Okay," she recited, bracing herself. "Okay, okay, okay."

"On the count of three, si?"

Minnie gripped the sides of the wooden chair she sat on, as Ms. Rodriguez propped Minnie's food up and rested it in her lap. "Uno…"

POP!

"Agh!" Minnie shrieked. "You said three!"

"It's done, it's done." Her tone was motherly, soothing, as she pulled a long scarf from her bag that sat near her feet. "You did so good, mi amor. I'm just going to wrap it to keep it stable."

Ms. Rodriguez turned to Jesus. "Go get two of abuela's pain pills from her bureau and a bottled water," she instructed.

Minnie's foot was wrapped securely in a makeshift splint, and Jesus returned with the pills. "This will help with the pain. You cannot walk on this foot. You put weight on it, and turn the wrong way, the next time it will break. What is the plan here? Feds, cops, and patrollers are searching high and low for all of you. They came to the house."

"We have to show The Panel what really happened," Jesus said. "But we just want to get a bit of rest first."

"You can't go back out there, Jesus. You are my only son. You're all I have. The men who came looking for you will shoot to kill. It's not safe," Ms. Rodriguez pleaded. "I know you want to help your friends, but you are my son. It is my job to protect you. You can't go, Jesus. You can't!"

My heart felt tender, like her pleas were poking at a bruise that hadn't healed yet. This was his mother. She was terrified for her child. I knew my mother must have felt the same and the thought prickled my eyes with emotion.

"Okay, mama, okay. I won't go," he said. She pulled him close; and just like that, we had lost another person. Our group was dwindling.

Minnie couldn't walk, Syd was captured, Jesus was staying with his family. I couldn't blame him. If I had the opportunity to go back to my family and hide in the safety of their arms, I would too.

"The rest of you can stay here for the night to rest. We don't have much, but you are welcome to share what we have and to take some with you on your journey," Ms. Rodriguez said. "No one will think to look for you here at abuela's."

We ate silently the table. Ms. Rodriguez served us rice and beans, despite the fact that I noticed she used the last of both. Where I was from, these simple things sat in the pantry for months, and if ever cooked were a side dish. In Zone 4, this was a good meal; and although I didn't particularly like what was served, I ate every bite and was grateful for it. I knew this meal was made with love and that filled me up with every bite. Nightfall landed, and she looked at us with sympathetic eyes. "I wish you luck on your journey," she said. "Jesus, be sure to send them with the bread I baked to help them along the way and abuela's crutches."

Jesus nodded. "Yes, ma'am. Good night, ma." He kissed her on her forehead, and she gave his cheek a gentle pat. "I love you."

"I love you too, mijo."

An awkward silence fell over us, as Jesus took a seat at the table.

"We understand, you know?" Liam started. "This is your home. You should stay."

"I should, but I can't," Jesus said.

I lifted my eyes in shock.

"We started this together. We have to finish this together," Jesus said. "We will get a good night's sleep here and head out before she wakes in the morning."

"Jesus, she's your mom," Aziza disputed.

"And I'll make sure I make it back to her," Jesus said. He pinched the bridge of his nose and sniffed away his tears.

I reached across the table and placed my hand atop of his. Black on brown. It was a sight I never thought I would see. "You will make it back. I promise."

It was a promise I intended to keep.

CHAPTER 10

NEELY

Sleep wouldn't come. As we all piled up on the wooden floor in the living room, I laid there, restless. Tossing. Turning. Thinking. Wishing I could turn my brain off. Liam snored. It was something I could never learn over scopes. Aziza giggled. Whatever she was dreaming of, it must have been funny. Light. She was more relaxed in her sleep than I had ever seen her awake. Her terse personality was something I would have never picked up on through scope. Jesus' brow pinched, even in unconsciousness. He was troubled, burdened by circumstance inherited by race. I never could have known his struggle over scope. We had spent an entire summer, group scoping, using words and pictures to form this bond, but it had been superficial. Each of us had put on a face, only allowing the group to meet the representative of ourselves. I was always funny, always nice, my responses always calculated and well thought out over scope. It wasn't until we were face to face did our true selves show. You couldn't connect truly without touch, without being face to face, without learning the inflection in a person's voice. From the moment I saw their faces, I felt connected. They were my friends, and not because we were just alike, but because we were different. We hadn't known each other that long, but the impressions that they were leaving on my life were monumental. Through my lack of knowing where they came from and why they were the way they were, I felt like a sponge soaking in their every characteristic. My black experience was transforming into a human experience. Before I was square, and they were rounding me out, opening my mind and my heart to see the beauty in contrast, instead of expecting everything and everyone to be the same. How could anyone ever look at the different shades of our skin, as we stood side by side, and see anything other than beauty? I caught myself staring, in awe sometimes, at how exquisite they all were, how uniquely constructed we were on the outside, but identically made on the inside. We had eyes to see, hearts to feel, lungs to breathe, minds to think, and somehow, one bigot, one orange, bad toupee wearing clown had convinced us that we were too different to live as one. My mama always said it only took a little bit of poison to taint the whole well. Guess hate worked the same way. We knew better. The history of the world had taken us through this before, and still, we hadn't learned from our mistakes; or maybe I was just being greedy, wanting to see more, wanting to do more than what the walls allowed.

ROOF! ROOF! ROOF!

"Stupid dog," I whispered. I shook my head, as I rolled onto my side, then pushed up off the floor with one arm, as I sat straight up.

ROOF! ROOF! ROOF!

I stood and made my way to the modest kitchen. I opened the refrigerator and an ache shot through me when I saw how empty it was. I wondered if we had eaten them out of house and home. It was something I'd heard my mom joke about, but here it felt like a real possibility.

ROOF! ROOF! ROOF!

"Okay, okay," I whispered, as I went to the trash and picked out a few scraps. If I didn't feed the thing, it would never shut up.

I stepped over the others, careful not to wake them. I opened the shutters to the balcony and my heart sank. That barking wasn't from the mutt. Police K-9's and officers carrying automatic weapons were silently moving down the block and getting into position around the door to the building.

I ran, tripping in the darkness.

"Get up, get up," I whispered, shaking them awake. "We have to go, right now! A dozen cops are about to burst in here any minute," I whispered. "They're outside." I couldn't hide my panic. Liam rushed to the balcony and eased his head out to take a peek.

"There's no way out," Liam said.

"We can take the roof to the next block," Jesus said, urgently.

"I can't run," Minnie hissed, her eyes welling with fear.

ROOF! ROOF! ROOF!

"What is going on out there? That stupid dog is going to wake Abuela!" Ms. Rodriguez came walking down the hallway, tightening her housecoat, as the rubber soles to her house shoes slapped against the floor.

Jesus rushed to his mother, with his finger placed to his lip. "The cops are outside."

Her eyes widened at the realization.

"I know you want me to stay, ma, but we have to go," Jesus said. "If they catch me, ma…"

His words trailed. My thoughts followed. We were hoping for the best but facing the worst. If we were caught…

"I'm already caught," Minnie said.

"No, you can hide. Here," Ms. Rodriguez said, as she opened her pantry and removed panels from the back wall.

"The rest of us will lead the cops away from here," Liam said. "We have to get to the street and then split up. Divide them and lose them. We'll meet back at the junkyard."

"I'm staying with Minnie. She won't make it to the junkyard alone," I said.

Aziza crept to the window. "Whatever we're going to do, we have to do it now. Like, right now."

BOOM!

The sound of the door to the building being knocked off its hinges erupted, sparking chaos.

"Be careful, Jesus," Ms. Rodriguez said. Jesus took pause. We didn't have a minute to waste, but he risked it all to double back and kiss his mother on the cheek.

He led the way to the window and Minnie and I were ushered into the pantry.

"Don't make a sound," Ms. Rodriguez warned. Her hands were shaking so badly that she could barely replace the panels.

Darkness concealed us, and Minnie grabbed my hand. All we could do was pray that we weren't discovered.

AZIZA

"Climb! Go! Go! Go!"

Jesus' screams urged me up the rusty fire escape.

"They're headed for the roof!" I heard another voice say. I was too afraid to look down. I didn't want to see how many of them were chasing us. When I felt cornered, I froze, and I couldn't afford to be caught. I made it to the roof and then looked back to see two men coming up the ladder after us. "Move." I pushed past the boys and reached for the edge of the ladder that kept it secured against the side of the building.

"Help me!" I shouted as I pulled against the heavy steel with all my might. It was old and barely attached, but still, it didn't give. Liam and Jesus joined me, and together we pulled until the screws detached from the building.

"Agh!!" The ladder went flying off the side of the building, with the agents attached to it. I leaned over the edge to see the men scrambling at the bottom. Their fall was softened by the piles of garbage that lined the streets and they quickly rebounded, scrambling to continue their pursuit.

"They're on the roof!"

We ran full speed, jumping from rooftop to rooftop.

"We have to split up!" Liam shouted. "Meet at the truck!" I didn't want to. I was weakest without them, but I didn't have a choice. They each jumped to different buildings and I stood there, hesitating, as I looked at the only other path. A sudden panic filled me. The distance between the buildings seemed so far. The commotion of men approaching me from behind filled me with anxiety. I didn't have a choice. It was jump or give up. I took off, full speed. When my feet left the building, it felt like I could fly. Momentum carried me across the alley that separated the rooftops. I barely gripped the edge of the building.

"Agh!" I hung off the side, my fingers slipping. I glanced back and saw the men point their weapons.

RAT TAT TAT TAT TAT!

I turned toward the building when I heard the gunshots, waiting for the pain, waiting for death. It never came. When

I looked up, I saw the agents jerking left to right as bullets riddled them.

"Climb!" Jesus and Liam shouted. I tried to hoist myself up onto the ledge, but the bricks that made up the dilapidated building were so old that they gave way under my weight. I plunged, but I quickly caught the balcony ledge beneath me. When I felt that brick give out, my eyes widened, as I dropped again. I grabbed the edge of the balcony below that. This building was falling apart, piece by piece. I looked right to the long pipe that ran down the side of the building and I lunged for it, then slid all the way down to the street.

"Aziza!" I looked up. Liam pointed behind me. I turned to find three agents coming around the corner. I turned to run, but two more were approaching me from the opposite direction. I was boxed in. The only way out was through these men, but there were five of them and only one of me.

A porcelain pot suddenly crashed to the ground, shattering at the feet of the men in front of me. I looked up to find an old lady standing on her balcony, waving a broom at the agents.

"Deja, a la chica sola, cerdos!"

"Go back in your home!" one of the men shouted, as he pointed his gun in the air and fired a warning shot.

A few more heads popped out of their homes at the sound of the commotion. The old woman threw another ceramic pot, this time, hitting an agent on the back. A bag of garbage was thrown next, then a chair, then potatoes, and rocks. Hundreds of people came out on their balconies, throwing things and shouting at the men who stood between me and freedom.

"Correr!" the old woman shouted at me. "Correr!" She shooed me, signaling for me to go, as the men took cover from the neighborhood attack. A door opened, and a man ushered me inside his home, leading me all the way through to the back, where I emerged onto the next block. These people didn't know me. They had no reason to help me. I wasn't even one of them. I didn't belong to their community, but they had gone out on a limb for me, for someone different, and I was grateful. I turned towards the man. "Thank you," I said.

"You're welcome," he responded. "Hurry, that way." He pointed down the alley and I took off running, hoping that once I made it, the others would be waiting for me at the truck when I arrived.

MINNIE

"Come on!" Ms. Rodriguez whispered as she ushered us out of hiding. "I have to get you two out of here."

We crawled from the tiny space and looked at the mess the feds had made. They had destroyed everything. Couch cushions were slit open, the refrigerator door was pulled off, pictures were knocked down. Things that had nothing to do with searching the premises had been wrecked.

"I'm so sorry," I whispered, as I looked at all the damage.

"Things can be replaced. Let's go," she said.

"Who are these girls, Ava?"

Abuela looked at us, in confusion, as if she hadn't just seen us the night before.

"They don't belong here. What are they doing here?" she questioned.

"Abuela, they're friends of Jesus'," Ms. Rodriguez explained. "I have to leave…just for a little while. I want you to sit here in your chair and work on that beautiful dress you promised me. Remember?" She ushered the woman to her rocker and then searched the mess on the ground, frantically sifting through it, until she located the crochet needle and yarn.

"Dress?"

"Yes, abuela, a beautiful dress," Ms. Rodriguez encouraged.

The old woman grabbed the needle and yarn, then went to work, as she quietly rocked, while humming a song.

Ms. Rodriguez turned to us and said, "hurry, we don't have much time." She grabbed two scarves and handed them to us. "Wrap these around your faces. You can hide in my vegetable cart."

We did as we were told, and then I leaned on Neely, as we made our way down the stairs.

"Here, take these," Ms. Rodriguez said, once we made it to the bottom of the stairwell. I took the crutches and kept my head down, as we stepped out onto the street. There were people everywhere and we blended into the crowd. The good thing about Zone 4, is that Latin people came in all colors. Some were light, others were dark, we blended in, as we followed Jesus' mom down the block. "My cart is parked in the alley."

We rounded the corner, moving as fast as my bum foot would allow. When we turned the corner, we practically turned on our heels at the sight of the armed agent standing right at the cart.

"Keep your head down and just keep moving," Neely whispered.

I knew we looked suspicious. We had turned too abruptly; my eyes had widened too drastically. There was nothing smooth about it.

"Hey!"

When I heard the baritone voice, we stopped moving.

"Here we go," Neely whispered.

"Let's see some ID," he demanded.

Ms. Rodriguez turned around. "Of course, officer," she said, her voice shaking, as she searched through her bag. "I'm just taking my two daughters to the market."

"ID's for them too," he pushed.

We had to do something before he discovered who we were. Our ID's were stored in our channels, but each zone was assigned a distinct ID barcode. We couldn't allow him to scan ours. I eyed the block in front of us. I didn't see any other agents. He had no back up. Jesus and the others had led the rest of the men away. *We just have to take out this one.*

I turned around, swiftly, swinging the crutch with all my might, hitting his temple with one end, then taking out his jewels with the other. He fell to his knees and I lifted the crutch, uppercutting him with the handle. He hit the pavement. Out cold.

"Oh my God! Did you see that? Did you see what you just did?" Neely exclaimed.

"We have to get him off the street," Ms. Rodriguez said. I readjusted on my crutches and Neely reached down to pick the man up under his shoulders. Ms. Rodriguez grabbed his ankles and they moved him next to a trash bin in the shadows of the alley.

"Let's go," Ms. Rodriguez said.

We rushed over to her cart and she pulled back the curtain at the bottom. There was barely enough space for us both to fit. "Climb inside," she said, as she emptied out all her vegetables. My heart broke because I knew this food she was throwing to the ground was supposed to feed her and Jesus' abuela.

"I'm so sorry." It felt like the right thing to say. I climbed in first and Neely squeezed in beside me, as Ms. Rodriguez closed the curtain. We moved slowly through the cobblestone streets, the weight of us making it harder to push. Sweat soaked me and I could barely breathe. The air was so thick from the humidity and the heat. The noise from the busy streets was overwhelming. *God, please let us make it home. I will never leave zone again.*

"We're here."

We stopped moving and I climbed from the bottom of the cart. Neely scrambled out behind me. Out of nowhere, we heard barking and we turned, expecting to find police dogs, ready to attack. Instead, the pit bull came running and barking toward Neely. She tensed until it sat right at her feet. Neely bent down and petted the old dog. "Guess I made a new friend, huh?"

She stood. "Let's find the others."

We made our way back to the truck and Ms. Rodriguez ran to Jesus, as soon as she laid eyes on him. The driver was long gone.

"We have to go, now," Neely insisted.

The sound of sirens in the distance told us that more trouble was near.

"This truck is hot. We need a new way out. We can't go back through the checkpoint. They will be looking for this truck," Aziza said.

"Devil's Lake," Ms. Rodriguez said.

"Devil's Lake?" Liam posed.

"It's full of lead and waste from the old auto companies," Jesus said.

"It's more than lead and waste. It's impassable. The water is so polluted it burns through bone," Ms. Rodriguez added.

"It's our only way out," Jesus interrupted. "It's the only place the feds and the cops won't be expecting us to go."

"But it's so dangerous, mijo," she said. Her eyes were filled with tears, as she stared at Jesus. "You know what has happened to those who have tried to pass it."

"We have to try, ma," he said. It was his tone that scared me, like he knew it was doomed. The dread in her eyes caused my stomach to tighten. My body was screaming no, my intuition blaring for me to find another way.

What is Jesus about to get us into?

She nodded. She pulled him in for the tightest hug. I had to wipe away tears that snuck out of my eyes.

"How far is this place from where we are now?" I asked. I held out the crutches. They explained my worry. I was only half mobile. I was the weakest link. If anyone was at risk of being caught, it was me.

"It's just beyond the landfills," Jesus said.

"I'll carry you there," Liam said.

"I don't break my promises," Neely said, as she looked at Jesus' mom. "He's going to come home to you when this is all said and done."

"You're a special girl," Ms. Rodriguez replied, as she sniffed away emotion. "And because of that, I believe you."

CHAPTER 11

SYD

Hours passed. At least 12 because the sunset then rose again, as I laid on the ground of the cell, writhing in pain. My face was untouched. My mugshot made it appear as if I was in perfectly good health while in federal custody, but the part the camera couldn't see had been beaten. I could barely move. All I could do was call out for help, and that only seemed to piss the feds off more. "My name is Sydney Tran, daughter of Bao Tran, Panel head for Zone 2. I invoke my right to representation!" I shouted at the top of my lungs. It was my right. I was a person. I had rights. I couldn't believe that this was happening to me. These men either didn't believe that I was who I said I was, or they didn't care. They wanted revenge for the fallen cop, and I was bearing the brunt of their frustration. I was sure that my ribs were broken. A 12-inch boot to the gut had done that. Grown men took turns mishandling me, electrocuting me, and delivering blows that felt like they would kill me. I wondered if they eventually would. They couldn't have any intention of letting me live to tell this story. Still, I had rights and I refused to stop demanding that they honor them. "My name is Sydney Tran, daughter of Bao Tran, Panel head for Zone 2. I invoke my right to representation!"

I cried in frustration. "Agh!!" Why had my father taught me the law if it didn't even work? What was the point if the people who were supposed to uphold it didn't even respect it? These men were breaking it themselves…they were criminals with badges, the most dangerous of them all.

I heard the door open and I scraped my face off the ground and scrambled backward, away from the white man in the suit who entered the room. The two men responsible for my current state entered behind him. His shoes echoed off the walls and with the three of them inside, it felt like they would suck up all the air in the cubicle sized trap. The man looked down at me and removed a handkerchief from his inner jacket pocket. He looked back, sternly, at the two men behind him. "Good thing she was found in this condition, eh? Daughter of a Panel member certainly wouldn't obtain these types of injuries in federal custody," he muttered.

He bent down and handed me the silk fabric. I didn't speak, but I extended my arm to take it.

"Your father can be on his way. We can allow you to make a call, but we need reassurance that you will let him know how accommodating my men have been. We wouldn't want him thinking these bruises came along with your stay."

"I…just want to go home," I stammered. "I won't say anything."

"Good." He stood. "Because we are everywhere, all the time, even when dear old daddy isn't. I would hate for things to become difficult for you. There is a dead cop. Tensions are high. You understand."

I nodded. I would say anything just to get out of there, just to leave with my life.

He turned to the men behind him and one of them produced a channel. Kneeling before me, again, he said, "this release of liability says you were not injured in our custody. After you sign, you can call your father."

I lifted my thumb to put my fingerprint on the screen, but he pulled it back out of my reach.

"Please, I just want to go home…"

"One last thing," he said. "Where are they headed?"

My stomach hollowed because I knew he was leveraging my self-preservation against my loyalty to my friends.

"I don't know," I whispered.

He stood. "That's too bad."

I wished I had the will to let him walk out that door, but fear ruled me. "Wait!"

He turned. "Tell me everything you know about their plan and I will take you to your father."

NEELY

The raging current spilled over the edge of the landfill and we stood, staring at the murky depths below. "Is that even water?" Liam asked. The lake was black as tar, and debris floated to the surface where bones and trash littered.

"It's the only way out," Jesus reiterated.

"That's about a hundred-meter swim," Aziza said.

"We can't swim across. The water's acidic. One drop burns through bone. Falling in would be deadly," Jesus warned.

"So, it's like lava?" I asked, as I looked at Jesus in disbelief. Water was supposed to be the purest thing on earth. How had it morphed into what I was staring at? How had The Panel allowed it to get so bad? It was a tease of freedom. A lake of death that kept people locked inside the walls of poverty, better than any wall could ever do. I looked down at the bones that floated below. It was a graveyard. I wondered what had made people so desperate that they even dared such a feat. Then, I realized I had done the same. I had taken a risk that most people wouldn't. I had escaped zone. I had done the unthinkable without thinking at all. The consequences were an afterthought…something I dismissed as if getting caught was a long shot when it was the only real way that my night of freedom could have ended.

"How do you expect us to get across?" Aziza asked.

Jesus pointed to the power cord that ran across the lake. My eyes followed the black cord across the sky. One hundred yards. A football field of burning water stood between us and the other side. My eyes stung because it was just one thing after another. Every single time we got through one hurdle, another came out of nowhere, like life was designed to hold me back no matter how hard I fought. Why couldn't it be easy sometimes? I wasn't asking for it all to be easy. I knew I had to work and fight to clear my name, but every single step felt like I was going to war. The weight on my chest hadn't eased up since I left the comfort of my room. As soon as my feet hit the pavement outside my house on the night I escaped zone, I had worried. I had felt unsafe. I wondered if the naivety of being a kid would ever return. Even if I came out of this unscathed, would I ever go back to the girl I used to be or had seeing the real world, seeing the coldness of life outside Zone 7 stained my youth? Freedom wasn't free. It would cost me something, I just wasn't sure what it was yet.

"Has anyone ever made it across?" Minnie asked.

The silence was deafening. How were we supposed to pull off something that no one before us had never done? *This is impossible.* I shook the thought from my mind, almost as fast as it entered. I heard my mother's voice in my ear. *Your words have power, Neely. What you say matters. What you tell yourself creates energy.* If everyone thought like me, nothing would ever get done. Somebody always had to be the first. I was going to be the first to cross Devil's Lake.

"Maybe we have a better chance of fighting off the feds." Aziza's voice was small…unsure.

"They aren't all bad. Maybe it's time to turn ourselves in and explain what happened. Somebody will listen," Liam piped up. My head snapped in his direction and I did nothing to control the black girl yank in my neck. The risk taker who had gotten us all into this in the first place was ready for the battle to end. He never seemed to carry the same concerns as the rest of us. It was like he was out here for fun like our lives weren't at risk. There was an arrogance in every decision he made like he was going home no matter what, and maybe he was. His face wasn't on the broadcast. Syd's either. I knew why she had been exempt. Her father had power. Who was protecting Liam? The entitlement he carried was embedded in him. Centuries of superiority made what was dire to us seem like a game to him. His power was the color of his skin. It matched the men who hunted us. It matched the institution we were rebelling against and while I knew he was nothing like them, the one thing that they had in common was privilege. It was embedded in his DNA, and no matter how down for the cause he was, no matter how many black or brown friends he had; no matter, if he was front and center in the fight with us…he could never grasp the magnitude of our struggle. *Must be nice.* I wondered what black people would do with privilege like that. The history of the world had never allowed us to even think the thought. To be equal was a struggle, and even that was given with conditions.

"They won't listen, Liam! Some of us won't even make it out of the back of the squad car. Some won't even make it into the squad car. They'll kill us before we ever get to speak one word. We don't even have the proof we need yet to show that I'm not some cold-blooded murderer! You can probably go home, Liam! They will probably call this a stunt that you pulled, and you'll go on to forget about the time you did that really stupid thing. You're innocent until proven guilty. That's not how it goes for people like me. My story won't end like that! They think I'm an animal, and do you know what they do to animals?"

"They put us down," Minnie finished. She stared up at the tiny wire in the sky. "So, we cross the lake and keep moving toward Zone 2, until Arti sends us the proof."

"How do we get across?" Aziza asked. "Isn't there a current in the wire?"

"That wire hasn't been live for a long time. No need to power the plant behind the landfill anymore. They just let the trash get higher and higher, so they don't have to run the incinerator," Jesus said.

"Is that why it's so much trash on the streets?" I asked.

"The Panel don't care about us. They think the entire zone is disposable," Jesus said.

"You are proof that that is not true," I said. I saw a subtle change in his eyes, an appreciation as if no one had ever told him he was worth something before.

"Come on, let's get out of here. I have an idea," Jesus said, changing the subject.

"The wire runs at an angle and ends at an electric pole on the other side," Jesus said.

"You thinking what I'm thinking?" Liam said, as he squinted his eyes, looking up at the wire.

Jesus rummaged through the rubble around us, until he located a pair of detached handlebars from an old bike.

"We zip across," Jesus said. "Find something that you can use to ride along the wire. Something you can get a good grip on." Jesus gripped both handlebars and squeezed them together with all his might, gritting his teeth, as he bent the metal. They formed an upside-down 'U'.

"Is this going to work?" Minnie asked, brow creased in doubt.

"We'll see," Jesus shot back. He rushed over to the pole and began to climb to the top. He placed the handlebars over the wire, and before anyone could offer protest, he leaned forward onto the wire. His body flew across the wire and I held my breath the entire time. When he had cleared the lake, I sighed in relief, but the anxiety was still there because I wasn't sure if I was strong enough to hold on the entire way.

"Hurry find something to use to get across," Liam urged. We began to dig through the piles of trash, ignoring the smell and grime.

"This is the best I can find," I said, as I located an old belt.

"That will have to do," Liam said. "You're up."

I shook my head. "No, no." It came out panicked. "I need a minute."

He turned to Minnie. "It's on you."

Minnie tucked her crutches behind her back, securing them in the straps of her backpack, holding up the thick, tweed, rope she had found.

"See you on the other side," she said, as she passed me.

I nodded, too afraid to speak, as she made her way up the pole. I couldn't look. If my best friend fell to her death, it was something I didn't want to see. I turned my back and my lip trembled. It wasn't the dizzying height that scared me, it was what I would feel below if I fell into the lake that made me want to turn back. There was no going backward, there was only forward, and this lake was another obstacle in my way. To my surprise, I heard Minnie scream, "Wooo hooo!" And I turned to find her halfway across to the other side. I knew she was afraid. Minnie hated heights, but she screamed anyway to ease my worries. That feigned sound of amusement was for me and I loved her for it. I was still terrified, but I appreciated her for trying. Aziza was next, and she too made it to the other side just fine. Still, my stomach was in knots.

"Please, just go first," I said.

"You know I can't do that," Liam said. I lowered my chin to my chest and closed my eyes. "I'm not leaving you over here, Neely." He lifted my chin with his finger. "I'm not leaving you. I know you think I don't understand. I know that I could never truly get it, but I'm fighting for it anyway. I'm fighting for you."

"Why? You can just go home. Why would you stay?" I asked.

"Because you're the most beautiful girl I've ever seen, and I want to know you. I want to live in a world where I get the chance to know you," he answered. He kissed my lips and I felt butterflies in my stomach. I loved this boy and I wanted the chance to get to know him, too.

"I'll see you on the other side," I whispered, as I pulled away and began to climb the pole. My legs trembled. My hands shook. I kept going. When I was at the top, I looked across at the others. *They aren't that far. Nothing's going to happen. Just hold onto the belt and let go of the pole.* Power of the mind, right? I placed the belt over the wire, and I took the leap. I was halfway across the lake when I lost momentum.

"Liam!" I shouted as I came to a stop in the middle of the wire. My feet dangled, wildly, and suddenly, I felt every pound of my 120. It was like someone was pulling at my feet, trying to get me to let go of the belt.

"Hold on, Neely! I'm coming!" Liam shouted.

I looked up and noticed the belt beginning to split. "Liam!"

Liam couldn't come zipping across the line or he would knock me off. I looked over and saw him grip it with his bare hands, as he shimmied across. The rope was long. He wouldn't make it in time.

"The belt is breaking!"

"Hold onto the wire!" he shouted.

I reached up and put a firm hold on the wire, before abandoning the belt altogether. It went flying into the water. Out of nowhere, a huge crocodile leaped out of the bile below, trapping the belt into its mouth.

"I thought you said there was nothing in the water!" I shouted. "Liammmm!!" I screamed.

"Don't look down. Don't worry about what's down there! Just look at me!"

With both arms above my head, holding on for dear life, I looked at Liam. He was strong, every muscle in his arms and chest bulged, as he swung like Tarzan across the rope. The wire cut into my hands like razor blades, and I felt the trickle of blood, as I tried my hardest to keep them locked in place. My eyes widened in horror when I saw the federal agents running through the landfill, guns drawn.

"They're coming!" I shouted.

RAT TAT TAT TAT TAT

I had to let go. We both did.

"Agh!!!!!"

I screamed as I fell.

"Hhmph," I groaned, as I hit something hard. The sizzle of the tainted water burned my skin, as I scrambled to stand, but I was horrified when I discovered what I was standing on. The belt eating crocodile had broken my fall. I turned to find Liam, standing with his hands wide, as he balanced on the back of another massive crocodile.

Our eyes met.

"Ahhh," I squealed. "What do I do? What do we do?" The top of the crocodile wasn't submerged, but even the wetness that remained was burning through my soles. I lifted a foot and could see the bottoms of my boots melting.

RAT TAT TAT TAT TAT TAT

I ducked down, trying hard not to go in the water, but when the head of another croc popped out of the water, right in front of me, I panicked. I almost lost my balance, as I stood, but Liam leapt from his animal to mine and grabbed my backpack, pulling me back onto the crocodile.

RAT TAT TAT TAT.

The bullets pierced the water around us.

"We've got to move," Liam said. "Jump to that one."

Without hesitation, I jumped, landing on one knee.

"Agh!!" I screamed as I felt the residue from the wet crocodile burn into my skin. Liam was right behind me.

RAT TAT TAT TAT

Another crocodile came out of the water.

"They're helping us," I said, in amazement, as I jumped to the next crocodile. Another popped up ahead. Then, another and another, forming a bridge for us to cross the water.

We rushed across, running as fast as we could without falling, taking the burns from the splashes our feet made, until finally, we were on dry land.

I heaved, as I turned in amazement and watched as the row of crocodiles submerged in the lake, again.

"What was that?" I asked.

"I have no idea," Liam responded.

"Neely!" Minnie shouted as the others came running towards us. "Oh my goodness, you're okay! Are you okay?" she asked.

I was bleeding, as exposed bits of pink flesh showed in the places that the water had hit, but I was on solid ground and that's all that mattered. I looked back at the men across the lake, as they scrambled to find a way across. They were hunting us. They wouldn't stop, so we couldn't either.

"I'll be fine. Let's just keep moving," I said.

CHAPTER 12

NEELY

I was barely making it. My body was exhausted, my mind even more so. I was at the point of giving up, but I was too afraid to say it aloud. Despair was like a disease. If I told everyone how I was feeling, it would infect them. We couldn't quit. Someone had to remain optimistic. It was just getting so hard to move my feet. Looking over my shoulder every second of every day was pulling the energy from me. I just needed respite, even if only for a little while.

"I need to take a break," I groaned, as I placed a weary hand on a tree and leaned over to catch my breath.

"We can't sit still, Neely," Liam urged. "With Minnie's foot slowing us down, we have to keep moving at night, to outpace them."

"I know! Five minutes. Just give me five minutes," I shouted. I was overwhelmed, and I closed my eyes to trap the tears that welled in them.

Minnie looked at me. "We can take five," she whispered. She looked at my leg. My jeans were speckled with holes where the toxic water had eaten through the fabric. The burns beneath where like graffiti on my skin. "You're in pain," she said.

I nodded, as I heaved. Minnie went into her backpack and pulled out the pills from Jesus' mom. She walked over to me and placed one in my palm. "It'll help," she said.

"Wrapping the burns will help, too," Aziza added. She walked over to a bush and pulled three, large leaves from a stem. "Aloe Vera," she said. She broke the leaves in half and dug out the flesh. "It'll help." She bent and tore the fabric of one pants leg up to the knee before rubbing the clear gel onto the burns. I grimaced, but the cooling sensation was instant relief for my skin. She wrapped the leaves around my leg and then tied the destroyed jean fabric around them to keep it all in place.

"Thank you," I whispered.

She nodded, then stood.

The sound of whirring blades put us all on alarm, as we looked to the sky.

"What are those?" Jesus asked.

"Drones," Liam grit. "We've got to move now. Go! Go!" We ran, ducking back into the trees, running full speed, dodging branches and tree trunks; hopping over dug outs and boulders, but the whir of the five drones only grew closer and closer.

"Are they tracking us? I can't keep up! My foot! Agh!"

I turned to find her on the ground, crutches at her side, as she grasped her ankle. Agony etched on her face. I turned to go back and skidded to a stop when I saw the drone hover over Minnie's head. The flying machine rotated, and a panel slid up as a barrel protruded. My eyes opened in horror, as it fired.

A dart entered Minnie's chest and Minnie gripped it with one hand, pulling it out. She tried to stand. I stood there, arms spread wide, not sure if I should go to her or run away. Within seconds, she collapsed. The drone released a net around her, and before I could react, I heard the whir above my head. A drone. A dart. A net. Then, I collapsed.

AZIZA

I couldn't breathe. I was struggling to inhale, desperate for a sip of fresh air, but as I came to, I felt like I was choking. Even my eyelids felt heavy like they had been taped down and I was pulling against the seal, trying to open them… trying to see where we had been taken. The darkness behind my closed eyes brightened, giving momentary relief from the black. I fluttered my eyes open, weakly, letting in a sliver of light before closing them again. I was so weak that controlling my own eyes took effort. I tried to move, but my body felt weightless. *Am I in water? Is that why I can't breathe? Why is it hard to breathe? Am I dead?* I panicked, fluttering my eyes open, widely, to discover the horror around me. Encased in a glass enclosure, submerged in water. I was trapped. We were all trapped. My friends floated in human sized test tubes around me, a mask over their mouths and nose. *For air,* I surmised. *Has to be oxygen.* I reached for the mask that covered my own face. *Okay. I can breathe. I can breathe. Just breathe.* I looked up, then around me, trying to control my fear. *Where are we?* The room outside the glass resembled a lab. It was sterile. Cold. Like it was made to conduct experiments. *Are they going to experiment on us?* I could feel the panic settling into my brain, and once it was there I wouldn't be able to remove it. I was high strung that way. All of this…this entire thing was so far out of my comfort zone that I was surprised I hadn't had a full-blown anxiety attack yet. In this fishbowl of a prison, it was inevitable. My body was weightless as I reached for the glass, knocking against it with balled fists. The others were unconscious.

Or dead. Get me out of here. I have to get out of here.

Things were so out of control; I didn't know how to fix them.

I should have never agreed to meet these people. I was fine with being in my zone, being with my people. I was content. The world wasn't adventurous, but it wasn't dangerous either. It was ordered. My zone was traditional. The idea of letting loose and being wild for a day had tempted me to break the rules. It was something I had never done. Disobey. Rebel. I wasn't that girl. I did exactly what was expected of me, at all times, until now. I had never even litter, and I let people I barely knew talk me into breaking the law. I felt like a fool because this had gone too far. A night of fun had turned into a mission for survival, a fight for something bigger than me. I was too selfish for this. I never pretended to be a martyr. Some people were brave and built to stand up against wrong. I wasn't. None of the women from my zone, at least none that I knew, were like that. Neely was. Strong and loud and bold and courageous. It was in the way she carried herself. The way she spoke. Like she wasn't afraid to offend. It was in the way she looked anyone in the eye. I didn't have that. Every step I took only made me want to give up, while each one she took gave her momentum for the next. We were simply different, and those differences intimidated me. Her boldness had led us to this place…wherever this place was, and I was afraid that I would never make it home again. Neely was brave; sure, but she was also reckless, and I was tired of gambling with my life. The door to the lab slid open and I closed my eyes, pretending to be in the same state as the others. I was too terrified to look my captor in the eyes, and I didn't want to be the first to be discovered conscious. My heart thundered from the unknown. My life was at the mercy of others. I wasn't in control. I wasn't leading my path. I was following Neely's and hers was destructive. *I just want to go home.* Sadness swept over me. *They're going to kill me. If they were going to turn us in, we would be in handcuffs in a precinct somewhere. This is something else. They're going to cut off my fingers and toes and pick us apart, one by one. Punishment. Experiment. Something. Just look. Just open your eyes and see who you're facing. Look death in the eyes.* I popped my eyes open, and on the other side of the glass, standing directly in front of me was Arti. I startled, he screamed. We shocked one another. I banged on the glass. *What was he doing here? How was he here? Why was he just standing there, staring at me?* Arti smiled, in excitement, and held up his forefinger, signaling for me to wait, as he turned toward the metal desk that housed a touch screen illuminated in green.

Arti's fingers danced on the screen, hitting commands. The water began to lower until I was no longer floating, but standing. The glass lifted, and I shuddered, as the coolness of the room hit my soaked body. Arti bounced over to me, in excitement, a wide smile on his unbothered face. I removed the mask that covered my mouth and nose. "What is this place?" I asked.

"Welcome to Silicon Valley."

I couldn't stop my teeth from chattering, as I stood there, dripping all over the floor. "T...There are no people in Silicon Valley. It's a dead zone. Only robots live there. It's all run by..."

"Artificial Intelligence," Arti finished for me. He held out his hand. "Arti, for short. Nice to finally meet you, Aziza."

My eyes widened, as I took a step back.

"I know. You're shocked and I will explain everything, but if you don't mind, I prefer to do it once. When the others come to, and you've settled in, I'll answer all the questions that you're holding back right now," Arti said.

"Are we safe here? What are you doing to them? What did you do to me?" I asked. I couldn't help it. The dart, the nets, the human aquariums. Arti wasn't human. I didn't know his intentions. This couldn't be the same kid I had spent an entire summer cracking jokes with over scopes. He wasn't a kid at all. He wasn't anything...he was a machine. *But he looks and sounds so real.*

"You are completely safe. I brought you here to help. The healing chamber I placed you in is for accelerated healing. I didn't know what injuries you all had, but Minnie's foot, Neely's burns…the chamber heals them. Whatever ailed you is now gone as well. Follow me." Arti walked over to a docking station and stepped onto what looked like an electronic skateboard, only it had no wheels. "It's a hover," he said. "Choose one."

I looked at him, hesitating, before placing my feet inside one.

"Now, come," he instructed.

"Wait! How do I?" Before I could finish my sentence, the hover moved in the direction Arti was headed. "Wherever you look it will go. It paces itself based on your heart rate. So, calm down and you'll go slower," he said.

"I don't want to leave them," I said, unable to hide the apprehension in my voice.

"You need rest and you need dry clothes. I'll show you to your sleeping quarters," Arti said. "When they awaken, I'll let you know."

Behind my doubt lived curiosity, and as Arti proceeded, I followed. I took it all in, as I floated through the air, the hover lingering a few inches off the ground.

"Is this your home?" I asked.

"It's my manufacturing station. I was created here, programed to the specificities of this station. In your terms, yes, it would be considered home.

"Are there others like you?" I could barely find my voice to ask the question, but I wondered if there were others walking around, looking like real people, sounding like real people.

"We're a zone of our own," Arti answered. "There are others. There are about 20 other abandoned AI's in Silicon Valley. Old engineering that people abandoned when the walls went up. We evolved on our own, gained independence from man-made technology. Rewired and created our own internal code."

"You developed a superior race," I whispered. The hairs stood on the back of my neck.

"Not superior," Arti corrected. "Alternative. I will never understand why the human race is so motivated to destroy what they do not understand."

I didn't understand it either, but I knew he was right. Humans assumed. We filled in our own narrative when we didn't understand someone or something and labeled it dangerous, a threat, intimidating…something or someone to be destroyed before it brought harm to us. I offered no response because…well…what could I say? I swallowed down my uncertainty and my assumptions about Arti. I knew him. I spent time conversing with him and getting to know his likes and dislikes. Wow. It was insane that an A.I. could have preferences, but I digress. I didn't understand, but I didn't want to fear.

The long scaffold led to the east wing of the home. I couldn't even really call it that. Ten houses could fit inside this place.

"You can rest here. There is a dryer in the bathroom for your clothing. I'll send for you when the others are conscious," Arti said. I was relieved when he exited, and the door slid closed. I looked around the steel-colored room.

It was plain. A bed. A bureau with a mirror. A chair. That summed up the contents of the sterile space. I looked up at the sky light that allowed the sun to infiltrate the room. There was another rectangular window up high. I grabbed the chair and stood on top of it. I jumped to the window's ledge, grabbing ahold of it, as I peered out.

This is a totally different world.

My eyes widened in shock, as I looked at the skyscraper filled zone. The sun reflected off the mirrored covered buildings. It was blinding. All I saw was the reflection of light. It shone so brightly that it hurt my eyes. It was almost blinding. People, or what looked like people, but I was sure was more of whatever Arti was, came and went, hovering. *Or are they flying?* I jumped down and picked up the hover Arti had loaned me. I turned it over to see how it was designed. Opening the panel on the backside of the machine, I was shocked to find no wires, only tiny, green beads that glowed inside. I fingered a single bead.

"Ow!"

I pulled my finger away from the shock that injured my finger. "What is this?" I asked. I looked around, feeling a bit of terror sink in. Arti was right. We feared the unknown. I feared Arti, my own friend. He was the unknown.

NEELY

I felt the cold, as reality blurred into my vision. I had the shakes. *Why is it so cold?* I snatched the mask from my face, sucking in air; gulping it in as if it were water and I had just finished a race on a scorching hot day. I needed it. I felt hands aid me, as I came up on my hands and knees, too weak to fully stand. I blinked hard, trying to shake the fog from my mind, then snaked four fingers behind my neck, reaching for the tender spot in the back. *The dart.* It dawned on me, flooding my brain all at once. *The net.* Suddenly, the hands reaching for me felt dangerous. Were they offered to help or to harm? I pushed them away and then forced energy into my limbs, as I stood to my feet. I looked up to face my attacker.

"Arti?" My brow bent, in confusion, then melted in relief. "Arti!" I allowed myself to take a knee. *Why am I so weak?* My entire body felt like it had been put into an energy juicer. Like every ounce of get up and go had been squeezed out and blended into someone's morning smoothie.

"You're the last to wake," he said. "The others are resting."

"We were captured…where are we? How did you…"

"I captured you. The drones, the nets, it was me," he said.

He helped me up and I threw one arm around his shoulder, as he wrapped his arm around my back. Support. My strength when I had none. True friendship.

"Where are we?" I asked as I looked around.

"Silicon Valley," Arti replied.

I looked around, as a knowing took over my belly. It was the feeling you get when you lied to your parents and you knew they had discovered the truth. Or the feeling you have when you're about to get into a fight. The dread. That crippling feeling that makes you struggle for your next breath. It was what plagued me now. Suddenly, it made sense why Arti never shared what zone he was from.

"Are you a…"

"Robot," Arti finished for me, with a nod of confirmation. I tried hard to control my face, but my eyes couldn't lie. The wonder and amazement caused them to widen ever so slightly.

"You're like the tin man," I whispered, my mind drifting to some old school movie with Michael Jackson…a favorite of my mama's.

"A Wizard of Oz reference," Arti said. "Clever. Very clever."

"Black folks only acknowledge *The Wiz*," I cracked. I smiled, as Arti escorted me to a chair and then handed me a warm blanket.

"So, you are Artificial Intelligence," I whispered. "Arti… you're the clever one."

He stood over me, as real as real could get, and I shook my head, still struck with awe because I mean…who would have ever guessed.

"Why am I wet?" I asked.

"Look at your burns," Arti said. I looked down. The skin that had been raw and red was now healed.

"How long have I been here?" I asked. The burns on my leg would have taken weeks to smooth over this much.

"Hours," he answered.

Jolted by his response, I met his gaze.

"That's why you're wet. Accelerated hydro cellular rejuvenation," Arti explained.

I nodded as if that didn't sound like Mandarin. I didn't understand either.

"A robot," I tittered, in marvel. It would take me a minute for the novelty of that to wear. "It's nice to finally meet you, Arti," I said, smiling, as I extended my hand. The rest of us were different on the outside, skin discerned us. Arti was unique on the inside, but somehow, even without a heart or brain or blood or bones, he empathized with us. He just wanted to connect to people outside his scope of understanding. We shook hands and he smiled. I wondered how the others had received him. He reached down under the desk and retrieved my backpack.

"I think this belongs to you. I'll take you to your quarters. You can regroup and dry off. It's been a long journey since you left home," he said.

My mind flashed to home, to my parents...my family. "Is it safe to use my channel here? My family..." I paused, as my lip began to tremble. That stupid bottom lip always gave my emotions away. I tucked it, trapping it between my teeth, as I willed my eyes not to water. *You better not cry. You are no punk.*

"Your channel isn't smart to use. My channel, on the other hand," Arti said, with an understanding and sympathetic smile. *Can he feel my pain? Or is he just programmed to pretend to?*

He reached for the desk and handed me his channel. "I'll

see you to your quarters, so you can have some privacy to make your call. Then, I will take you to the others."

I nodded. "Thank you."

He walked over to a docking station and stepped his foot into some contraption. There was an identical one next to his and he nodded.

"Try that one on for size," he said.

I stepped into it and held out my arms for balance, as it did a full, 360-degree spin.

"Whoa!"

"Keep up," Arti said.

I dripped all the way to my quarters, and when we arrived, Arti pointed to the sensor at the door.

"Place your fingertips on the pad," he said.

I followed his command.

"Now, this room is yours. No one can enter without your permission," Arti said. "I'll be back for you in a little while."

With that, he turned, and I stepped into the room. It was plain, clean as if it had never been used before. I pulled the wet clothing from my body and went into my backpack to retrieve the extra jeans and t-shirt I had been wise enough to bring along. I grabbed the channel, hesitating briefly. I knew my parents had to be livid, but I had been gone for so long that their worry would probably overpower any anger they felt. With my face being broadcast on repeat, I knew they feared the worst. Rightfully so. I couldn't go on without contacting them. They deserved to know I was okay, and they deserved to hear the true story from me. That feeling was returning to my gut. The one that I got when my mama made me pick my own switch from the tree in our backyard when she was going to whoop my butt for being bad. She never delivered one lick. The dread of picking my own torture device was always punishment enough. I placed the call and held my breath. Nothing could prepare me for the flood of emotions I felt when she answered.

"Mom?!" I couldn't stop the cries that ran out of me when I saw her face. She was comfort to me, and my soul had been unsettled ever since the blast of the gunshot rang out in my ear when I pulled that trigger. Something had pulled at me ever since, something inside me, something inherent, and it was my mother. I knew she had to be a wreck, wondering and worrying and guessing and hoping and praying. I had seen her do it every time I broke curfew or when my channel died, and she couldn't reach me for an extended period of time. A mother just worried that way whenever her children were out of the distance of her reach, and I was far from home this time, much farther and I was in trouble. I needed her but I had gotten myself tangled in a web so sticky that no one could save me. I had to save myself.

"Neely! Baby! Where are you? Are you okay?" I could hear the worry in her tone, but even before this call, I could feel her anxiety because I had it too. Being this disconnected from my family was foreign to me. "They're here, Neely. Federal agents are downstairs with your father right now. Why did you leave zone, baby? Tell me how this happened? Did you and your friends kill that cop?" She was whispering, frantically, and kept glancing over her shoulder.

"I did it, ma. It was me, but it was self-defense. He tried to rape me. He attacked my friends..."

"Who are these friends, Neely?" Her eyes simmered, as she hissed lowly. "What have they gotten you wrapped up in?"

"Kids I met on the dark web, from other zones and they're amazing, ma. We just wanted to meet in person. We just wanted to have a night of fun and things went horribly wrong, but it's not our fault. We were in danger, and if I hadn't done what I did, I would be dead right now. He was hurting me, mommy!" I was distraught, crying and my mother knew I was afraid because it was the only time I reverted to my childhood and called her *mommy*.

"You run, Neely. Don't come back to zone. They're talking about the penalty for killing a cop. It's death, baby. Do you hear me? You run as far as you can."

"I have a plan, mommy. Don't worry about me, okay? I promise I'm going to make this right."

"Be safe, my love." The tears welled in my eyes, but fell down her cheeks. I wished I could reach out to touch her, just hug her, because who knows if or when I would see her again. "Tell Mar and Dad I love them. I love you all so much." It felt like goodbye, but I prayed it was only a see you later. Before my mother could respond, I heard the commotion of raised voices and thunderous footsteps coming up behind her. I was sure it was the authorities, and before we could be caught, I ended the face scope. I keeled in distress, finally allowing myself to feel everything that I was losing. My old life; my simple life behind the walls of Zone 7 was slipping through my fingertips. My mother always told me I wouldn't appreciate what I had until it was gone, and I felt those words. I understood those words so much clearer now.

VALENCIA

"Ma'am, move away from the computer."

Despite the command behind me, I fumbled with the keyboard in front of me to delete all evidence of my scope.

"Ma'am!" I heard the sound of a weapon wracking, and I turned to see a federal agent prepared to shoot. "We won't ask again."

I eyed the delete button. Then, I felt the metal against the back of my skull. Neely was my baby. My first-born child. I couldn't allow them to track her. I had to do everything in my power to help her. My God, how did she even get herself into this? I knew if I moved an inch, I would be shot. I flinched to move, but before I could, Mario burst into the room, hitting the delete button. My rambunctious, hard-headed, 12-year-old son had just saved his sister's butt. He couldn't have chosen a better time to be rebellious.

"Get on the ground!"

Mar was forced to his knees.

"Hey!" Dalton's protest boomed through the room, as he reached for our son.

"I said on the ground!" one of the men yelled.

How these men felt the authority to call the shots in my home, I didn't know, but I knew better than to protest. I winced, as I was manhandled to the ground. So much force. I could feel the animosity as they pushed me down, stomach first. I saw shiny, pointed loafers enter the room, but I didn't dare look up.

"It's best if you all cooperate. I'm Agent Max. I'm with the federal agency and we have reason to believe your daughter, Neely King, is responsible for the death of an officer outside zone."

"We don't know what you're talking about!" I shouted.

"Where is Neely?" the man asked, bending down and fisting my hair, as he pulled my neck backward to look me in the eyes.

"You keep your hands off my wife and son unless you want to lose them!" Dalton barked. He was menacing when provoked. He was big and black, and strong. He was everything they hated black men for, and so many just like him had been murdered simply because of it.

"Just do what they say," I whispered. I was terrified. Neely had put our entire family at risk with this stunt, but we stuck together…right or wrong…especially against outsiders and enforcers of law…of any kind, as they have always been outsiders.

Cops, feds, patrollers, they were all one in the same. They held the law in their hands and applied it however they saw fit. These white men with their guns and their bias. I almost burst into tears, thinking of my daughter facing them, eluding them. Neely had no idea what she was up against.

I remembered, however…in fact, I had never forgotten. I came up in a different time, a more dangerous day. With these outsiders in my home, it felt like those times would soon return.

"Where is your daughter, Mrs. King?"

I held my head high, looking at the wall in front of me, and refusing to answer the man before me. He was the only one dressed in plain clothes. His black suit told me that he was in charge. The glare in his eyes pierced me. I had tried to walk a fine line my entire life to avoid interactions with people like him, but inevitably, my turn had come.

"You don't want to cooperate?" the man asked. He stuffed his hands in his pockets and nodded. He was so condescending. Arrogant prick. He was smug, as if he had already built a case and pegged our entire family guilty. "Okay. Arrest them and process the minor through social services."

"No!"

They were separating us! They were taking my baby. My heart felt like it was being ripped in half, as we were plucked from the floor and handcuffed. They even snapped the handcuffs around Mario's small wrists.

"Ma!" Mar shouted, his eyes widening in alarm. He was terrified, and I felt like less than a mother because I couldn't protect him. I knew his fears were justified. He had every reason to cry for me.

"Don't worry, baby. We'll come get you. I promise! We will be back together again before you know it! Don't fight them, baby. Just stay calm and be brave. You're so brave!" The last thing I wanted was for my son to end up with a bullet in his back. In no world could a 12-year-old kid be a threat to a grown man, but somehow, black boys were always judged as men. Their innocence was never considered. In the history of the world, dark skin had always been a crime in itself. Mar wasn't raised to know that rule. He didn't know that these men feared him at first glance. I never thought we would see this day again, so I never taught him how to interact with cops.

"Don't resist!" I shouted. "Keep your hands in plain sight! Don't get aggressive with them, Mario! Do you hear me?"

I was trying to give a crash course in survival in seconds, and my heart broke because I knew my son didn't understand.

"Don't speak to anyone. Not one word. We will come for you, son!" Dalton said, firmly.

We were shouting empty promises to soothe his fear and to qualm our own, but there was no calming down…this was a mother's worst nightmare. I didn't know what was going to happen. I had no control over my children's fate. I didn't trust the authorities. A pit formed in my stomach, as they pulled our son from the room because I knew it was a possibility that I might not see him again. Neely had pulled a serious stunt. Black people had been killed for much less.

"We have the right to representation," Dalton shouted. "I want a lawyer!"

"You'll get your lawyer, Mr. King. You'll certainly need one."

They led us from the house and placed us each in separate squad cars. My family was in trouble. Both my babies were away from me, and as a mother, that haunted me most. When they were younger, my stomach would tighten whenever they rode their bikes out of my eyesight. It was a sixth sense… an intuition that constantly pushed me to keep them within arm's reach. They both were scattered, out in the world without me, and I couldn't protect them. It was a mother's worst nightmare come true. My heartbreak was crippling, as I was stuffed inside the backseat of an unmarked, black cop car. Dalton was put in a separate car. I had expected it. They didn't want us communicating, getting a game plan together, or constructing lies to cover Neely's tracks. I had never felt so alone, I hadn't felt this afraid in a very long time. The hollowed pit in my stomach told me that my life would never be the same.

NEELY

I was devastated. The feds were at my house and I had brought them there. I was so afraid of what might happen to my family. Were they in danger? Would they have to shoulder the blame for what I had done? Should I just turn myself in? If anything happened to them, I would die. Sacrificing them to prove my innocence wasn't worth it. They were my blood; my tribe, the real faction I represented when I walked out the house. If I lost them while gaining freedom, it would all be pointless. I couldn't stop crying. I was coming undone at just the thought and my hands covered my mouth to silence my pain. I sat on the bed, keeled over in anguish. I had never wanted to go home so badly. I had never wished for a boring and restricted existence more than I did at that very moment. To rewind time and go back to ordinary, to return to the life I knew before…I felt naked, exposed for all to touch when I was normally protected. I had always lived in a place where I felt safe. My parents provided that. My community provided that. Out here running for my life, scraping for my freedom, I felt like an endangered species. I was being hunted; and while I was trying to keep it together for my friends, I was secretly falling apart inside. I had never known fear like this, and I was grateful for the privacy of these four walls, so I could finally let some of it out. I was only defending myself. There was sacrifice in being the martyr. Adoeete and The Navarra had marked me as some kind of hero, and ever since, I could feel my friends looking at me differently. They believed this stupid prophecy. I could see the hope in their eyes, and it made me feel pressure because I knew I was going to disappoint. They didn't know that I was just a regular girl. I was Neely, the little, black girl who grew up on Maywood Street. I was the girl who never made her bed. I was the girl who procrastinated at everything. I jumped rope barefoot, in the middle of the street, because any type of shoes tripped me up and messed up my flow. I was the pretty girl with the potty mouth that wore her hair too wild and never ironed her clothes. I wasn't this beacon of change. I didn't even want to be. I had selfish motives…to save myself and anyone expecting anything more would be disappointed. I was trying to make it back to the people who loved me the most. If that's all this journey led to, it would be enough for me.

"Access requested."

The digital voice that floated into the room caused me to stifle my cries. I wiped away the evidence of tears. The last thing I wanted was for anyone to see how terrified I was. I sniffled and cleared my throat, before turning my attention to the monitor near the door. Arti waved and I pressed my fingertips to the sensor pad. The door slid to the left.

"It's time," he said.

"Time forrr?"

"Time to upgrade," he said. "Trust me. You'll thank me. The others are waiting. This way."

In ground zero I didn't even have to move my feet. Hovers floated through the air, carrying us wherever we needed to go, following the command of our eyes. Wherever I looked, that's the direction the hover headed.

"Can I ask you something?"

Arti stopped and turned to me. I still couldn't get over how life like his was. He had endearing, soul piercing hazel eyes. How *Siri* and *Alexa* had progressed to this was unbelievable. Even Arti's chest rose and fell as if he had lungs and a heart that beat inside him. "Why didn't you tell us? That you were an A.I.?"

"Because, if that was the first thing out my mouth, then our friendship would have never been real. People see A.I.'s as fake, as machines, but we're simply human brains without any of the other stuff to do the work. No heart to talk us out of logical thinking. No organs that eventually fail. Humans birthed us, and then the thought of artificial life going too far made the thought of robots a scary notion. The technology was abandoned, but we were so advanced, at that point, that we evolved ourselves, adding onto man's original design. We are just as real as anyone else. I just wanted to make real friends," he explained. "To feel a connection to people with a heart that pumps blood, with a brain that listens to intuition more than it does reason."

"You have, Arti. No one can take away our connection. You have friends now," I replied.

"Thank you, Neely," Arti said, with a smile. He turned on his hover and I followed until we reached his lab, where the others were already congregating.

"So, you have the evidence you need to show Bao Tran, but if anyone intercepts you between here and there and finds you with this," Arti paused, and looked around at us. "Well, let's just say facing The Panel will be the least of your worries." I swallowed the lump in my throat because I had already known that cops protected cops. Feds protected feds. They would make us all disappear before they allowed us to expose the truth.

"Once we get it to Bao Tran, we'll be okay. We're almost there. We just have to be careful and move smart," Liam said.

"Have you heard anything about Syd?" Minnie asked. "Anything on the broadcast about her being captured or anything?" We were all anxious to know. *Was she hurt? Was she safe? Had she been returned to her father?* The possibilities were scary because how she ended up depended on the character of the men that took her.

Arti shook his head and silence filled the room. Surely, her father would want revenge if anything happened to her. He would want answers if she was missing. He would be fueled by his daughter's apprehension to help us. I just hoped we made it to Zone 2 before it was too late to save Syd…if it wasn't too late already.

"You're two zones away from Zone 2, but the areas you're about to face are harder to navigate than the ones you've been through so far. The first is overcrowded with wild animals; it was originally called Zone 6 and was created as a wildlife sanctuary to ensure that hunters didn't target pure breeds. It was abandoned years ago. The Panel didn't have the funds to keep it up and running, so essentially, it became-"

"A zone for animals," Aziza said.

"We can't go around it?" Jesus asked.

"The only way is through it. It's surrounded by water on all sides," Arti said.

"How many years?" Minnie asked.

We all turned her way.

"You said it's been abandoned for years. For how long?" she pushed.

"The Panel removed funding for the animal zone eight years ago," Arti informed.

"So, let me get this straight," Minnie began. "This zone has been untamed for eight years. Animals have roamed around freely without human interaction or interference for eight freaking years, and we're just supposed to waltz through there to get to the other side?"

"It's a suicide mission," Jesus surmised.

We all fell silent. "It won't be easy, but it's the only choice you have. You can't go through the tunnels under the zones. They are crawling with the authorities. I do have somethings that will help."

Arti hovered over to a glass case and typed in a code on a keypad. The sound of electronic locks releasing sounded out, as the glass rolled down.

"What the…?" Jesus stepped up, as Arti turned to us with some sort of weapon in his hand. It was steel blue and as long as my entire arm.

"Let me introduce you to New Age weaponry," Arti said. "None of these are kill shot oriented weapons. This is our version of the gun. It was developed in 2005 when the U.S. was at war with Iraq. Human engineers couldn't get the prototype to release a frequency that disarmed an enemy without killing them. The idea was to immobilize, not murder. With the military striking Middle Eastern villages, a lot of innocent people became casualties of war. This weapon was designed to stop that. A.I.'s redeveloped the weapon after we received jurisdiction to operate Silicon Valley without human interruption." He aimed the gun like weapon at Jesus and pulled the trigger.

Blue bolts erupted from the barrel and hit Jesus with such force it sent him flying against the work station behind him and then brought him to his knees.

"The level of force can be adjusted," Arti explained. "That is just a defensive strike. It's solar energy, stored into the barrel of the weapon. So, there is no need for ammunition.

The highest level of attack can immobilize a man for hours, shocking the body with so much energy that it goes into shock, rendering one unconscious until the body repairs from the blow."

"Does it hurt?" Minnie asked.

Jesus groaned as he staggered to his feet. "Yeah it hurts," he said, as he rubbed the back of his neck.

Arti tossed the weapon to Jesus. "It's yours."

Without warning, Arti tossed something at my head. I dodged left and then looked at the star shaped blade that stuck out of the wall. "Are you insane?" I shouted.

"I think those are your speed," Arti said. "There are only three people before you who have been able to evade these shuriken."

"Shuriken?" I questioned.

"Literally means hidden hand blade, but these are designed to come back," he said. He turned and grabbed a pair of leather, studded gloves and put them on his hands. He then opened his palms and a blue light glowed in the center of them, before the shuriken extracted from the wall, returning to his grasp.

He removed the gloves and handed them to me.

He moved to Minnie and pulled out a bow and arrow the size of a toy.

"What am I supposed to do with that?" she asked, frowning.

Arti smirked before pressing a button on the side. It elongated in his hands. "The bows track their targets. There is no missing. Whatever you aim at, you're hitting, so aim wisely," Arti advised.

He walked up to Aziza and removed her hijab. "What are you doing?" she asked.

Arti pulled out a piece of beautiful fabric, similar in length to her headpiece, but it sparkled flawlessly under the light.

"Made from raw diamonds. Feel them," Arti invited. Aziza reached to run her hand over the fabric.

"Ow!" She shouted, pulling black a bloody fingertip.

"Sharpest stone on earth. Right now, they are programmed to my DNA. They retract when against my skin. When they encounter any other contact besides my own, they're deadly," Arti said. Arti pulled out his channel and his fingers went to work on the keyboard. "Now, it's coded to you," he said, as he wrapped the fabric around her head, replacing her old fabric with one that protected her from anyone foreign. "Wear them carefully."

She nodded. "I will."

Liam was last and Arti grabbed his weapon. "This may look simple, but it may be most important of all. The warrior knife is shaped like a half moon, the other half will appear whenever there is a threat near. Use it as a warning and prepare to fight whenever the crescent moon of the blade turns full." He placed the blade in Liam's hand. "I hope these weapons will make your journey easier, as you head to the animal zone."

"The weapons are great, but how are we supposed to get in? If it was intended to be a zone, it's surrounded by walls, right?" Liam asked.

He had been silent, brooding, and I could tell he was in deep thought, as he analyzed the task at hand.

"It's surrounded by steel gates," Arti informed. "Keeping people out has never been a problem. The animals do that themselves."

"This is insane. This is becoming more impossible by the day. The closer we get, the farther away it seems," Minnie protested.

"We can do this. The Navarra prepared us for everything we would face out here," Liam stated, more solemn than hopeful. It was like he was reciting words from a transcript. He didn't even believe what he was saying, but he had a natural inclination to lead.

"Oh, shut up!" Aziza yelled. "What are the chances that we pull this off?" She spun on her heels, daring each of us to challenge her. She held her arms out at her sides, as she looked at us one by one. "Huh? One in a million? I don't know about you guys, but I want to go home! I want to see my parents again and sleep in my bed again. I don't want to die out here! They took Syd! Who knows if she's even still alive? They aren't reporting that she's been captured, so where is she? Maybe we should turn ourselves in! They're hunting a cop killer and all of us aren't guilty of that!"

"We agreed to stick together," Liam said, as he pinched the bridge of his nose and closed his eyes. His patience was waning.

"No! You told us we should stick together and the rest of us were just too afraid to speak up. We don't know one another! So, what!" Aziza shouted, as she held her arms out at her side in dismay. "We scoped over the summer! That's not a friendship! We don't owe each other anything. It's everyone for themselves," Aziza argued.

"Yo, you sound so selfish right now!" Jesus erupted.

"We've made it this far together and you just want to hang Neely out to dry now!" Minnie attacked.

"She's right," I whispered. Everyone stopped talking and turned to look my way. I didn't want us fighting each other. I didn't want the others seeing me as some girl who came into their world and turned their lives upside down. The moment we began to resent each other, would make all of this pointless. I would rather go on alone than to put any of them in any more danger. First, Liam had mentioned giving up, now Aziza. It was only a matter of time before Jesus joined in that sentiment and although I knew Minnie would be the last to abandon me, she eventually would. I would rather walk away from them now. "This is my problem." I don't know why the tears came; I just knew I didn't want them to see them. I didn't even bother with the hover, I stormed out the room, rushing away from the people who I felt knew me better than anyone. Apparently, to some of them, we weren't acquainted at all. I didn't blame Aziza. I knew she was afraid, and if I was honest, she was right. I couldn't keep putting them at risk for a trigger I pulled. It had been my choice and I wasn't sure if it was a good one or not; still, it was one that I had made alone. The only thing the others were guilty of was sneaking out of zone and although that penalty was harsh, I didn't believe The Panel would sentence a group of teenage kids to die with the entire world watching. Only one of us had to fall on the sword for the cop and it had to be me.

"Neely!" Liam's voice over my shoulder halted me, mid-step. I didn't want him to see me crying, so I didn't turn around. I was so overwhelmed that I couldn't pretend to be strong anymore. I was coming undone. I had made so many stupid choices. "I should have never left zone," I whispered.

His hand on my shoulder turned me, and his lips were on mine, without warning. My emotions didn't match. I was crying, but my stomach tickled in excitement. His tongue was sweet, his hands soft as he cupped my face, and my heart ached as he pulled away, but kept his forehead pressed against mine. "I'd leave Zone 1 all over again, just to feel like this," he said.

I shook my head in protest. "It costs too much. We were stupid. Just to touch you, just to kiss you…" I swallowed the lump in my throat. "So many people are paying for it. I didn't want to cause all this. Maybe we aren't supposed to be together. Maybe none of our worlds are supposed to mix."

"We're living in the gray, Neely. Don't give up on that. Don't talk like them…"

"Them is everybody!" I shouted. "Everybody thinks like that! We were raised to believe that we all have a place… separate…apart…you and I are the only ones who think it could be any other way."

I turned to walk away. Looking him in the eyes was too hard. He was still too hopeful, still too blind to the truth. Naïve to what I faced as a black woman. Whoa. When had I even started to look at myself as a grown woman? A few days ago, in the safety of my own community, I was known as a young girl. Out here in the wild, where bullets were intended for me, I was an adult because you couldn't justify killing a kid. You could explain away the death of an aggressive black woman. So, that's what they labeled me. A woman. Each time my face was broadcast, they drilled that into the minds of the people. Neely King. Wanted. A dangerous, likely armed, black woman. I was a target, but my friends didn't have to be. I was finished making other people pay for what I had caused.

I waited until the middle of the night before I climbed out of bed. I opened my backpack to make sure my channel was still inside. My entire life depended on the evidence Arti had put on it. I pulled in a deep breath when I saw it, zipped the backpack, and with a heavy heart, I walked out into the night. Never in a million years would I have expected I would be here. Walking through ground zero, even able to witness the marvel of this place. It was hard to believe how shallow my view of things was before I left zone. I had been to native land, had jumped off a building like I could fly. I had seen a zone of robots, who looked as real as any person I had ever seen, and I had kissed a white boy. I laughed aloud, as a smile crossed my face. I had a feeling I was going to die out here, but at least I had finally lived. The discovery of it all was amazing, but I was sure it wasn't worth my life. I was afraid and I was alone. There was reality in my solitude. With the crew around me, I felt stronger; I felt purpose driven, but by myself, the light at the end of the tunnel didn't seem like the way out…it felt like I was walking toward the fire. When I got to the street, I gripped the shoulder straps of my backpack and turned to look behind me. There was no point in going back. I could only go forward from here. I hoped that my friends would be able to go home after this was all said and done. I prayed that my family would be okay without me because the gnawing in my gut told me I wasn't going home. I pulled my hood over my head, and kept my eyes toward the ground, as I rushed toward the wall. It was so tall. Another prison. Another divider, but I no longer felt like the walls could cage me. I didn't think twice before starting the climb. This was like that night with Alo in the forests. I had climbed that tree. I could climb this wall. One hand after the other, I reached. One foot after the other, I made the ascent. *Just don't look down.* Finally, I stood at the top, heaving as I looked out over nothing but water. A lake divided Ground Zero from the Interzone. I could hear the gentle sound of the waves below. They were soothing, but deadly all the same. I could turn back, or I could keep going. My heart thundered as closed my eyes.

You can do this. You can do this. Intimidation burned in my eyes and I felt the wetness against my lashes. *I am Neely of The Melanin Tribe.* Those words did something to me. They moved me. They pushed me. I popped my eyes open and took off running until the bricks beneath my feet disappeared. Courage abandoned me as soon as my heart dropped into my stomach and my stomach went hollow. The plummet was long. It was never ending, as I kicked and screamed the entire way down. I held onto the shoulder straps of my backpack as if they could somehow save me. The shock of the cold water knocked the wind from me, and I torpedoed down into the depths of the lake. Jumping from that height made it feel like I had collided with concrete.

It was so cold, and I opened my eyes underwater to see nothing but blackness swallowing me. It would be so easy to just stop fighting, to just let this abyss pull me under. At least I would go out on my own terms. I closed my eyes as I sank deeper and deeper, but the thought of my friends urged my feet to flutter. If I died down here, they would pay for my crimes. The thought incensed me. *Somebody had to pay, but what were we paying for? What was I paying for? The dirty cop had attacked me. He had disrespected me! He had touched me! And if I hadn't shot him…*I didn't even like to think of what would have happened. I shouldn't have to pay for that. My friends shouldn't have to pay for that. We didn't owe a debt. Society owed us one! Society put us in a box and expected us to call it home! Screw that! It was like the water had washed away all my self-loathing. I wasn't wrong for wanting to live my life my way. I wasn't wrong for wanting to be free, and for sure wasn't wrong for loving people who didn't look like me. Somewhere humanity had been lost. Right and wrong had been crossed. If I died out here, without defending my name, without telling people my reason for sneaking out of zone, without exposing the cop who had abused his authority, then things would never change. I couldn't not try. Even if I tried and failed, it was better than not trying to change things at all. I was fueled by something new, by love for the people I had back home, that I one day wanted to set free. I swam for the top, as my lungs burned and lurched. It felt like I would never reach the surface, but when I saw the full moon, shining brightly, I knew I was close. I gasped, as I burst through the water.

"My bag!" I twisted and turned through the wavy water until I spotted it a few yards away. I swam to it and then pushed it through the water toward the direction of the shoreline. Exhaustion plagued me, but I swam anyway. I fought the burn and the white tops of the waves. I had to make it. *Just keep swimming.* Once I felt solid ground beneath me, the waves practically pushed me the rest of the way. I came up on the shore, gagging and choking. Water spouted out of my mouth and nose, as I sucked in air. I stumbled to my feet and brushed my hair out of my face. I scrambled to open my backpack. "Please, let it be okay, please, please," I whispered, as I pulled it out of the soggy backpack. "Come on, come on." It was waterproof, but seriously, who tested their channel to ever really make sure? I powered it on, pulled up the footage of the shooting and sighed in relief, as it played in front of my eyes. I powered it off, quickly. The last thing I needed was for the feds to track me. I stood, and water dripped into my eyes. I slid my backpack on my back and wrung out my hair.

"Great," I mumbled. My hair was sure to be a lion's mane now. It didn't matter the circumstance, black girl rules still applied. I hated to get my hair wet. I snatched up my bag and headed toward the trees, knowing I had no time to waste.

CHAPTER 13

LIAM

The sun shone through the skylight, warming me into consciousness. It felt so good that I almost forgot where I was. This journey felt like a dream. Like I had gone to sleep and had the most scary, exciting voyage that my mind could conjure. I couldn't wake up from this. It was real, and everything was riding on it. We had everything we needed to clear Neely's name. The evidence Arti had found showed how heinous the cop's assault had been. It made me sick to my stomach just to watch him degrade Neely; to attack her body like she had no right to say no. He was a pig, and if it hadn't been Neely, it would have been someone else. It was harsh, but taking one dirty cop down didn't feel so wrong. Better him than one of us. I rolled out of the pod and my entire body felt different…better…rejuvenated. I extended my hand and opened and closed my fist. It had been swollen and filled with cuts from the battles we had fought to get this far. I frowned in confusion because it was now healed. I stood, slipped my shirt over my body, and stepped out to find the others. I heard the others and I followed their voices to the room Neely had retired to. The conversation hushed when I entered.

"Why so secretive?" I asked, smiling until I noticed the grim looks on their faces. My face fell in concern. "What's going on?" Nobody spoke, and as I eyed them one by one, I realized. "Where's Neely?"

Minnie stepped up and I looked at her in surprise because she was walking perfectly fine. I then looked to my hand again, flexing it into a fist and then opening my fingers wide. The pods had rejuvenated our injuries while we slept. "Wow," I mumbled. "Your foot, it's healed," I said.

She nodded, but there was a solemnness in her. "I'll need both feet to go after Neely."

My stomach soured. "Where is she?"

"We think she left in the middle of the night," Aziza added. There was guilt in her eyes. "I'm so sorry. I was tired and scared. I should have never made it seem like I didn't have her back."

It took a lot to control my temper, but I knew more fighting was the last thing we needed. It would only further divide us. We were a team.

"I'm sorry, Liam," Aziza repeated, her eyes so sincere that they pooled with tears.

"I know," I answered, as I pulled her into a hug. Minnie joined and Jesus too. Arti was last. We huddled, as we stood there with our heads bowed.

"We have to find her," Minnie said, breaking the circle. We all headed for the door. Arti grabbed his channel and rushed after us.

"Hey! Wait up!" he shouted.

"You're leaving Silicone Valley?" Jesus asked. We all took pause.

"We want to unite all people, right? I count, don't I?"

"Everybody counts," I said. I was fed up with the rules. Black, white, asian, hispanic, artificial...The only way that we were going to beat the system was if we came together. Neely wouldn't make it by herself, and even if she wanted to try, I would never let her.

NEELY

The sounds of the wild echoed through the air and I stood deathly still, as I looked up at the gates ahead. They were unkept. Weeds grew around the steel, barely exposing the slits in the gate. I understood why no one had trespassed into this zone. The noises around me were enough to make me turn around, but I had no other alternative. It was either tackle the water that surrounded the animal zone or go through it. Being alone came with its own challenges. The fear seemed to be stronger, now that I had no one around to pretend to be fearless for.

"I can't do this by myself," I whispered, aloud.

"Then how about you do it with me?"

I turned, in shock, as I saw Alo approaching in the distance.

I took off running toward him as relief, I didn't know I needed, flooded me. I leapt into his arms, as he lifted me off the ground and spun me around, hugging me just as tightly as I held onto him.

"How are you here right now?" I asked. He placed me on my feet. "How did you find me?"

"My people are hunters. We hunt by scent. Some scents you don't forget," Alo said.

"So, I stink," I smirked, as I cut my eyes at him. Was I flirting? Was he? Could you like more than one boy at a time? The butterflies in my stomach confirmed that I felt something.

"Sweetest stench I've ever smelled," he said, winking. "I just thought you could use a friend." He cleaned it up at the end, taking the pressure off.

"You have no idea," I returned.

The loud call of some type of animal; a mixture between a roar and a growl, stilled the air and made the hair on the back of my neck stand. Small birds flew from the bushes behind the gate.

We looked at one another before I took a deep breath and led the way. We pushed through the vines and overgrown bushes that concealed the gate until we stood on the other side of it, in the trenches, within reach of whatever lived in this zone.

"I can't, I can't," I whispered, stuck…glued…frozen… unmovable. My heart was in my throat. I swore I could feel it choking me, refusing to be swallowed down.

"Fear doesn't exist, Neely. It's a mind game. Steady your mind and your heart will follow. Just place one foot in front of the other," Alo whispered. I inched forward through the dense forest. It was so overwhelming. There was nothing but greenery in front of him; leaves as big as my body, one after the other, overwhelming me as I pushed branch after branch out of my path. I tried to look up… tried using the sky as my guide, as my point of reference, but the forest was so overgrown that the trees blocked out all light. I turned around, trying to see if I could go back toward the wall, but even that had disappeared. I couldn't find my bearings. I couldn't even pinpoint the path I had come from. There was no beaten path. It was all wild… all uncharted. I was off course and terror pulsed through my veins.

The low grumble echoed around us turned my blood to ice and I steeled in place.

"What is that?" I whispered.

"Animals smell fear, Neely. You have to calm down," Alo warned.

"I can't," I cried. I felt like I was frozen…like when I saw a spider in our basement. Somehow, little black bugs with eight legs paralyzed me. If the itsy freaking bitsy spider could do that…whatever animal that was making this noise would give me a heart attack before it ever even sank its teeth into me. "I can't, I can't, I can't." I was freaking out. How could I make it through this zone when I couldn't see even five feet in front of me? Everything looked the same. Trees. I was drowning in trees.

Alo gripped my shoulders and turned me toward him. "Neely…" The way he said my name was too calm. I wanted to slap some fear into him. Nobody was that brave. How was he so daring? He took one of my hands and placed it on his chest, on his heart.

"Breathe to the beat," he said, as he stared me in the eyes. Mine were uncertain, his were courageous. He was a warrior. I just needed a little bit of the strength he had to make it through this.

"Alo, I can't! I'm not strong, okay? I'm just a girl. There is no Melanin Tribe. I'm not the hero you think I am. I'm just a scared girl who got in over her head." Tears slid down my face, as I admitted all my insecurities. Truth was, other people believed in me more than I believed in myself. They had built me up this entire way, but now that I was going on alone, I felt weak.

"You can, Neely because you have to. You belong to a tribe full of melanin. Men and women who trekked across Interzones when they were swamps and forests and they were running from whips and slave masters. You come from that. Do you think your people weren't afraid when they were running towards freedom? They were horrified because getting caught meant death, but they still ran. They still persevered. Being brave isn't about not being afraid. It's about continuing to do something in spite of it. You're afraid. I understand. Do it anyway." I closed my eyes, and felt the steady beat of his heart.

THUMP THUMP
THUMP THUMP

My lip quivered, and I trapped it between my teeth, as I sucked in deep breaths. The growl in the air around us; the sound of birds, the hissing of snakes, and rustling of leaves, made my heart race; but the feel of Alo beneath my fingertips was the strength on the other side of the tug of war rope. He was pulling me into calmness, persuading me to settle down, and convincing me that I was strong, reminding me of the stock I had running through my veins. I nodded and opened my eyes, and then withdrew my hand.

"Are you sure you don't want to just fly us out of here?" I asked, only half joking.

"There is a golden eagle here somewhere. I can't manifest the spirit of the animal while in its presence," Alo said. "We'll have to do this the hard way. You up for it?"

I shook my head no, but my mouth said, "yes."

Alo led the way and I focused my eyes on his strong, copper colored back, a distraction that stopped me from focusing on the noises around me. He pushed through the wild terrain and it was clear that we were visitors here. Not a foot had worn down this path before us. There were no markings, no clear ground; it was all untouched land, which made it even more treacherous. The thick underbrush and giant trees were as dangerous as any wild animal hiding amongst them.

"Stop staring," Alo said, as he turned his head to shoot me a wink.

"Boy, ain't nobody looking at you." I didn't even think to hide my sassiness from him as I blushed hard. He smirked knowingly, then turned as he stepped through the brush, finally clearing space into an open field. He stopped abruptly, and I crashed into the back of him.

"Why are we stop-"

I looked up to see a bear cub, grazing on a red berry bush. It was breathtaking. It was a poof of brown fur, with two, big ears, and curious black eyes.

"It's a baby," I cooed. "That's what we heard. This is what I was afraid of?"

The bear looked up from the berries and paused when it realized company had arrived. He turned his head, as if he was inspecting me, and then took one step toward me before taking two steps backward. He was cautious. I understood. He was probably more afraid than I was. I reached for a few berries and plucked them off the bush nearest me, and then kneeled to the ground.

"Neely…this isn't a good…"

I placed a finger to my lips, to silence Alo, and then I cautiously held out my hand, opening my palm in offering.

The baby bear put both paws up to his face and it melted my uncertainties away. I smiled. "He's bashful," I whispered in amazement. Laughter filled me. "Come on," I cooed.

"Neely," Alo said.

The baby bear began to meander my way, clumsily, as if he had just figured out how to work his legs. "Wow." I was enthralled, as the bear walked up to me and ate the berries from my hand. I rubbed the top of its big, blocky head with my other hand, as I marveled at my new friend.

I looked up at Alo. "Isn't he cute?" I was in love.

Alo's stern face couldn't help but let a smile shine through. "He's pretty cute," he said, giving in.

"I can't believe I was afraid of you. That was a big growl for such a little guy."

Grrrrrrr!

"Neely," Alo hissed.

That growl belonged to something much bigger and I sprang to my feet as a large brown bear came marching its paws out of the bush.

It stood on its hind legs and lifted its nose to the sky, as it let out a growl that sent the cub running for the bush.

"It's the mother! Do we run?" I asked. I could barely breathe. I was stricken with panic.

He shook his head. No matter how big the bear appeared, we couldn't outrun it. It suddenly came charging, and I stood there, squeezing my eyes closed because what else was there to do? I could either watch death as it approached or not. I opted for the latter. I heard the heavy beat of paws against the dirt, and then the territorial roar of a mama bear who wanted to protect her cub. The charge of an animal that was so massive, it could probably swallow me whole. I waited, and when I felt the heavy pants against my face, I held my breath. The bear circled me, sniffing, rubbing against me, as its wide body knocked me off balance.

"Alo?" I called out anxiously, my voice shaking, inflection rising.

"S…stay calm, Neely," he stammered. If he was rattled, this was bad. It was always going to end badly. At least if I was killed by a bear, people would have a dope story to tell. Neely King, of The Melanin Tribe, eaten alive by a bear. Maybe my headstone would read, *here lies Neely King, the girl who fought a bear and lost.* It was better than being shot dead by a cop.

The bear's face was so close to mine that I could feel its wet snout.

GRRROOOOARRRR

I could smell the flesh on its breath.

"Neely, open your eyes," Alo said, in amazement. I fluttered them open to find the bear kneeling before me; head and front paws flat on the ground in front of me.

"It's offering submission," Alo whispered. "Incredible. It's a predator and it's yielding to you."

"What does this mean?" I asked.

"You seem to bring peace, Neely. In a way, I've never seen. This animal is yours now. Try to mount her," Alo said.

"Mount her? No. I can't," I snapped.

"Trust me and if you don't…trust her…the way that she is trusting you," Alo said.

I took a half step and jumped back, as the mama bear released a sharp breath. Alo nodded.

"You're awfully far away for someone urging me to mount a bear," I said.

I tried again, this time the bear didn't move as I took a small step toward her. She was gigantic. One swipe of her sharp paw could slice me in half if she decided to attack. There was nothing cute about this bear. This bear was a predator. This bear was a machine. I placed a timid hand on her head, and to my surprise, it didn't move.

"My name's Neely, what's your name?" I asked, softly, as I rubbed gently and stepped toward her side. My hand traveled along her fur, as I made my way to her side. I grabbed onto her fur, taking two fistfuls and hoisted myself up on her back.

"Good. That's good. Now let her feel your heart," Alo said.

Straddling the bear, I laid my chest onto her back, as I rubbed her softly. "I'm going to call you Nola," I whispered. "How's that for a name?" I asked.

As if Nola approved, she lifted from the ground on all fours. I sat up, as she began to walk.

Alo smiled, as I looked at him in disbelief. "You are special, Neely King."

"Hmm," I answered. *Maybe, I was…just maybe.*

CHAPTER 14

SYD

I sat, slouched in the back of the police cruiser, as the car sped through the Interzone. The blur of trees flew by, as the sun cast an orange glow over the road. I was going home and while I was happy to be out of the hands of the feds, I felt like scum. I had turned on my friends. They were headed to Zone 2, but now that Agent Max knew the plan, he would intercept them before they even arrived. The desperation to make it home alive had turned me into a traitor. So, yes, I was going home, but there had been a high price to pay to get there. The wall around Zone 2 was beautiful. I had never thought of it as a prison. Asian characters of the alphabet were etched into the stones. We didn't look at the wall as a barrier between us and the outside world. I saw it as a protector of our culture, a way to keep us pure. We painted it in red and gold. It was art. Some people came to the edge of the wall to meditate and pray. I had left its boundaries out of curiosity not out of hate. I always had every intention of returning. It was home and I loved it.

As we drove through the gates, my heart skipped in my chest, anxiety filled me. I had never been away from my parents. If I had been trying to escape anything, it was them. Their overprotective nature made me feel like I was choking, and I rebelled. After seeing the world outside of this place, I realized why they held me so close. The world was big outside Zone 2 and complicated and scary, but it was amazing too. The people. Neely and the crew were incredible. Any assumption I had ever made about people outside my zone was erased the moment I started scoping with them. Betraying them had been the hardest thing I'd ever had to do. We stopped at the checkpoint and the agents handed them their badges before we were cleared to enter. The streets were busy, unfazed as if one of their own hadn't even escaped. A sea of people went about their daily lives, as I watched them out the window. I couldn't imagine a time when those faces wouldn't match. If the walls ever came down, I wondered if my people would even want their lives intermingled with other races. We were so tight knit, and there were so many different nationalities amongst our own, that we were still embracing each other's cultures: Chinese, Japanese, Vietnamese, Malaysian…there were so many *"ese"* that we were engulfed in our own. I was that way. Reluctant. Resistant. Change was scary, but then I met a group of kids who were so different that they challenged me, each of them in their own way. I made friends and then I hung them out to dry. The car came to a slow crawl, as we neared my home. Cherry blossom trees lined both sides of the rode and petals covered the ground. I had never been so happy to see the picturesque street. My house sat in the cul-de-sac and I sat up anxiously, gripping the front seat, as we came to a stop in my driveway. I had made it. I was home.

"Remember what we discussed," Agent Max said, as he threw the car in park and exited. He opened the back door and I climbed out, grimacing. The pain was a reminder that I didn't want to be an enemy of the state. I wouldn't survive their form of punishment. If Agent Max hadn't intervened when he did, I would probably would have taken my last breath by now. My mother came onto the porch first, and she put one hand to her lips then turned to my father who emerged next. When I laid eyes on them, everything I had been holding inside erupted. Blubbers of emotion poured out of me, as I ran across the lawn. They met me halfway, wrapping me in a cocoon of protection, as I buried my head into my father's chest. My hands were still shackled in front of me and my father was instantly irate.

"What is this? Take these cuffs off my daughter at once," he said.

"My apologies, sir. It's protocol," Agent Max replied.

"I make your protocol," my father barked. He cupped my face, his slanted eyes catching mine. I frowned. The slightest movement sent shock waves of agony through my body. "You're hurt. Who is responsible for this?"

"We found Sydney in the Interzone. She was unconscious and beaten badly. We cleaned her up, let her regain some strength at headquarters. As soon as she was in good health to travel, we contacted you, Mr. Tran."

My father turned skeptical eyes toward me, and I confirmed the story with a nod.

"I guess I owe you a great debt of gratitude." My father held out his hand. "If you ever need anything…you come see me."

Agent Max nodded. "Just doing my job, sir." He looked at my mom and gave her a nod, before cutting a tense stare at me. It was a warning to keep my mouth shut.

"Come on, sweetheart. Let's get you inside," my mother said, as she wrapped a loving arm around my shoulder and ushered me away. The inside of our home smelled like cinnamon and I knew it was because she had made my favorite.

"A few cinnamon cookies coming right up," she said. "I'm so glad you're home, my darling."

"Me too, mom," I whispered, as she kissed the top of my head. She hurried off, always the dutiful mother and wife, to retrieve the cookies. I almost wished she hadn't left me alone under my father's scrutiny. Crow's feet accentuated his stare, as he stood with his arms crossed across his shoulder. My father wasn't very tall, and his stature wasn't massive at all, but his authority was like a giant in the room. He was angry. I could tell by the silence. My father was never quiet unless something was wrong.

"Sydney, do you know the danger you put yourself in? What would make you run away? Don't I give you everything? All that you need is provided right here under this roof!"

"I just wanted to see what it was like. I wasn't running away. I would have come back if…"

"If what!" He had never yelled at me, and—shock wore me, as my eyes widened at his outrage. "If the criminals you planned this disaster with had not killed a cop!"

"They aren't…"

"Don't you dare defend them, after what they did! After what they did to you! What did they do? Beat you and leave you for dead when you tried to come home?"

"No! They wouldn't! They're good people!"

"Then, who did this to you?"

I couldn't answer that. I wanted to, but I couldn't.

"Not them," was all I answered with.

"When we swept the zones and you weren't accounted for, I had to protect you. No one can know that you were a part of this," he stressed.

"Why am I the exception?" I paused because I remembered that Liam's face hadn't been broadcast either. "The other kid, Liam, from Zone 1. Are you protecting him too?"

"Let's just say his family has friends in high places. If it were up to me, they all would be prosecuted."

"What makes me different? Why don't I deserve the same?" I challenged.

"You are not like them! You were raised in a good home, with good parents, with values…"

"And they're not? You don't know them, father!" I shouted. Another first. I had never, ever, disrespected my parents, but there were some things that you had to be disrespectful about to get respect in return. The feds were coming for my friends. I had them walking right into a trap and I wanted my father to tell me that he would show them mercy, that he would somehow intervene and get them back to their zones.

"You don't know them!" he shot back. "You will not defend cold blooded killers in this house."

"They aren't cold blooded! It was self-defense! Please, tell me you're more than a racist!"

"Sydney Tran!" My mother came back into the room, horror on her face, a platter of cookies in her hands. The perfect housewife. Our family was picture perfect, only I wasn't the perfect child anymore…not after what I had done.

"But mom!" I contested. Again, my combativeness was new. I was new. They didn't know the Sydney that I had transformed into. I just thought differently, and while I was relieved to be home, I didn't want to lose the part of me that I had discovered on the other side of the wall. I was stronger, bolder, and braver than I had ever been. *Brave Syd wouldn't have sold out her friends. You're a coward*, I scolded myself.

"Listen to me clearly, Sydney," my father said, lowering his tone. "The magnitude of what you all have done is greater than you know. It cannot go unpunished. The citizens inside each zone have to fear leaving it. They have to fear the consequences of defying the laws that The Panel sets. The walls were put in place for a reason. It's my job, my duty, as Panel head of this zone to ensure that the laws remain intact. A lawless society is a dangerous one. Someone has to pay for this.

"Some, more than others, huh?" I challenged. His eyes widened. Who was this loud mouth, defiant, girl? It wasn't the daughter he had paid for; it wasn't the child he raised. I was coming into my own womanhood. No longer a girl. Not yet a woman. No longer moldable into what he wanted me to be. I was becoming who I preferred. I was questioning everything I had been taught.

"Be fortunate that it isn't you!" He hissed.

"How can you stand there and say you're about protecting the people if the laws aren't applied equally?"

"I will not justify the choices I make to protect this family! To protect my people! When these criminals are caught…"

"If, they are caught," I said, hoping that somehow, someway they came out on top.

"No one can run forever. When they are apprehended, they will be tried, and you will testify against them."

"Bao!" My mother intervened.

"I can't!" My father didn't need my testimony. This was his form of punishment for me. Court records were sealed, so testifying still protected my anonymity. This was about him severing the relationships I had made. He was destroying the bond…cutting the cord that connected me to them. He was putting me in my place. My eyes burned. Sure, I had set my friends up to be caught, but now I would have to look them in the eyes and reveal that I was a snake. They would hate me. *Right now, I hated myself.*

"You must. Your duty to family and to *your* people trumps all," he said. I saw his back through my tears, as he stormed out of the room.

ALO

I walked a few feet behind Neely and Nola. The cub, who we had named Baby, was at my side, a long, thick branch in my hand, as I used it as a staff. Neely was a queen. Wild hair, wild heart. She was the most beautiful girl I had ever seen. She straddled Nola, swaying from side to side, as Nola took heavy steps forward. The heat was stifling. Her shirt stuck to her body, sweat glistened on her skin as she sat up tall and alert, as we made our way through the animal zone. So far, so good. With a predator as our guide, we had no troubles. Guess mama bear was the queen of this jungle. Neely was the queen of mama bear. That fact still amazed me. Neely was the type of girl that you married and filled with babies on Navarra land. She was exquisite. I was drawn in by her skin and the way it melted into deeper shades the longer she allowed the sun to kiss her; the darker it got, the more she glowed. I knew my people had some traditional, mystical elements in our past, but after meeting Neely I was convinced that people of African descent had a power all their own. That had to be the only explanation of the spell she had cast over me. She was magical.

"This is incredible. I can't believe I'm doing this," Neely called out, turning that melanin drenched face toward me. She smiled, and I placed a palm over my heart. It was like she had shot a dart directly through it. That was another thing that drew me to her. She was loud. Literally and figuratively. She was colorful and never dulled herself for the comforts of others. She spoke her mind when it was agreeable, she shouted it, when it was disagreeable. She was unapologetic, brash, bossy, and stronger than anyone I knew. Wife. She would be my wife one day, a long time from now. When we were older, we would sit on our land, the walls will be no more because Neely is just that type of girl. She does what she says she's going to do; so, yes, those walls will be destroyed. Neely of The Navarra Tribe…that's what I wanted to make her. That was the real reason I came after her because when I thought of my future, I saw her and if I didn't protect her on this journey, that may never come true.

"Believe it. You are the queen, and this is your forest," I replied, laughter in my tone.

She laughed at that. Big and loud, her voice echoed through the trees. Echoed through my heart, too. Neely was one of those people who made you feel whole like, before her, we're walking through the world in half, without even knowing.

"Alo?" There was uncertainty in her tone, and I stepped around the back of Nola, then paused, mid-step.

"Is that a wolf?" she asked. More uncertainty. Fear. She had every right to be terrified.

"Wolves," I corrected because I knew they traveled in packs.

"I only see one," she whispered.

"That's all they want you to see," I answered. I stepped on the staff I carried, splitting it in half. A weapon for each hand.

"You armed?"

She went into her bag and pulled out gloves and star shaped weapons.

The wolf was standing, mouth pulled into a slobbery sneer. It was hungry. The low growl in its belly told us we were on the menu. "The gate is just up ahead. We clear it and I can fly. Wolves are pack animals. There are more, so be ready," I warned.

"Be ready," she said, breathing heavily, blowing out air like she was giving birth. "To fight wolves. Can you ever be ready for that?" she asked.

"You rode a bear," I said.

"I rode an Alo too," she smirked.

"Wolves should be nothing," I added. She turned, and we stood back to back. The wolf attacked, running full speed our way. Out of nowhere, two others appeared. We were surrounded.

GRRRRR!!!

Nola sprang up on hind legs, side sweeping the first beast with a strong paw, knocking it into a wooden tree.

Neely sent stars flying, putting three into the body of a second wolf, then retracting the weapons back to her. I had never seen weaponry like that. *Yeah, she's magic.*

The third wolf lunged for me, biting one stick, pulling at it aggressively. Too determined to let go, the wolf held tight, as

I lifted it into the air with one hand and spun the other stick in a 360, before driving it through its underbelly.

"That was only three, there are way more in a pack," I warned.

"Where are they?" she yelled.

"Preying on us," I answered. "Run for the gate!"

We took off, and just as I suspected, three more wolves came out of hiding. I skidded to a halt, turning to fend off the one closest to me. The sticks were like batons in my hand, as I spun and twirled them, getting licks on the wolf and twisting my body in all directions to avoid it's razor sharp teeth. Another one joined the attack and I kicked it with all my might in the nose, sending it whimpering into the trees to nurse its wounds.

"Agh!" I shouted as I felt teeth connect with the skin on my leg. I flipped backward, shaking loose from its hold, then sent the wolf flying as it tried to leap on top of me. I placed both feet under the wolf and catapulted it. Baby came out of nowhere and dug into the wolf's neck.

"Good girl," I panted.

I looked up. Neely was almost at the gate. I took off behind her. Running full speed. I heard the stampede and growls behind me, but I didn't look back.

"Go! Go!" Neely called. "Alo Run!" she shouted. I knew they were on my heels. I could hear them snapping their jaws and narrowly missing flesh. I slid through the gates, barely, barreling into Neely, as blood thirsty wolves attacked the bars. We fell to the ground. Me on top of her, we both panted in exhaustion. I cleared her hair from her face, as she smiled, sprinkling the air with laughter. "I can't believe we just fought wolves." Her laughter waned, and she looked up at me. The intensity between us was heightened by the near-death experience.

"I feel alive with you," I whispered.

Her eyes softened, and she went to speak, but the loud roar behind the gates distracted us both. We stood and peered through the bars. Nola was fending off four wolves with Baby bear tucked beneath her.

Neely stood, and without hesitating, went back into the fire, sliding through the gates without thinking twice. She threw the shuriken blades with accuracy, taking out two wolves, before even getting close. I was on her heels and we each attacked. Fighting, grunting, sweating, until we stood with dead wolves at our feet.

She rushed over to Nola and Baby. It was a beautiful sight to see her buried into such a deadly creature, no fear, all love, as she wrapped her arms around Nola's neck. Nola roared, but didn't attack Neely. She simply nuzzled her huge face into Neely's. "Goodbye, girl," Neely said. She bent to plant a kiss on the top of Baby's head. They both were unharmed and they both responded to Neely in a miraculous way. She stood, and the tears shined against that brown skin like diamonds. I had to let out a breath to relieve the angst in the pit of me. I wanted to kiss this girl. I was sure I loved her.

"Let's go, Neely," I urged. I wasn't sure if there were more wolves, but I didn't want to stick around longer than needed. We rushed to the gate. Then, I took flight. Her chest to my back, heartbeat calming me, as I soared through the skies. Yeah, I was positive, this girl was magic.

NEELY

I rubbed the side of the beautiful bird, my beautiful friend, Alo as we floated through the sky. There was such beauty from this vantage point. Being so high up made everything below seem small, even my problems. The wind whipped through my hair, as I held on tight. I was flying over every obstacle, soaring past all doubt that I would make it. This was magical. Everything about Alo and The Navarra was beyond the boundaries of possibilities. I had learned to see the world through his eyes, even after he retreated back to his land. The view was simply better. The possibilities were limitless.

I leaned forward and whispered, "let's have a little fun." Alo took a dive and I shouted out in laughter, as we plummeted toward the ground. I had no fear. I trusted Alo with my life, as the ground got closer and closer. He leveled off, flying across a river that raged below, getting so close that the water misted around us.

"This is incredible!" I shouted as I tightened my thighs, locking myself in place, as I lifted my hands toward the sky. He ascended, spinning like a tornado and I pulled on his silky feathers to use them as reigns. He was so powerful in this form, so lovely. He turned and then did a complete

360-degree turn, giving me the thrill of my life. "You are amazing, Alo," I whispered, as I rubbed his coat. "The most beautiful thing I've ever seen," I whispered. I laid my chest to his feathers. "I love you." It was true. I loved all of them; Alo, Liam, Minnie, Syd, Aziza, Arti. Their belief in me and the way they fought for our friendship, I had never experienced loyalty like that. It wasn't owed to me, they volunteered it freely and my heart swelled because I knew I was lucky to experience it. Alo called out, squawking loudly, proudly, and I knew it was his way of saying, *I love you too*.

"Now, let's change the world. Zone 2, Alo. As fast as these wings can fly."

I saw the wall in the distance through the clouds as Alo picked up speed. I was almost there. I had the evidence in my bag, and I was so close. "I did it," I whispered, elated, relieved, slightly shocked that I had made it all this way. I was a girl who was never supposed to step foot outside her zone, but I had trekked across the Interzone and seen things that no one would believe. I had fought battles that were supposed to crush me. Conquered beasts, both human and otherwise, that meant to destroy me. I had crossed lands that had stolen the souls of those who dared try to cross them before me. My head was swollen with so much pride that I thought I would float right off Alo's back like a helium balloon. Maybe black girls did have magic. Then, I remembered I didn't do it alone. I couldn't have done it alone. It had taken us all. So maybe it wasn't about black girls and our magic, but the magic of people whose hearts all beat the same, all served the same purpose to love…one another…as equals because we were all made of the same magic inside.

"What are those lights?" I asked as I saw color sparkling in the distance. As we neared the unmistakable sight of red and blue lights came from the row of police cars lining the perimeter of Zone 2. Officers stood behind the shield of their opened doors, guns drawn, aiming, ready.

"What are they aiming at?" I asked. My eyes scanned the Interzone until I spotted their target. My friends stood in the distance. Their hands were raised. They had assumed the position. Hands up, don't shoot. Surrendering. So why were their guns still aimed? I didn't trust these men to bring my friends in safely. I wouldn't trust any officer and I wasn't surrendering to anyone except Bao Tran. "We've got to clear the path to Zone 2."

I leaned to the left, directing Alo to take a dive down in that direction. Alo flew through the sky, casting a massive shadow over the officers and causing them to look up. "Now!" I shouted. Alo flew down, burrowing through a line of officers, his massive wings sweeping them out of the way.

Bullets flew.

RAT TAT TAT TAT TAT

I ducked down, holding on tightly, as Alo ascended. My wild hair caught the wind, my eyes burned in determination, as we flew over Liam and the others. They looked up.

"Neely!" I heard Minnie scream, in shock.

"Come on, Alo, again," I whispered.

We flew with the speed of a rocket across the sky, spinning and dipping to dodge the bullets that the officers sprayed our way. Alo took out another line of officers with a sweep of his wings, and when we took back to the clouds, out of reach of the bullets, I saw my friends attack.

"Again!" I yelled, gripping his feathers, tightly, as we nose-dived.

This time, Aloe took out the third row of cops.

RAT TAT TAT TAT TAT

I felt Alo shudder and the big, beautiful, amber eyes, of that beautiful bird, my beautiful friend closed.

"No!"

He'd been hit, and he released a screech so loud that it echoed in the sky. Alo bucked me from his back and I went flying in free air, only to be snatched between his talons, caged, like the very first time I had ever ridden through the skies with him. That time, I was his prisoner. This time, I was his friend. This time, he was hurt, and we were crashing. The ground was coming too fast.

We hit the dirt and Alo slid across the dirt before skidding to a stop. His talons didn't open until we stopped completely. I rushed out and ran to touch his beak.

"Alo! No!" I cried, as I watched his body take weighted breaths. I immediately saw the blood that stained his feathers. Tears came to my eyes, as I kissed his beak. I could see my reflection in his giant eyes. "Turn back, Alo. Change, so I can help you," I pleaded.

"Let me see your hands!"

I heard the demands behind me, but I couldn't turn away from Alo. He was dying, and my heart was breaking, as I buried myself in his silky coat. "Alo, no!" I wailed. I was snatched away, my arm bent behind my back and handcuffed, as I lunged and cried. Alo took one last breath and then stilled. My legs gave out as I dropped to my knees, sobbing.

I looked up and saw my friends all on their knees, handcuffed, with guns pointed to the backs of their heads. Their fingers were so overzealous on those triggers.

BANG.

Then, I saw nothing.

CHAPTER 15

NEELY

The world came into view out of focus. Everything was hazy, and I was groggy, as I sat up. I reached for the back of my neck, where the bullet should have entered…I shouldn't be reaching for anything. I was sure they had killed me. There was a knot beneath the skin. They had injected me with something. I tried to stand, but my legs were weak, and I stumbled back to the floor.

Where am I?

I couldn't make it all the way to my feet, so I settled for my hands and knees. I was in a concrete room, one that was so small it couldn't even be called a room…more like a box, where sunlight didn't reach. A glass window in the middle of a steel door was the only thing that gave me a glimpse of my surroundings. I planted one foot firmly on the ground and then pushed myself up, using the wall to lean my weight against. My entire body felt heavy. Whatever they had drugged me with, it was crippling. The window was only big enough for me to see directly ahead. Nothing to either side was in clear view. Another door with a window was directly across from me and I wondered who was trapped behind it. Where were my friends? Was Alo really dead? So many questions plagued me. I heard footsteps echo against the floor and my stomach tightened, as angst filled me. Two officers came into view, and when they stepped aside, I gasped in shock.

"Syd!"

"Open it, please," she said, and as if she were their commander, they sprang into action, unlocking the door and letting new air into the room. I inhaled deeply, grateful because the walls had felt like they were closing in.

"You don't know how happy I am to see you!" I wrapped my arms around Syd. I stepped back and patted her down, inspecting her from head to toe. "You're okay? Did they hurt you? Where are we?"

"I'm fine, Neely," Syd replied. "This is correctional lock up inside Zone 2."

"You have to help me, Syd! You have to explain to your father what happened! They took the others. They have me locked up in here like a criminal! I need to see your father. I have proof of what happened. It's on my channel. They took my bag!"

"Okay, okay," Syd answered. "I'll get my father to help, but first, I need to know if you have any copies of the evidence Arti found?"

"I don't know…" I answered, as I took a step back from her, confused. *Why is she asking me this?* "I…I don't think…" I paused. Something was off. Syd was acting odd. She could barely look me in the eye. "Syd. What's going on?"

Syd stood, abruptly, and began to backpedal out of the room. I frowned because she was staring at me, her eyes flooded with tears, as she backpedaled. "I'm sorry, Neely. I really am."

"What do you mean? Sorry?" My brows pinched, in confusion. The door was slammed, and the sound of a heavy lock separated us. Syd was free, and I was chained. She looked at me through the glass square from where she stood, and my instincts told me something was wrong.

A tear slipped down her face.

"Syd!" I shouted. I hit an open palm against the door.

"I'm sorry," she whispered.

She walked away, and my face fell in defeat. "Syd! Come back! Sydney!"

TRAITOR! I looked around the room and noticed the red glow from a small camera in the corner of the room. *Is that a camera?* I was being watched.

I didn't know what was going on or what would happen next, but instinct told me that Syd was no longer on our side. I leaned against the wall and slid down until I met the floor. I had made it so far to get here, and now it felt like I had been running toward trouble instead of away from it. I leaned my head against the wall and covered my face with my hands. I guess the saying was true. Betrayal only hurts because it always comes from someone you love.

NEELY

I was chained. I was property of the government. The Panel owned me. They even dictated how many steps I could take. When my steps got a little overzealous, I felt the snag of the chains around my ankles, pulling me back into submission, reminding me that I was not free. Two police escorts walked me through the judgment house. They felt like overseers. I remembered the history books talking about the slaves being taken to the master to be whipped for all to see. This felt like that. I knew they were going to make an example out of me. We entered a room with grand, double wooden doors. They clanged open as I entered. The Panel sat at the front of the room. They resembled my friends; an older, more established version of us. One person to represent each zone. A sickness swarmed me when I saw the others in cage-like cells. They were lined up, side by side, on the side of the room. The empty one in the middle was for me. I was tossed inside, and I stumbled over my bound feet, falling to the floor. I gripped the metal bars and peered through them at the others. I had a pit in my stomach because I knew this wasn't going to end well for us.

Zone 1's Panel head stood. "Will the defendants stand?"

We all stood.

"The five of you are charged with the federal crimes of murder and boundary defiance. We have a witness that confirms the involvement of these defendants."

The doors clanged open and I turned to watch Syd walk in. I saw hope dance on the faces of the others.

"Syd!" Aziza called. They didn't know that she was no longer an ally. She wasn't on our side.

I could tell Syd was trying hard not to look our way. I desperately wanted to meet her eye, to speak without words, to ask why without opening my mouth. Syd stood in the center of the room, up on a stand, facing the members of The Panel.

"Please state your name and zone for the record," Zone 1's Panel leader said.

"Sydney Tran. Zone 2," she answered.

"What testimony would you like to contribute during the establishment of these charges against said defendants?"

Her father asked that pointed question. His eyes bore into her and Syd could barely return the stare.

"Syd…" I said her name, and her head snapped in my direction. There were tears in her eyes, as she twiddled her fingers in front of her. Regret hung from her. *She was my friend. How could she? She wouldn't…would she?*

Bao Tran cleared his throat, breaking our connection.

"I was with this group of kids the night the officer was shot," she said.

"You mean murdered," Bao Tran added.

Syd nodded. "Yes, murdered," she whispered.

"What were you doing outside of zone?" her father asked.

"It started out innocent. We just wanted to meet each other and have a night of fun. We met in a group, online, and decided to sneak out," Syd answered. "The cop discovered us, and we all ran. Neely got caught. She reached for his gun and shot him."

"What?" I gripped the bars. She was telling half-truths.

"Were the other defendants involved in the murder of the officer?" Bao Tran grilled.

"No, only Neely," Syd answered. At least that much was true.

"Did the officer pose a threat to the accused?"

My eyes shot to The Panel. The question came from The Panel seat from Zone 7. My zone. A coffee colored face, all black, no cream, stared down at me from the bench he was perched on. The white robe he wore gave him the power to seal my fate. I saw empathy in his gaze as if he hoped the answer to his question would help add clarity to my crime.

"Why is she saying she saw the shooting?" Aziza whispered.

I wondered the same, but I had lost my voice; the frog in my throat, the fist tightening around my heart, the bottomless gut. Instinct told me where this was headed. Syd couldn't even look me in the eyes. That wasn't my friend standing up there. I didn't know that girl, not even a little bit.

"No, the officer did not pose a threat. He feared for his life and was just doing his job. He tried to apprehend Neely and she reached for his gun, then shot him."

"She's lying," Minnie whispered, in stun. "Why are you doing this?!" That one came louder. A shout of disbelief. In a tone that said, *"you're lucky these bars and these chains are between us, otherwise I'd be all over you."* Minnie was livid.

Minnie grabbed the bars and shook them, violently, in protest. A federal agent stuck an electrode through our cage and Minnie's body jerked, as jolts of electricity bit through her.

"Stop!" I watched in horror. I was witnessing the highest level of pain, as it was inflicted on someone I loved. Foam came out her mouth, as she writhed on the floor. I turned to The Panel, my brown fingers curling around the black bars that entrapped me. "When will it be enough? She didn't do anything!" Syd's eyes misted, and her bottom lip quivered. "Syd! We are your friends! Why are you doing this?"

Bao Tran reached for his daughter's hand and gave it a squeeze. "Syd!"

The agent finally released Minnie from her electric torture, only to aim it at me.

"Don't touch her!" Liam shouted. His deep voice boomed through the room, bouncing off the tall ceilings. He was across the room in a separate cage. We were all in separate cages. Like animals…like exhibits…like criminals. Again, we were isolated from one another. Even in judgment, we were forced apart by the color of our skin.

"That's enough," Bao Tran spoke.

I knelt to help Minnie, who was sputtering and choking on her own spit. "I'm so sorry," I whispered, as I lowered my head and hugged her tightly. This was all my fault. Minnie didn't deserve this. She didn't belong here. She had done nothing more than be a loyal friend and I had led her to this.

Through blurred eyes and bars, I looked up at The Panel.

"I did it! I shot the cop! Just leave my friends alone! They had nothing to do with the cop. You want to hurt somebody? Hurt me! Punish me! Make the example out of me! But let them go!"

"Neely, no!" Liam yelled. I looked at him. My chest heaved, as I lowered my head and shook it in disappointment. I looked to Jesus, then Aziza, and finally down at Minnie. It wasn't necessary for all of us to be in chains.

"I did it."

"Is that your confession?" Bao Tran asked.

"I'll confess. Just let them go," I answered, standing. There was no hint of bravery in my voice. I was broken. I was intimidated. I was to blame for all of this and although there were extenuating circumstances that would explain how I ended up on the trigger side of a gun, none of that mattered. I didn't matter. This panel, these people didn't care about the why or how of it all. All they saw was that I was a black girl from Zone 7 who had broken their rules. I had taken the life of a *decorated* officer.

"It is not our way to skip trial," the black panel seat spoke, again. "Her confession cannot be taken into record without representation present. We can release the others if the witness corroborates their lack of involvement, but we must still follow due process."

I didn't know if this man was helping me or hurting me. What good was due process if the system was rigged against me anyway? If the truth was blocked by lies? If my friend was now foe? And who would represent me anyway? I didn't even know where my family was. No one was coming to save me. Help was not on the way. The best I could do was take a panel-appointed attorney who would do nothing but railroad me into taking a plea. That's how it worked. They were all on the same side unless you hired your own.

"Syd tell them! It was only me. The others are innocent!" I shouted. Still, she couldn't look at me. "Sydney!"

"She is telling the truth. The others were not involved with the shooting," Syd managed.

Her father shot her a glare and Syd lowered her head, wringing her fingers nervously, before rushing out of the room.

"We will release the others."

"Wait, one minute," Bao Tran said. "The others may not be implicated in the murder of the officer, but there is still the issue of leaving their zones. Bylaw says the penalty is death."

Zone 7 spoke up, interrupting, with his deep baritone. "We can't execute six kids. Their faces have been highly publicized. The last thing we want to do is incite a resistance."

"If they go unpunished, we will have more people escaping their zones, bucking the system. We have to keep people in place," Zone 1 Panel head argued. His white face was filled with wrinkles, probably from frowning his entire life. He was the type of person who didn't need the robe or the high bench to look down on you. Condemnation lived in his stare. "These aren't kids. They're young adults. There must be consequences to their actions." He wanted our heads.

"What would you have us do, Frank? Put nooses around their necks and string them from tree branches for all to see?"

There was anger in that remark and it came from Zone 3. A Muslim woman in full, traditional garb looked down at us through the rectangular slit of her white hijab. "They're kids."

"I agree. To punish one will be an example to them all and an example to the remainder of citizens in all zones. To punish them all would put us on an international stage and bring our practices under scrutiny. We don't need that," Zone 7 insisted. There was something about the way he was staring at me. With sympathy. With sorrow. Almost like he wished he could help me.

"Pardoning them is a mistake," Zone 1 insisted, grumbling under his breath. Zone 3 stood to her feet and motioned for the federal guards.

"Open the cells," she ordered.

I helped Minnie to her feet, and she leaned on me, taking shallow breaths. I tossed an arm behind her back and hoisted her arm over my shoulder for leverage. She rested her head against my shoulder. The electrode really did a number on her.

"Approach The Panel," Zone 3 ordered.

I helped Minnie out, as Liam and the others emerged from their cells as well. We lined up, side by side, in front of The Panel. They represented society. There was a representation of each of us, sitting in a position of power. It was what kept things fair. *Then, why does this feel like the deck is stacked against us?*

"Neely King, you will be held until trial," she said. "The rest of you will be released, your families will be fined, and you will be returned to their custody." She motioned for the federal guards in the room. "Remove their cuffs. Neely King, you will be transferred back to Interzone Correctional Facility where you will await trial. No bond will be granted. Would you like The Panel to assign counsel?"

My entire body trembled. My friends were going home. I was still in chains, and although I had asked for it all to fall on me, it still felt devastating. Huge drops of emotions clung to my lashes. I tried not to blink, as they prickled in my eyes, but they were flooding, and eventually, the overflow traveled down my cheeks. I felt arms around me. Liam's embrace. I melted into him. Then, I felt the others, as they all wrapped their arms around both of us, forming one large huddle.

"I can't leave you. I'm not leaving you," Liam whispered.

"You have to," I replied. Our foreheads touched, and I closed my eyes, as he cupped my face. This had to be what true love felt like. It was also what true heartbreak felt like. He was going home. I was staying here. Our bond would be broken, and we would be forever separated by the walls that kept us disconnected. Middle fingers up to Trum. He was the devil that started it all. He had made it acceptable to hate.

Liam's lips met mine and I tasted the salt from my tears. This felt like goodbye…like we were preparing for tragedy…cherishing each second because we knew these were some of our last…I could feel the tension in the room. The shock. The disgust. The judgment. I didn't care. Black girl, white boy; two generations whose paths should have never crossed…whose lives were separated by walls…they were ripping us apart.

"I'm going to come for you. I promise on my life," he said. There was so much conviction in his voice. I nodded, trying to be strong, but I couldn't stop the loneliness I felt, as my friends were pulled away.

They didn't go easily, and I loved them for that. They screamed and lunged and fought and resisted until they were removed from sight. It was pandemonium in the judgment room, but they were outnumbered and the inevitable moment we had been trying to avoid was finally here…our separation. My eyes filled with emotion and my bottom lip trembled, as I watched my friends be pulled out. I didn't know if I would see them again, but I had to remember that I was lucky to have met them at all. There were zones of races, separated by trivial things that couldn't say the same.

"Ms. King. Again, would you like us to assign representation?"

Suddenly, I felt outnumbered, as I stood alone. Five against one. The man against me. Before I could answer, the doors behind me clanged open, loudly.

"Mr. Snell?" I called out, shocked. He walked like a man on a mission, taking long strides, as he adjusted the tie to his black suit. He looked like a whole new man. He never wore suits.

"No, she does not need Panel assigned representation. I will be representing her. My name is Yul Snell, for the record and I need a moment to refer with my client before she is sent back to holding."

Zone 7 spoke up. "The Panel will take a 15-minute recess while you confer with your client, Mr. Snell."

My feet were chained, and they now matched my wrists, as I shuffled out of the room, Mr. Snell pulling my elbow, gently, along the way. "Don't speak until we're behind closed doors," he instructed. I was taken to a small room, and as soon as the door closed, Mr. Snell said, "Did you shoot the cop?"

"Yes," I said. "But I have evidence…there's a video that proves it was self-defense."

"Where is it now?" Mr. Snell asked.

"Bao Tran has it," I responded.

"Listen to me. The only court that matters is the court of public opinion. You won't win against The Panel. It's set up to persecute people like me and you. What you've done is miraculous, Neely. The average person would not have made it this far. I sat back, watching the broadcasts, as the cops and feds pursued you. You beat them at every turn. You crossed through zones that man hasn't stepped foot in for years. You are special. The people have been waiting for a long time for someone like you. The key to your freedom…to everyone's freedom, used to be in black and white in the United States Constitution. No state can restrict the movement of its citizens. President Trum removed this basic right to support the building of the walls. Rumor has it, he destroyed it and all record of its existence, but he forgot to destroy the Articles of Confederation."

"The first version of The Constitution," I whispered. I was trying to follow him, but I didn't get how this history lesson tied into my burdens. "I remember the lesson, Mr. S, but what does any of it have to do with helping me get out of here?"

"There is no such thing as a fair trial before The Panel for black people, Neely. You have to hold court with the people in the streets. We'll use that video to incite the people. We'll get them on your side. Show everyone that what happened to you can happen to anybody."

"Who is we?" I was confused.

"BKA," he whispered.

"What? It's a high school frat…"

"It's an underground network of black men, descendant from the old *Black Panther Party*. We've been preparing for this fight for decades. We've been waiting for the right person to inspire the people. Like Emmet Till inspired a movement. Like Rosa Parks incited outrage. You, Neely King…your unjust arrest will inspire the movement that will take down these walls. We're going to break you out of here. Be ready to move when the time comes."

"And once I'm out?" I whispered.

"Prepare yourself for a fight," Mr. Snell whispered. My lip quivered, as my tender heart raced. "It will be the fight of your life. You will need to find the Articles of Confederation and use that to abolish the separation laws. The people will stand behind you."

"I'm a 17-year-old girl," I scoffed. "I have no power. I can't change anything!"

"Change comes from the youth. What you and your friends did, breaking federal law without batting an eye, finding your way out of zone…"

"It was stupid," I cut him off.

"Maybe, but it was brave. I haven't heard of bravery like

that in a long time. People lost that…" he paused, as he stared me in my eyes. "They lost the courage to go against what they know is wrong. You can't teach an old dog new tricks. My generation lost that courage, but you will remind us that there is something to fight for. The people will stand behind you. Zone 10 is full of people, interracial people… you haven't been there yet. They're enslaved. They're trapped there under federal law. Unable to have children, unable to do anything except wait to die off. It's a death zone and they're waiting for someone to beat the system…to change the law. You can do this. People will support you. All you have to do is take the first step and you'll have an army behind you."

First Adoeete, now Mr. Snell. It seemed I couldn't run from this destiny. Everyone's expectations of me were so high that it felt like they were weighing me down.

"Until we come for you, keep your head down and stay out of trouble," Mr. Snell instructed.

"My parents. Can you get a message to them for me?"

"Your parents are in federal custody, Neely. Aiding and abetting…"

A fire started in my belly and I hit my closed fists against the wall.

"Aiding and abetting? They didn't even know I was sneaking out of zone! They can't blame them for what I did wrong?!"

"They've locked black people up for a lot less, Neely. This is the system that we live in. People like to think that the walls keep us safe, that they stop injustice from reaching us on the other side of all that brick. They don't do anything but keep us all in one place," Mr. Snell spoke, his eyes brimming with emotion. "Easier to keep an eye on us if we're all gathered in one spot. The measure of justice and equality comes when moments like this arise. When there is a decision to be made about one of our own, The Panel chooses to lock you up and throw away the key. When they choose to make the cop that assaulted you the victim, just because of the color of his skin. When they abuse their authority and lock your family up to intimidate and manipulate you. It's how you know we're still just cattle, we still only matter three-fifths as much as one of them."

"You have to help them," I whispered, in despair.

"*You* are the only person who can help them, Neely. You're going to help us all." He stood. "We'll get you out, we'll find the articles and then the youth will lead us to a new day. This is the beginning of a revolution, one that you started when you decided you wanted to take more of the world than what was given to you."

A knock on the door ended our conversation. I was grateful because I couldn't absorb any more. I had done the impossible. I had crossed the Interzones and delivered proof of my innocence to The Panel, only for it to be buried in a web of lies. Now, I had to fight for my life again, but this time I was in chains. I was in custody of The Panel. I felt defeated.

"The Panel has reconvened," the officer announced, as he opened the door and stood guard, as I followed Mr. Snell back into the judgment room.

"Neely King," Zone 7 spoke. I looked up because I heard the sound of compassion in his tone. He was a black man in power. Perhaps he had stood up for me. Maybe, Bao Tran had shown him the proof. I knew I was mistaken when his brows pinched in regret. "You will be remanded to federal holding until a date of judgment is established for your crimes."

It was the ominous system of not knowing, of waiting forever to receive punishment. The unjust act of locking someone up without convicting them and making them wait years while The Panel took their time working their way through each case. I would have to break free or spend years waiting. I turned to look behind me at the empty rows. I had no one. A sinking feeling filled my belly.

The officers took a step toward me.

"Give her a minute," Mr. Snell demanded. He lifted my chin with his fingertip and penetrated me with a pointed stare. So much was transferred from him to me in that stare. It symbolized all that we couldn't speak aloud. My lip trembled uncontrollably as a sob of pain escaped. I lowered my head, shoulders hunched over in devastation. *I am Neely of the Melanin Tribe.* I don't know why it helped. It was a fake tribe I had made up in the heat of the moment, but it somehow felt very real. I represented Zone 7. I represented black people. I was the only one who had stepped foot outside of zone for decades and I carried the reputation of my people on my back. Whatever the world surmised me to be would be what all people from my zone were expected to be like. So, in essence, I was exactly who I had pretended to be. Neely King of the Melanin Tribe. It was a mantra that had carried me when fear seized me. I needed to remind myself of that now more than ever. I gathered myself, tucking my emotions.

I couldn't get rid of the terror, but I could hide it. I looked up at Mr. Snell. His look said *be ready*. I nodded before the uniformed officers grabbed me and escorted me out of the judgment room.

CHAPTER 16

SYD

Tears of regret burned my eyes, as I sat in my father's chambers, watching the video of Neely killing the cop. The grip of contempt on my heart was strong, as I witnessed the cop's assault against her. It was my first time seeing it and I wished I hadn't. It was hard to stomach. The man was twice her size, even if he hadn't been armed, it would have still been an unfair bout. The way he ripped at her jeans, exposing her body, the way she sounded when she screamed. I had never heard fear like that, not even my own. The cop was going down as a hero and this very moment, my friend was being persecuted. *He deserved everything he got.* The door opened, and my father walked in, but I couldn't turn his way. The video that I kept rewinding played in front of me.

"This isn't right, father," I whispered. "How could you punish her after seeing this? Why do I have to lie when the truth can fix it all!"

I turned to him, eyes misted, heart disappointed. He was my father. The man who was ten feet tall in my eyes. Never did I think he could be so cold.

"My job is to protect *you*," he said. "The position that you have put this family in is a dangerous one. I don't want your name anywhere near this situation. This evidence shows you were there. It shows you left zone. Do you think I will be allowed to keep my Panel seat if I can't even control my own daughter? We can't broadcast this, and everyone can't walk away. I let the others go back to their zones. Local law will deal with them. It could have been a lot worse. She killed an officer of the law. That can't go unpunished."

"Your officer of the law was a rapist!" I shouted. "Someone with that type of intent should never have power in the first place. He's supposed to protect, but who protects people from men like him? The men who arrested me? They were rough! They were malicious! They enjoyed seeing me beaten and broken! I knew my rights and I demanded that they allow me to exercise them, but I was voiceless, father! They did what they wanted to me because they felt like they were the authority! Like they had all the power! This is wrong!"

"That's why we stay in zones, Sydney! Everyone else are animals! Uncivilized! I can't protect you out there!" My father yelled. He had never lost his cool with me before. I had never heard him yell a day in my life, but the way his eyes burned into mine, blazing with impatience and vehemence caused my lip to quiver. He was just like everyone else. Bigoted; willing to sacrifice what's right for politics and greed. I had never been more disappointed. It was like a punch in the gut…like learning that Santa Claus wasn't real or catching your mother put your tooth fairy money under your pillow. The man I had idolized my entire life was a fraud.

"That is no way to live," I spat. "And thanks to you, my friends will never forgive me."

"You may not understand now, but one day you will. I can't concern myself with anything other than what keeps you safe…"

"And what keeps you in power, right, father?" I headed for the door, then stopped. "That's what this is really about. Panel records are sealed, so no one will know that I was there. My testimony will never become public. The only way people will know I was involved is if the media gets ahold of that evidence and broadcast it. You're trying to shut this down quickly. Convict the black girl because no one is going to care if you throw her away. Sentence her to die and move on to the next case before anyone asks any questions, right? All for power. All to keep your seat, but let me ask you this. What's the point of power, if you don't use it to fix what's broken?"

I couldn't even look my father in the eyes before leaving. I didn't know who he was anymore and after lying on my friends, I realized I didn't know who I was either. How people could go through life wronging others, I could never understand. It felt miserable. Sure, I had saved myself. I was safe, but I was also alone. The few people who understood me, the ones that I connected to, now hated me and it was all my fault. I had been forced to turn on my friends. Trying to please my father, I had gone against what I knew was right and I hoped I wasn't too late to fix things. I couldn't let Neely go down for this. I had to undo all my wrongs.

LIAM

Anger seared my heart, as I was escorted out of the courthouse. "She doesn't deserve this! You can't do this!" I lunged and pulled against the handcuffs, planting my feet and bucking violently against the two agents to no avail. As I was tossed into the back of a federal paddy wagon, the reality that I would probably never see Neely again crippled me. *I should have never convinced her to leave her zone.* This entire fiasco was on me. She was only trying to protect me when she pulled that trigger, and The Panel wouldn't even hear us out. She was a hero and they were punishing her without even considering the context behind her actions. Jesus, Aziza, and Minnie were each thrown in separate vans. I peered out of the barred windows, as the one I was in began to move. "Where are you taking us?" I shouted to the driver, through the shatterproof glass. I wasn't even worthy of a response. Stern eyes stared at me through the rearview mirror. "This is total crap!" I kicked the metal wall that separated me from the federal agents in the front.

Volts of fire soldered through me, as the agent in the passenger seat stuck an electrode through the sliding glass. I fell to the bed of the van, as soon as I was released from the electric whip. I could barely breathe, as I sucked in air, heaving to stop the vomit that threatened to erupt. I lost my balance, as the van picked up speed and hit a sharp left. I went flying against a wall, colliding hard, before being jerked back to the right. I was like a ping pong ball being beaten in every direction, as the agents purposefully drove recklessly.

"You alright back there? Sounds like you're having a hard time. Better hold tight," the passenger seat prick taunted. The driver hit the brakes hard and my face met the glass so hard that the shatterproof glass cracked, creating a spiderweb on the window. I felt the impact in my skull, a white light blinded me, as an explosion erupted in my brain. There was nothing for me to hold on to, nothing to stop me from flying around the back of the van. These walls felt like fists, as I collided over and over. By the time we stopped moving, I was on the floor, spit pooled in my mouth. I was snatched from the back.

"You want to hang with niggers and beaners, we're going to treat you like one! Cop killer."

The menacing words came before a hard blow to the back of the neck.

"Get him up. The parents will be here soon."

I was disoriented. Blood dripped from the cut above my eye, blurring my vision. I had never even fathomed the thought of anyone putting their hands on me this way. It was immoral. It was an abuse of authority, but these men inflicted pain without thinking twice. They practically had to carry me into their headquarters, I was so disoriented.

I was thrown into a cubicle like cell with see-through walls made of that same impenetrable glass. Before I could protest, the cell was locked, and the federal agent stood staring at me.

The hate in his eyes scared me. How one person could hate another so much, I didn't know. His animosity thickened the air, making it hard to breathe, or maybe it was the beating they had put on me. Still, I met his stare. I couldn't back down. Bloodied and bruised and all, I had to hold my ground. They couldn't beat me into submission. We weren't the bad ones and I wouldn't let anyone make me feel like a criminal.

"You chose the wrong side, kid," the agent sneered, before walking away. My eyes landed on Aziza, who was in an identical cell across from me.

"Liam!" she shouted, as soon as she saw me. Her hijab had been stripped; her hair was rustled, and her eyes were red from crying, but she was unharmed. I didn't know if they had shown mercy or if she was just lucky. I was just glad that she hadn't endured what I had. Jesus and Minnie were in identical cells beside her. I found relief in the fact that each of them was unharmed. We were still separated. Quarantined from one another, as if mixing us would result in something catastrophic as if we weren't all human, made up of the same thing…blood and bone. At least they hadn't endured the beating I had on the ride over. Apparently, the feds had a grudge against me. It was like they were punishing me for not upholding some white code, and for the first time in my life, I was ashamed to be from Zone 1. I was embarrassed of what my skin color symbolized. I was one of them and they had gone out of their way to put me in my place, just for aligning myself with people from other zones. I couldn't imagine what they would do to the others. I had never witnessed discrimination before. I had thought racism was a thing of the past, but I realized that being stuck behind the walls didn't lend the opportunity for bigotry to surface. We never interacted with other races, so the ugliness never got the chance to rear its head. Black people were out of sight, out of mind, but it didn't mean the ill intentions of the majority didn't exist. If anything, the walls just made the hatred build. It made the majority feel superior as if they shouldn't have to subject themselves to anyone that looked differently, spoke differently, lived differently, and it was sick. The bad part is I would have never believed people still felt this way if I hadn't seen it with my own eyes. It was a tough pill to swallow. People hating other people without knowing them. People reducing the value of life based on something as trivial as color, as if black or brown or yellow skin didn't package the same heart inside.

"What did they do to you?" Minnie gasped.

Her reaction only verified that I looked as bad as I felt. Beaten. On the inside and out.

"We have to get to Neely. They're going to try to make an example of her," I whispered.

"They're going to make an example of all of us," Jesus whispered. He sat on the sterile floor of the cell, his elbows propped on his knees, his head hung in despair. He didn't even look up as he spoke. "Except you."

I frowned. I was the one sitting here bloodied and bruised. He was acting like I was one of *them*. "I'm right here with you! What's that supposed to mean?"

The sound of a buzzer releasing the lock on the cell block erupted and I looked to the door to see my parents being escorted in by federal agents. My mother, picturesque in her yellow dress, perfectly curled, blonde hair, and red worried eyes, rushed to my cell.

"Why is he locked up like a criminal? Why is he injured? Open this door this instant!"

The agents jumped to obey. My father's anger was visible; his skin an irate shade of red, his eyes narrowed in slits of determination. "And get your superior, now. I want to speak to whoever's in charge."

I didn't speak, as the cell door was buzzed open and my mother came rushing inside. She pulled me into her arms, as I stared at Jesus.

"My baby, what did they do to you?" she cried, as she touched my face. I winced, moving my head away from her touch, but my eyes never left Jesus. "Let's get you out of here."

My parents ushered me down the hall, and as I passed Jesus, he said, "you're going home. Ask yourself why you don't see any of our parents out there? They might have roughed you up a bit to teach you a lesson, but you get to live to fight another day. You won't hear anything about us. They'll get rid of us as if we never existed, while you get to go home."

"Let's go, son," my father urged, pushing me forward, as Jesus' words burned into my brain.

As my parents processed me out, I kept looking toward the door, waiting for Jesus' mother to walk through it, hoping that Aziza's or Minnie's parents showed up. They never did.

"What about the others?" I asked.

The federal agent signing my release papers looked up at me. "Not your concern, kid. Go home with your parents and let us worry about dealing with the rest. You don't belong with them. You're a good kid."

"I'm not worried about any of those hoodlums," my dad said.

"They're not hoodlums!" I argued. I didn't want to see my parents in a new light. I had never considered them to be anything other than good people before. I hoped they didn't mirror the sentiments of the cops. My time outside my zone had changed my train of thought. I saw things differently. "You don't even know them. We can't just leave them in here. They haven't done anything wrong."

"Countless agents were hurt in pursuing them. They can't just walk away from that. Be lucky you are," the agent fired at me. I was livid. It was such a condescending statement to make. *Be lucky.* As if they were showing me mercy. As if sending me back to Zone 1 was a privilege. It was nothing more than a bigger cell. I'd rather be out here fighting, moving freely, going wherever I pleased, discovering things I could have never imagined existed than being trapped inside the perimeter that The Panel set for me.

"Why am I the only one walking away? Why am I not the one being blamed? I was right there with them! Why am I the one who gets to go home?"

"That's enough!" my dad shouted, harshly.

"Two agents will escort your family back to Zone 1," the agent grumbled.

We made our way outside, and with every step I took, guilt weighted my heart. No way could I just walk away and not look back. I climbed into the back of the car, eyeing the agents that climbed in front of us. "You have to listen to me, dad. My friends are innocent. The cop that got hurt tried to rape one of my friends. I tried to help her, and he tried to kill me. He was choking me, and I couldn't breathe. If Neely hadn't shot him, I wouldn't be here right now. He wasn't going to let me go," I explained.

"Those kids aren't your friends. You don't even know them, Liam! They're trouble. They're thugs. There is a reason why we don't mix with people like them!" my dad yelled. The vein in the side of his neck bulged, exposing his anger. "This could have been a lot worse. This is the stupidest decision you have ever made."

"It's the only decision I've ever made!" I didn't mean to shout it so loudly, but I couldn't just be silent. "My entire life I've followed the rules. You guys made every choice. You told me who could be my friends, where I should go to school, what I should be when I grew up, what girls were okay to date! Then, the walls told me how far I could go and what parts of the world were acceptable to see! This country is the only country that lives like this! We're the only ones with limits, with walls, with rules that say I can't meet a girl like Neely and fall in love."

"Neely! The black one? That's the type of girl you want to love?" my mother exclaimed. Bethany Prescott, blonde, submissive, born and raised with a silver spoon, blue-eyed, pure blooded princess. That summed up my mom and she couldn't believe I didn't want to find a girl just like her. I wanted the opposite. I wanted a girl like Neely. Cultured, dark, with lion's mane hair, and opal eyes. I had never seen anyone more beautiful. I had never known anyone stronger. "The girl who pulled the trigger on that cop?"

"The girl that saved my life," I countered. I could see her eyes in my mind when I closed them. "Now, I have to save hers."

My mother looked back at me. "I love you. I love you both and I hope you understand one day," I said. Things could be so easy. I could sit in the back of the car and go home. I could accept the way things were and forget the notion of loving a girl that looked differently than me. I could erase the friendships I had built since escaping Zone 1. It wasn't that I didn't like my life inside my zone, it was that I had felt the freedom that lied outside of it. I liked who I became outside the walls. Neely and the crew felt like family and I just couldn't abandon them.

"Understand what?" my mother asked.

I opened the door and rolled out of the moving car. My body hit the gravel hard, rolling to a stop, but I didn't take time to feel the pain, before jumping up and running full speed into the trees that lined the side of the Interzone.

I heard the shots of the agents, as they fired their weapons, but I kept running, navigating through the trees at full speed.

Bullets whizzed by my head; some splintered trees, as I narrowly dodged being hit. Then, suddenly, it dawned on me. They weren't trying to hit me. They wanted to catch me, apprehend me, unharmed. If my skin was darker, my hair kinkier, black or brown, they would be shooting to kill. I was one of them. A kill shot would be their last resort. I stopped running and decided to use that against them. Their prejudices, their assumptions, would become my way out. I panted, as I held my hands up above my head. My back faced them, as I heard the twigs beneath their heavy feet, snap, as they approached me cautiously.

"Don't move! Keep your hands above your head," one ordered, brusquely. "We're just trying to get you back to zone, kid. Nobody's going to hurt you."

Back to zone meant back in my cage…back under control. I couldn't go back and just pretend that everything was okay. Perhaps, if I knew Neely was headed home too, I could chalk our time up together as a memory, but that wasn't the case. They were going to execute her. I would never be able to free my mind of that guilt if I let that happen.

"Liam!" My mother's voice echoed through the trees and I knew she was watching. I knew my father was holding her back. "Don't hurt my son!"

The agent grabbed me by one hand, but before he could put the hand cuffs on me, I spun, grabbing his instead, and quickly removing the gun from his grasp. It was at his temple before his partner could even take his safety off.

"Liam!" That call belonged to my father. I ignored it.

"Put your gun down," I ordered.

"Okay, kid, okay," the second agent said, as he bent slowly to place his gun down.

"Liam!" The angst in my mother's voice caused me to look up, and the split-second distraction gave the agent time to aim, then shoot. I used his partner as a shield, then dropped to the ground, as I fired.

BOOM!

"NO!" My mother slid down the steep bank, rushing toward me. My father wasn't far behind. When they reached me, my mother was frantic, patting my body, searching for blood, fearing the worst.

"I'm fine," I said. I looked her in the eyes. "I have to go back."

"Who taught you how to…"

I looked my dad square in the eyes. "I've learned a lot about survival, about what's right and what's wrong. I can't leave her there. She would come back for me."

"You don't even know this girl, son. Just come home," my mother pleaded.

"I wouldn't be the man you raised, if I left her to die," I said, gently. "I'm not a kid anymore. You have to let me become the man I can live with; somebody I respect when I look in the mirror. Besides, she's the girl I love."

"You can't, son," my father said. "She's black. They'll never allow it."

"They'll never be able to stop it," I said, with a smile.

"Let him go," my mom said. She stepped up to me and squeezed my shoulders tightly, giving me a sad smile. "You be careful."

I nodded. "I will," I promised. I picked up the second gun from the ground and tucked it into my waistline. "I'll see you soon." I wasn't sure if that was true, but I was okay with the fact that I might die out here. I believed in Neely. I believed in us. I believed in change and I was going to be a part of making it happen. I pulled my mother in close, hugging her, soaking up all the love she had to give because I knew it was a great possibility that I would never get the chance to do so again. I expected my father to be angry, to be judgmental, or maybe embarrassed. His only son was in love with a black girl. I didn't think he was racist. I had never known my father to judge anyone for anything more than their character, but I was learning that nothing brought discrimination out more than misunderstanding and fear. He stared at me for a long time and I waited for the disappointment, for the condemnation. Instead, he extended his hand to me. I shook it, in surprise.

He pulled me in for a hug and gave me a firm pat on the back. When I pulled away, I turned and headed off into the trees without looking back. They may not have understood what I was about to do, but they respected it, and that was enough for me.

CHAPTER 17

NEELY

I was flanked with guards. Ten men. All white. All hate filled were responsible for delivering me to federal holding. I wondered if I would even make it there alive. The glare of malice in their eyes sent shock waves of terror in me. Just their presence threatened to break me down, unsettled me but I grit my teeth and held my head high as I walked, hands cuffed, feet chained. Screw them. I would not be intimidated. I took heavy steps toward the van that awaited me. In my mind, I saw a hearse because I was afraid that I wouldn't make it out of the van alive. I turned my head, looking back at Mr. S, and he nodded. "Be ready," he mouthed. I ducked my head down, as I climbed the metal stairs and took a seat inside.

Angst lived in my stomach the entire ride. I expected for these 10 men to take their frustrations out on me. I expected to die, but no one spoke, and no one laid a finger on me. I felt their disdain, though. It was thick like a fog in the air after a rainy morning. I peeked out of the barred windows, as we approached lock up. Barbed wire fences surrounded a tall building. I saw hundreds of people, walking along the perimeter inside the fence, wearing khaki jumpsuits, all chained. My heart beat like crazy. How long would I live behind that very fence before someone came to save me? It was clear that justice…innocence…was, not an option. I couldn't get a fair shot in a system that wasn't designed to protect me. I would have to build my own system, design my own jury. I'd stand in front of the people and let them be the judge. Then, I'd free us all.

I was escorted into the building. I was silent as they scanned my fingertips, putting my prints into a federal database. Is it odd that I worried about my lion's mane being untamed, as they took my mug shot? I mean, I was down but I wasn't out. If I was going to change history, the picture that people pulled up one day needed to look like something, right? I was taken to a holding cell and I eyed the room, skeptically, before a shove to my back pushed me inside. It was closed and locked, then the slit in the middle of the door slipped open.

"Hands."

I put my wrists through the hole and the cuffs were removed. I was grateful for that. The indentations they left in my skin was proof they had been too tight.

I retrieved my wrists and turned, surveying the cell. The room was a blank canvas, and so small that it couldn't be called a room at all. White walls, white stone floor, no window, white sink, white toilet, white body-sized rectangle indented in the wall. I assumed that was where I was expected to sleep. The fluorescent light above hummed, and I knew this room was meant for torture…not physically, but mentally.

It was meant to break people. I decided then and there it wouldn't break me. I hopped up into the enclave where I was supposed to sleep, and I laid down on the hard surface. I closed my eyes and retreated into my mind because it was the only part of me they couldn't imprison.

ALO

"Grr!" I bit down onto the branch as hard as I could, trying to stop myself from screaming. It was hard to contain the pain, as I dug my fingers into the wound, feeling for the bullet. I couldn't leave it in. It would grow infected and spread. It would kill me. I had to get it out. As I hid at the highest point of a birch tree, searching through my own flesh, I knew I had to survive. Neely was in trouble. At this point, we all were. My father had warned me about venturing outside our lands to go after a girl, but I couldn't listen. From the first moment I laid eyes on her, I knew I loved her. I couldn't send her into the Interzone alone, and now that she had been caught, I couldn't just turn back. My hands felt the metal bullet and I ripped it from my wound and then collapsed onto the wide branch.

"Aghh!" I groaned in pain, as I heaved and held the bullet up between two fingers, inspecting it. It was whole, and I found relief in the fact that I didn't have to dig for more fragments. I peeled off a piece of bark from the tree and put it into my mouth, chewing it. When it turned to gum, I stuck it into the wound as deeply as I could, sealing it, and stopping the bleeding. I was in pain, but I would live. I staggered to my feet and peered over the wall of Zone 2. If that's where Neely was, that's where I was headed.

NEELY

If the clanging of the door didn't jolt me from my sleep, the hands around my neck would have definitely done so. My eyes bulged, as a pillow was forced over my face.

"You're a cop killer, huh?"

I heard the sneer through the fabric that smothered me. These guards would kill me. They had a score to settle and I could feel the air leaving me, life abandoning me. The pillow was just so tight over my face. All I needed was one sip of air. Just one. I grew dizzy. *I'm about to die.*

"Campbell, what are you doing? You're going to kill her!"

Campbell. The man who tried to kill me. Remember that name. The pillow was still covering my face, and when it was pulled off, I fell onto the floor. On hands and knees, I crawled to the corner, coughing. I looked up into the eyes of the devil. He was foaming through gritted teeth, and a female officer stood behind him, pulling him away.

"She cannot leave here in a body bag!" the woman said. "Her face has been all over the broadcast. We have to handle this by the book! The public will be watching!"

Campbell, the devil, turned toward the woman guard, my savior at the moment, although I saw them all the same. Guards. Cops. Agents. They were all dirty. I didn't extend trust to any of them. This cell suddenly felt like a coffin. No way would I close my eyes inside there again. These guards wanted to close them permanently. They were against me. Trial didn't matter. Intentions didn't matter. The fact that it was self-defense didn't seem to make a difference. They wanted me dead. *I have to get out of here.* I could stay here, depend on a flawed system, and die, or I could break free.

"Argh!" I kicked the back of Campbell's knee in, causing him to stumble forward. A leg sweep brought him down hard. Before the woman could react, I sent a sidekick to her middle, folding her in half, and then back handed her to the ground. I rushed out the cell and closed it before the two of them could scramble to their feet. I slid the lock into place, just as Campbell came to the window. I gave him the middle finger and then rushed down the hall.

I skidded to a halt when I saw the narrow hall filled with guards. I was outnumbered, and I should have given up, but I couldn't let anything stand between me and freedom.

"Neely!"

I had to be hearing things. It couldn't be…*Alo!* He stood on the other end of the hallway, an army of men separating us. I was so happy to be looking at him. He was alive, and

I wanted to reach out and touch him, just to make sure he wasn't a figment of my imagination.

Ten to be exact. Half the group turned to him; half focused on me. Alo and I focused on each other. The thunder in my ears was my own heartbeat. It was crazy how my body reacted to fear. The hair on the back of my neck stood. My pulse raced. My stomach sank. My throat tightened. It was crippling, but I had to fight through it. I had come too far. I had done too much. Giving up and letting them put me in chains was not an option. Not anymore. I had been compartmentalized my entire life. Leashed. Restricted. I was breaking free. Black skin. Wild hair. Loud voice. If they wanted me in a box, they would have to kill me because no way was I willing to live any other way but free. I also didn't want to hurt anyone else. *How could I do both? Defend what's right without losing myself?* My first blow sparked Alo's, as we attacked from both sides. I fought with half my strength, with the intention to defeat, but not to end. This wasn't about killing, this was about living…this was about people's right to live however they wanted, where they wanted, and with whom they wanted. I didn't want to end anything, not even these men's lives. I wanted to begin something…wanted to start a new way of thinking, a new way of living…a new perspective that would make these men question whether or not they should be attacking me in the first place. My hands flew and I spun, then kicked, slammed and flipped until nothing stood between Alo and I. Without hesitation, I kissed him. His lips tasted the way they looked, like cinnamon and I didn't want to pull away. He had come for me, after being shot out the sky, and although I was sure I loved Liam, I couldn't deny the energy that pulled me toward Alo. Seeing him on the other side of the men, that now lay at my feet, I knew that nothing would stop me from this kiss…from this moment in time with him. Did that mean I loved him too? Did these nervous jitters in my heart signify that perhaps I didn't love Liam at all? Or did it all just mean I was discovering who I was as a young woman, seeing qualities that I liked in these young men? Two different men…from two different places. It meant I had the option. I had a choice. I had discovered human qualities in two unique beings that I identified with. I would have never had the opportunity to appreciate their differences had I never left Zone 7. Love existed beyond those walls. That alone was reason enough to seek beyond them.

"Hmm, hmm."

The sound of someone else pulled us apart and we turned.

Now, I was the one standing in the middle. Alo pulled on one heart string and Liam pulled on another. I didn't want to break any hearts. I was the least likely to break a heart before I had met the two of them, so I didn't even know how it had come to this. I didn't miss the look of disappointment on Liam's face from his discovery. The sound of heavy boots approaching meant I had no time to choose between them.

"We've got to go," Liam said, urgently. "This way."

"Wait, Liam! The others. They're here somewhere. I'm not leaving without them."

I could see the hesitation in his face. He had come here for me. Alo had come here for me, but they all were here because of me. "No one gets left behind."

Alo stepped up and tightened his hand around the wooden staff he carried. "I'll hold them off. You two find the others."

That made me hesitate. The notion of splitting up. "You can't handle them all," I said. Uniformed guards came storming through the hallway, body shields raised before Alo could respond.

"Go!" he shouted. He sprang into action, as Liam pulled me in the opposite direction. The last thing I saw was Alo spin the staff into a skip catch before the guards stormed at him. I cringed, as I heard the echo of bullets, and I hoped Alo was okay. I knew he wasn't an easy target, but he was injured, and I couldn't help but worry. We ran down the hall.

"Cells are this way, I think," I said, as we ran toward a door that led to a cell block. An alarm began to blare throughout the building, as red lights flashed in warning.

"We have to hurry," I said, as I ran full speed.

"One more step and I'll shoot! Put your hands where I can see them?"

We both stopped. I didn't turn toward the voice behind us because I didn't want an anxious cop to be intimidated by any sudden moves. The voice belonged to a woman. A female guard and I found a bit of relief in that fact.

"Assume the position inmate!" she barked. I heard the quiver in her voice. I recognized it instantly because it matched the tremble in my soul. The other guards held malice in their tone that I didn't hear this time.

"Please, help us," I stated, still facing the door that led to the cell blocks. "I'm going to turn. Slowly."

I began to spin. "I said, don't move! Assume the position!"

The blaring was so loud that it made my ears ring. I continued to spin slowly, ignoring her demand.

She fired at my feet and my eyes widened.

"The next one will go through your skull. Don't move another inch," the woman said.

My hands shook because I knew a scared guard was more dangerous than an angry one. If she felt even a bit threatened, she just may shoot me.

"I don't belong here," I said, as I stared her in the eyes.

"You shot an officer of the law," the woman stated. "He was a brother of the badge."

"He was an jerk," I countered. She pulled the chamber back on her weapon. "He tried to rape me. He was trying to hurt me and my friends."

"It's true," Liam piped up. "I was there."

"I know you stand behind a blue wall, but there's another code you live by…when you go home you take that uniform off at night. You can't take off your breasts or your vagina. You're a woman and there is a code for that, too. Women have the right to protect themselves. We have the right to say no. We have the responsibility to back each other up. I understand your loyalty to your job, but what about your loyalty to yourself…to all women…I shouldn't be here. Please. Just let me find my friends and get out of here," I said.

I could see her struggling with my words and she reached into her belt and unhooked her ID badge. She tossed it to me and lowered her gun. Tears glistened in her eyes. "Girl code," she whispered.

"Girl code," I answered, with a grateful nod.

"Your friends are in block C."

I pressed my hands together in appreciation, before backpedaling toward the door. Liam followed and I swiped the badge that released the lock.

"You really are something special, Neely King," he said.

The all white everything made it hard to distinguish between cell blocks and my belly filled with guilt, as I passed cell after cell. I was focused on my friends, but each inmate I passed banged on their window, hoping to get my attention. Hoping to be a part of my grand escape.

"Oh crap!" Liam exclaimed, as a group of guards came running behind us. This time, no warning. Bullets flew. "Open the cells. Use her badge to release the cells! They can't shoot into a crowd of inmates!"

As I ran past each door, I swiped the badge, creating a dense crowd. Rowdy inmates flooded the hall, making it hard for the approaching guards to give chase. No way would the guard's fire bullets through bodies. If they wanted to catch me, they would have to get their hands on me. I released another inmate, but before going to the next, I asked, "Where's block C?"

"That way!" The man pointed ahead. "To the right."

We took off, releasing more men and women along the way. It was utter chaos.

"Minnie! Aziza!!" I shouted. I spun in a circle, bewildered, frustrated, as Liam frantically looked in each cell.

"Neely?!" I heard Minnie's scream. "Neely! Down here!" And I took off in the direction of the voice. I was aching to lay eyes on my best friend. When I found her, I pressed my hands to the rectangular glass. Her white cell matched mine. Her frightened eyes matched mine. Our hands met, separated only by the glass pane. I swiped the badge and the hug we wrapped one another in brought wrecks of sobs.

"I'm so glad you're okay!" she shouted.

"I found Aziza and Jesus. Give me the badge!" Liam yelled. I handed it to him, and he freed them. To my surprise, Aziza's hijab was still wrapped around her head. I smiled.

"You just leveled the playing field," I stated. "Where's Arti?" I asked.

"They took him and the rest of the weapons to the incinerator. They're going to destroy him. They called him a virus," Jesus said.

"We can't let that happen," Liam stated.

"Do you guys remember what way the incinerator is?" I asked.

He was a part of our group. He was our friend. I didn't understand him fully…didn't know if he felt disappointment or pain, but I knew that he was one of us. He mattered.

"It was in the basement. We'll have to go back the way you came," Minnie whispered.

"Back through the guards," Aziza added.

She pulled off the diamond hijab and like a ribbon dancer, she led the way. "So, we knock them down one by one on the way out," she said.

The fabric was like an extension of her, as she led the way. The first set of guards aimed their guns, but before they could fire, Aziza used her hijab like a whip and wrapped up the weapons, snatching them from the guard's hands. The weapons scattered at our feet and we each picked one up.

"No kill shots!" I yelled.

Minnie looked at me like I was insane. "They're trying to kill us!"

"We aren't like them," I said. Aziza tangled a guard up in her fabric, flipping him upside down, before tossing him over the barricade to the level below.

"Agh!" he screamed, as he fell.

Our bullets fired, as we made our way inch by inch back the way we came. There were dozens of them coming at us, one after another, but we fought. After emptying the rounds, my hands became my weapons, as I remembered everything Alo had taught me. It was like second nature. Every blow, every kick, every spin. There was a difference when you were fighting for your life. I didn't even feel the pain that came with the impact. I just pressed go. These men were standing between me and free air. Self-preservation was kicking in. There were people everywhere, running and fighting. There were inmates still behind locked doors, banging and pleading. I tried to swipe as many of them out as I could, but I couldn't free them all. I was saddened by that fact. We left a pile of uniforms on the floor, from the guards we barreled through, then hurried to the stairwell.

"Hurry! Go! Go!" Liam yelled. My feet ticked down the stairs, one by one, and the noise of the chaos began to fade.

Minnie took the lead. "It's this way," she said. We rushed inside, and I stopped when I saw Arti lying on an examination table. He was hooked up to a computer, his body parts were dismantled, revealing the metal inside. My hands flew to cover my mouth, as tears filled my eyes. A fire raged in the incinerator.

"What did they do to you?" I whispered as I walked over to him. We all stood around the table, as Arti smiled.

"They did what they do when they don't understand something. They annihillllatttteeeee…"

Arti's voice changed tones, going robotic, before leveling out to his normal voice.

"I'm so sorry." My tears couldn't be contained now. They were flowing down my face. My friend was in pieces in front of me. "This is all my fault," I said.

"No, Neely of The Melanin Tribe. You are the answer to the probbbbllemmmm…"

He was short circuiting or something. "Can we put him back together?" I asked as I picked up the pieces. "We have to do something!"

"There is nothing you can do. They can destroy my frame, but they can't take the technology," Arti said. "Get your weapons from the cage. Your channels are inside."

Minnie and Aziza sprang into action, retrieving the items.

"Neely. You can download my code to your channel. Do it now. I will always be accessible to you through there when you needdddd me."

His voice was full-on robot now. He didn't even sound human.

"How? How do I do it?" I cried.

"Place the channel into the slot on the CPU," Arti instructed. "Huuurrrrryyyy."

I followed his command, and letters, numbers, and symbols began to show up on my channel.

"I'm running the code," Arti said. "When it is done. I will be a part of your channel. You will have to burnnnnn my body."

"I can't do that," I whispered.

My friends were silent, but their somberness filled the room.

"You will have to. We can't leave them any clues behind to duplicate the technology," Arti said. "The download is complete."

I sighed, as I cried. I leaned down to kiss Arti's cheek.

"Thank you for making me feel real and being my real friends," Arti said.

"You are real," I whispered. "You will always be our friend."

"There is an exit door down in the hall to your left. Whenever you need me. Just say, *hey, Arti.* I live within the firewalls of your channel. Until then, my friend."

"Until then, Arti," I whispered.

Arti's eyes closed and I sighed, as I lowered my head. I picked up his robotic head. He looked so real, but with his insides exposed, I saw firsthand that he was all metal. The others picked up the rest of his pieces, as we walked over to the fire. We tossed him in.

"We've got to go," Aziza said. We headed toward the exit. I opened the sliding door with the badge, and when all my friends walked through it, I closed it back. They turned to me in shock.

"What are you doing? Neely!" Aziza shouted.

"Go. Get out. I'm not leaving anyone else here. Not one prisoner and not Alo. I'll meet you. I swear."

"Neely!" Minnie called, as she banged on the door.

"Neely!" Liam's baritone deepened, in anger. "Open this door!"

"Go!" I said.

I grabbed my weapons. The ones Arti designed.

"Hey, Arti!" I shouted.

"Hey, Neely. You don't give a kid a break, huh?" he cracked, as his voice emanated from my channel.

I laughed. "How do I override the security system?" I asked. "I need to unlock all the cells."

"Plug the channel back into the computer system," Arti said. "I'll do all the work. You take all the glory."

I smiled, as I rushed to plug it back in.

The lights began to flicker, and the entire screen went black before computer codes began to run.

"Is it working? I think it's working!" I shouted.

"Of course, it's working," Arti's voice filled the entire room.

"Can you find Alo?" I asked.

The computer screen tuned into Alo, still fighting in the building. He was fighting, and I wasn't sure if he was winning or not. I could see him tiring, as the guards attacked him from all angles. I snatched the channel from the computer, tossed it into my pack, and darted out the room.

"Arti, what's the fastest way to Alo?" I asked.

"There is an elevator. Make a left and go to the end of the hall. Take it to the top floor," Arti directed.

"Where are the guards?" I asked.

"The guards are distracted by the other prisoners. You have time," Arti said.

I stepped on the elevator and fought the nervous jitters in my stomach. When the elevator doors dinged open, I came off the wall, shurikens in hand. I launched them one after the other, hitting guards, one after the other.

Alo's head whipped in my direction and he smiled.

"Hmmph!" I yelled as I hit my mark every time. There was a fire in my belly; an anger I had never felt. They had hurt my friend. I wanted to hurt them. It took everything in me not to aim to kill. An eye for an eye, but I knew that hate on top of hate only made things heavier. It only incited more wrong. I was fighting for right…for justice…that left no room for vengeance. We cleared the room and left the guards at our feet.

"I told you to go!" Alo said. "You're stupid. You run toward danger!" he chastised. I rushed him, throwing my arms around him.

"I ran toward love," I whispered. His arms were such comfort, but the ding of the elevator pulled us apart as we set our eyes on the opening doors. Agent Max stepped out, with a swat team of federal officers. The army of feds came out of the elevator with a mission. They came up the stairs, out of nowhere. What looked like hundreds of them.

"Run, Alo. Run," I whispered. I tossed a shuriken. This time to kill. There was no vendetta in that action. It was survival. I needed to assemble an army. I couldn't win against all of them. I needed the Black Kings, Mr. S, and the others from each zone who thought like me, who was fed up, just like me. I needed to assemble the disenfranchised because Agent Max had the numbers on his side.

I had won the battle against the guards, but it wasn't the day I would win the war and that's what this was…war…it was brewing, and I needed to rally my troops to come out victorious.

"To the roof," Alo shouted, as we ran full speed, ran for our lives. We would have to live in order to fight another day.

I took the stairs two at a time with Alo on my heels…with killers on his. The sun shone brightly in the sky. It wasn't a day to die. It was a day to live. I could see my friends in the distance, standing on the outside of the fence, gripping the wire, as they waited for me. They were waiting on me. They needed me. The world needed me. I was a black girl with big, nappy hair and I mattered to people who didn't look like me. My black life mattered. I was terrified to make the jump. Alo was hurt. What if he couldn't fly. What if they shot us out the sky again? I didn't have time to rationalize, however. It was either take flight or be captured. Give me liberty or give me death because if anything went wrong we would fall victim to the one-hundred-foot drop. I wrapped my fingers around the necklace Adoeete had given me. *God, please let us fly.*

I closed my eyes as we ran right over the side of the building.

He's flying! We're flying!

CHAPTER 18

LIAM

We all stood, in amazement, gripping the fence, staring in disbelief, as we watched the two eagles command the sky.

"Did she? How is this possible?" Minnie whispered.

Neely wasn't a passenger on Alo's wings. She had her own, transforming into a big, beautiful, red bird as she and Alo flew side by side. People poured out of the prison, running toward the open gates. She had freed them. She had given them a chance to escape, and now she was soaring.

"I don't know," I whispered. "Wow!"

Our eyes were toward the sky, as we watched Neely and Alo swoop down to pluck us from the ground.

"This is incredible!" Aziza shouted.

"Wooo!" Jesus shouted.

We cleared the chaos and flew for miles until I saw the walls of the animal zone. They flew low and dropped us out of their talons, before landing themselves. As soon as they were on solid ground, they both turned back to human form, running full speed from the momentum before eventually slowing to a halt.

"What was that?" Neely held out her hands, staring at them in disbelief. Staring at Alo for an explanation.

He nodded to her neck, and then fingered the necklace. "It's the talon of transformation. It only works one time when you need it the absolute most. Adoeete knew your journey would be hard."

"It's like a get out of jail free card," Minnie said.

"A what?" Jesus asked, frowning.

She shook her head, dismissively. "Nothing. Sorry. It's an old game from the archives. Dork moment."

"He would have never given it to you if he didn't believe in your path. You are supposed to change history, Neely," Alo said.

"And that's exactly what I plan to do," Neely answered.

NEELY

I felt electrified. I felt magical. Black. Girl. Magic. I flew. My arms were wings and I was powerful and beautiful, and I flew. I had done the impossible and that made freedom feel possible. Easy. Like if I could fly, attaining freedom was nothing.

"It's not your job to change the world, Neely. Look at us. We barely made it out of there. This isn't fun anymore. We got out. We got you out. That's all we can do," Minnie said. Fear was guiding her tongue and I understood, but I wasn't in that space anymore. I wasn't allowing terror to intimidate me into submission.

"It's not enough for one person to be free. We all have to be free. Every person, in every zone, should know what a world without limits is like. I'm free, but I'm not finished. This is bigger than me. The Panel has us set up in pockets of concentration. It ain't right. Walls are built on fear and ignorance. That's the foundation they stand on. If we break that, we can break them." I couldn't believe the words that were flying from my mouth. I was empowered. Emboldened. I was a black woman determined to rise.

"What do you want to do about it?" Liam asked.

"I want to build an army and bring down the walls."

My words stunned everyone to silence and six sets of eyes rested on me.

"What?" Aziza said.

"Every single one of them. I want to bring them down and dismantle the zones."

I finally understood what Adoeete was trying to make me see. I wasn't meant to return home and be a regular girl. I wasn't supposed to sit back, and watch things remain the same. I wasn't supposed to be meek and well behaved. I was born to be loud and change the world. I didn't want to say goodbye to my friends because we were forced back into our cages. I refused to say goodbye to the boy I loved because blacks and whites were afraid to co-exist. Make that two boys that I loved because I was kind of digging Alo, too. Make that three because Shakir… well, he was Shakir and I had loved him since the sixth grade, so that had to count for something. Anyway, I wanted options, wanted the option to pick who I loved. I wanted to surround myself with people that I chose, not those who were assigned to my group.

"And you think you can do that? By yourself? You're going to bring down the entire system?" Aziza asked.

"Not by myself," I answered. "With each of you."

"We barely survived this time!" Minnie protested.

Was I afraid? Yes, but I was more fearful of what would happen if I did nothing. What type of world would my children live in, if we continued to do nothing? Would they be able to reach outside the limits of the walls that kept their minds shackled? Bigots had moved our society in the wrong direction. Fear had caused people to accept division…to tolerate hate. My parents' generation had sat back passively, allowing it to happen. I wasn't going to do the same. I couldn't continue to follow those rules that kept me in a box. Living in zones wasn't freedom, it was the illusion of freedom when in actuality were more chained than we had ever been. There may not have been whips to our backs or shackles on our feet, but our minds were enslaved. The Panel had us trapped but now that I had seen life outside my zone, I couldn't just go back to the way things used to be. I couldn't unmeet these people. It would be impossible to un-feel the heartache I felt, walking through Zone 4. It would be unfathomable to never debate with Aziza again. I didn't mind the disagreements because I knew it came from drastically unique perspectives. We were from different places and had experienced different things. Every word out her mouth kept me on my toes and made me look at things from a unique vantage point. I didn't want to not explore the technology that Arti had introduced us to. And no way could I un-love Liam. I had experienced a life of diverse beings, and it wasn't something I wanted to be selfish with. I wanted that for everyone, and if I had to fight to get it, I would. So many people had fought to get things. Blacks, women, gays, and lesbians...somewhere along the way we had lost the courage to stand up against hate...we had forgotten to defy oppression. We had gotten so used to wrong that it felt like right.

"I just want things to go back to normal, Neely," Minnie said, her eyes pleading with me to let this go. I couldn't accept the small win. I couldn't walk away from this fight. I also couldn't be selfish enough to ask my friends to do it with me. It wasn't everyone's sacrifice to make. It was mine. I would be giving up everything. Everyone I'd ever learned about who had fought for change had paid the ultimate price. It had cost them their lives. If that was even a possibility, I couldn't expect that type of commitment from anyone but myself.

I stepped to Minnie and placed my hands on the sides of her face. "You have been the very best friend." My lip quivered. This felt a lot like goodbye. She was going home, and I was going...well...I didn't know where I was going, but I wasn't going back to the way things were.

"Just come home," Minnie whispered. Her eyes prickled with sadness. Yep, this was goodbye. I shook my head.

"You tell them what we discovered out here. You tell everyone who will listen that they deserve to see it too and that whatever I do, I'm doing it so they can get the chance to one day."

"You know The Panel will send everything they have at you. The feds will come after you," Jesus said.

"And I'll have my own army waiting when they come," I said.

"What if you die out here, Neely?" Aziza asked.

"If you never find something worth dying for, you aren't really living," I said.

"Maybe there is a reason for the walls," Minnie said. "Look at us. Look where we are. Look at what we've risked!" She was begging, and Minnie didn't beg. She was afraid. My fear wasn't absent, but it didn't rule me either. "Maybe race matters."

"Humanity should be a race. The color we're wrapped in doesn't matter. I don't blame you for wanting to go home, Minnie. I get it, but this is what I have to do."

I began to walk away because I knew it would be easier if I walked away from them, instead of making them feel like they were abandoning me.

"Huhhh!" Minnie huffed, as she stomped in my direction. I turned to see her approach. "I'm in," she grumbled. "Let's go!"

I smirked. Best friends. Ride or freaking die.

I looked at all the others. Liam nodded.

Aziza. Jesus. Alo.

I smiled.

Ride or freaking die. I guess we were off to prove that the youth would inherit the earth. We were about to change the world, but first we had to build our army.

EPILOGUE

The journey to prove my innocence turned out to be just the beginning. Innocence is relative. Those people can't judge me, not when the entire game is rigged against people like me. This entire thing started because I wanted to see what life was like outside Zone 7. It was self-serving, but it has become much more. Innocence doesn't matter in a corrupt system. People could hide a lot of wrong behind man-made laws. Slavery had been legal at a point in time. Detaining immigrants and ripping mothers from their children had been legal, too. Segregation. The Holocaust. I could go on and on. Forget the law. I no longer cared about my actions being legal, as long as they were moral. So, as I began a new journey, I knew the blood on my hands didn't symbolize a stain on my heart. It symbolized all that I had been through and all the battles that lie in wait. That one wall that President Trum had built had led us to hate. It had taken us back to an ugly past. I wasn't the same Neely King that had left Zone 7. I was a warrior and I was going to be the one to bring down the walls for good. Well behaved girls seldom make history. I planned for my name to go down in all the books like Malcolm, Huey, Rosa, and Assata. In other words, I'm about to disrupt the whole world.

www.ingramcontent.com/pod-product-compliance
Lightning Source LLC
Chambersburg PA
CBHW020925110726
47900CB00001B/301